The eight stood in a circle around the small fire pit. Outside the shelter, the rain poured so hard it was a steady, deafening sound. Cora stepped closer to the fire and stared into it. She glanced up and nodded to Leena. Taking Dade's hand, she whispered, "Let's hope the ancestors are available tonight."

Dade lifted her hand and kissed it before he let go. "I'll make sure they are." He picked up the instrument in front of him and gently began to shake it from side to side. His lips moved in a silent chant, and he closed his eyes.

Owen watched as Leena and Steven both turned their backs to the circle, facing the pouring rain. Raising their hands, they lowered their heads in concentration. If he hadn't seen it with his own eyes, he'd never have believed. As their heads came up, the wind circled the shelter and blocked out the pouring rain. He could no longer see, or hear, the heavy downpour. Not knowing what to expect, he looked at the others. Chris, Kasey, and Rachel were standing with their hands clasped and staring into the fire as the flames rose, flames that were nearly white now. He blinked just to make sure he wasn't seeing things.

Also by Jacqueline

Mystic Gifts Trilogy
Mystic Perception

Dreams

Curses

After the Silence
Volume 1 Bree

Animal Trilogy
Heart
Scent
Passion
Courage

Magic Seasons Romance
Beltane Magic
Solstice Heat
Harvest Dreams
Autumn Dance
Winter Mist

Single titles
Solitary Witchling
Cafe Serenity
Salvation

Beltane Magic

Book I
Magic Seasons Romance

By Jacqueline Paige

Published by Exordium Books FRP
Copyright © 2017 Roxane Kerr
Edited by Gaele L. Hince
Cover art by: Off the Wall Creations

Previous editions released in 2009, 2012

Excerpts from *Solstice Heat, Salvation,* and *After the Silence Vol. 1* by Jacqueline Paige copyright © 2015, 2016 by Roxane Kerr

ISBN: digital 978-1-7774682-8-6
ISBN- print 978-1-7774682-9-3

A note from the author

The Magic Seasons was my first (serious) step into the world of writing and like everything else I do, I jumped in full speed ahead! The first book was written in 2006 (as a prank and 'last' word with a friend) and then we discovered it was good and that I could write.

I spent the next few years writing more, finally having Beltane published in 2009. Then again in 2012. THIS edition is the final and best version.

Thank you to the editors and proofreaders for rounds one and two, I know it wasn't easy to correct for grammar and flow without losing how I saw my story and characters.

A huge thank you to Gaele who persevered and helped me take my story back to the way it started and working with and around my little quirks. It would be a mess of repetition and blurry lines without you.

Many thanks to those that have read each edition of this series, you are amazing! To those that are reading it for the first time – you're seeing the best version first.

Jacqueline

DEDICATION

For Meridian: for believing in me even when I didn't—
shocking us both when I wrote this.

ↂ **Chapter 1** ↂ

Leena drove slowly through the massive trees, their branches were like gnarled hands, long, pointing greyed fingers reaching toward the others across the road. Light sifted through, casting web-like patches of brightness on the road. Soon leaves would fill in the spaces, blocking the light. She wanted to stop and just drink in the scene.

A few lingering titian-colored leaves were sparsely scattered along the sleeping limbs; having determinedly held on through the winter. To some it would feel eerie, or a detail they wouldn't stop to notice, to her this was nature at her most beautiful time of awakening after the long, restful winter.

She sighed and glanced back to the road. Why was she the one to get there last, after driving through this middle-of-nothing alone? Oh right, she was the big supervisor; the one who needed to stay behind and finish up while her three friends and coworkers had piled into another car, four hours earlier. Well, at least they'd be sure to get a cabin in a good location. One close enough to everything to be easy to get to, but far enough away that private time wouldn't be a problem.

1

Leena glanced in the rear-view mirror before stopping the car in the middle of the road. Of course, no one would be behind her on this scenic route, which was beginning to look more like a path through an enchanted forest. She picked up the map to study it again. Somewhere there was supposed to be a bridge and slight incline. She was pretty sure the drawing with arrows pointing down meant downhill. She grinned. Justin made this map, and unless he'd changed since last year, she knew in her gut that his description of a thing and hers were not going to be even close.

Justin and his wife, Gwen, organized several small events throughout the year and they were never in the same place twice. The places were always completely secluded, and completely appropriate, for the small gatherings. She admired them for that.

She wondered how they managed to find some of the places; most were so remote that explorers were probably the last people to have set eyes on them. Knowing this made her look forward to this first gathering after the winter months, just for the surprise.

Double checking the printout from Gwen's email one more time, she started moving forward again. She held her breath as the car carefully crept around the corner. In this atmosphere, she almost expected a dragon or another fanciful creature from the fairy tales to jump out on the other side.

That was the bridge? It looked more like a few logs tossed in a line. She glanced in the mirror again. It had to be. There hadn't been anywhere to turn off from this road, it seemed to get narrower with each mile she traveled. She didn't want to think what she'd do if she met another vehicle at this point.

Driving slowly and hearing the crunching under the tires of her car did nothing to reassure her. Nor did she allow herself to look out the window and see what exactly was under this primitive bridge. She hadn't realized she was holding her breath, until it rushed out in a whoosh as the back tires cleared the last log and were once again on the dirt path that passed for a road.

Her stomach was knotted with tension from the drive, and fluttery with excitement. The Beltane gathering was finally here. Most called this a festival, but to her, it was more. Being reunited with those she saw only a few times a year, or some she'd only ever seen at an event.

For some this would be the only time they could be who they were inside, be how they wanted to be and feel accepted.

Leena felt she was luckier than most, she had three *true* friends. They didn't have the exact beliefs as one another, but in the last five years as the friendship grew stronger, they found ways to blend and merge those beliefs into something strong and unbreakable.

This was a slight incline? She almost hit the brakes but was afraid she'd slide off the road. It looked as if it dropped right off to nothing. The email said private and secluded. However, they didn't mention that people would be too afraid to venture over the bridge, and if they did, surely this hill winding down into a dark path of overhanging trees would deter them from going any farther.

It was probably breathtaking once everything was reborn and newly grown. As it was not yet May, it was still covered with the brown and grey of winter's slumber. She smiled, soon a thousand different shades of green would cover the ground, and life would breathe anew. Leena loved spring, loved the rebirth after long cold winters. Being of a pagan nature, she understood that winter was needed to revive the Earth, which supported so much life, but this still didn't stop her from being as thrilled as a child seeing the first signs of spring every single year.

This path would be eerie in the darkness with the trees casting shadows, and it would scare many, she thought. Well, those who did not believe as she did. Nevertheless, she loved nature in every form, as it chose to present itself.

These next three days would be spent with many of the same heart and mind celebrating the new season; celebrating Beltane and thanking the Earth for blessing them with the bounty of the seasons to come. The excitement of the gathering brought a smile to her face. Together again with her chosen family, not the ones of her blood, but with her friends and fellow pagans, she could revel in the seasonal change.

As she pulled through a gate covered with dry vines she smirked, because it left the impression of entering a haunted space. A short distance away was the best part of her pagan family. Coralee, Rachel, and Kasey stood by a little shed waving to her. Pausing, she took a moment to just sit and be thankful for friends such as the odd trio walking toward her.

The four of them together had all the bases covered in terms of looks. Coralee was a few inches taller than Leena's five foot ten, with long, dark red locks of "frizz," as Cora herself liked to call her own hair. Rachel, whose pale complexion seemed even lighter than normal next to Cora's dark skin, stood a little over five and half feet and had straight, jet black hair barely past her jaw line. Kasey was the shortest of them, and this week, wore her blindingly bright, wavy blonde hair in short spikes all over her head.

Leena glanced quickly in the mirror to make sure she didn't look as frazzled as she felt after the adventurous drive. Her scant makeup seemed intact, and her lifeless brown hair was, as always, perfectly flat.

Many on her spiritual path would spend a lifetime trying to find a close friend with similar beliefs. She had been lucky to find three five years earlier. And she thanked whatever forces were responsible for this every day.

Cora grinned and leaned in the door as she opened it. "How'd you like that bridge?"

"It seemed like trees that fell in place. My heart still hasn't slowed since I drove over it."

Rachel laughed. "We debated on parking and walking over, but didn't want to interrupt Kasey, who was praying to every goddess she could think of."

"It didn't help when you said if it failed, we'd be rafting instead." Kasey mumbled quietly, as she tried not to grin.

Leena got out and stretched. "I need the bathroom. Now. Then I'll go check in with Gwen." She watched as the three all smirked. "There is an actual bathroom here, right?"

Cora nodded. "Yep, there's one bathroom for the guys and one for the girls." She grinned when Leena's eyes widened. "It should be interesting with roughly a hundred people in attendance, according to Jean at registration."

"Let's hope they're mostly men then." Leena reached in and grabbed her purse.

"Yes! Mostly men works for me." Rachel grinned.

The others were laughing as Leena headed in the direction Cora pointed, shaking her head. "We'll take your stuff to the cabin and meet you at registration."

After exiting the bathroom, which she was sure at some point had been a storage shed, Leena paused to look around. The cleared area wasn't huge, but it was big enough to have a large open space with a few covered picnic areas in the center. There were small cabins around the outskirts of the clearing that looked much newer than the bathroom shed. They were far enough from the surrounding trees to give you a sense of privacy without having to hide in the bushes to get it.

She smirked as Charlie, the regular event handyman, walked past, carrying a shovel and mumbling to himself. Charlie was a familiar sight at the gatherings. Although in all the years she'd been coming, she never actually remembered saying more than a handful of words to him. She watched the older man attack the ground with the shovel for a moment.

Outside the clearing were trees of every size and type. It was almost as if they were holding the small area in their arms, keeping all those inside safe and protected. Perfect, as always. It would take a solid day or more to hike up out of this valley through all the trees, without getting lost; and you couldn't hear any traffic or unnatural noise. To the east, she could hear running water and made a mental note to find the time to check out the river. It was obviously swelling with the spring thaws and rushing madly between the banks. Smiling, she headed back toward the larger building. She hoped it held a kitchen that was a bit more modern than the bathroom.

With registration taken care of, the four headed to the cabin. Leena was surprised to see it was actually larger inside than it appeared. Dark and weathered wood on the outside contained a soft cream interior, making the area seem larger. One window at the back and the glass door allowed natural light to brighten the space. She was thankful when she noticed the wooden door to shut at night and they wouldn't have that "being watched" feeling. There was a set of bunk beds on each side of the room. Well, it wasn't the Hilton, but it would be dry and reasonably private.

The four women allowed themselves the luxury of a cabin at events. It was easier than hauling tents and other gear, they had all agreed after their first time sharing a tent. The tent came close to going up in smoke during one silly moment, lighting candles for a ritual.

Turning again, she noticed the little folding table they always brought was sitting by the door. "Shall we cleanse and protect our little space?" She grinned, because the others were already digging in bags and cases. Mixing beliefs and magic, always proved to be interesting among the four, for you never knew who was going to do what.

Cora stepped to the table first and placed a small cloth voodoo protection doll in the center, "To protect those who dwell within." She stood with her eyes closed.

Kasey opened her hand to sprinkle shiny dust around the table. "A touch of moon dust to see us safe during this full moon." She joined hands with Cora and waited.

Rachel stepped up to place a light blue candle on the table, then grinned and held her hand over it. As the wick burst into flames, Rachel smiled. "Blue light to protect us and ours."

Leena stepped into the space between Kasey and Rachel and placed an abalone shell onto the table. Smiling at Rachel, she rubbed her hands over the shell letting crushed herbs fall. They began smoking as they settled in the shell. "Lovage to cleanse, purify, and release this space of all negativity." She clasped hands with the others and smiled.

The air in the small cabin stirred and swirled lightly, taking the scent of the Lovage throughout. From one hand to the other, through the four, a tingle could be felt.

Leena dropped her hands and smiled. "At least you kept the snakes and critters at home this time, Cora. I wasn't ready to hold Kasey still again."

Cora laughed in her deep husky way. "I promised not to bring living things after that first time. It's tempting, but I'll save you from that fun." She bundled her jacket up. "I'm heading to see if they need any help in the kitchen before the opening circle. Anyone coming?"

Rachel picked up her poncho. "I'll head that way with you. I want to see if they expect any children this time around and if I can help with the kids' program."

Kasey flopped down on a bunk with her notebook. "I'll be here trying to describe that drive through the stalking forest."

Smiling, Leena found her warm cape and headed back to the door. "I'm going to wander. Don't forget to show up for dinner, Kase." She grinned when the blonde head didn't even lift in acknowledgment as the pen in her hand was already flying.

Ambling around the site, Leena was lost in her own thoughts and almost walked past someone talking to her.

"You don't say hello anymore?"

Leena turned to look up into deep green eyes. "Chris! Sorry, I was in my own little world." She accepted the hug from the tall, dark-haired man. "I haven't seen you since Kasey dragged me to your Wiccan church. How long have you been here?" He grinned down at her as she quickly stepped back from him.

"Got in an hour ago. Wasn't sure we'd make it over that bridge with the van. But we survived."

She followed his gesture to see his usual group of festival buddies. Tall, dark-haired, dark-eyed, brooding Dade. "Dade. Great to see you." She almost hesitated as he stepped forward for a brief hug.

"Let her go so she doesn't forget me!"

Grinning, she turned to see Steven, with his friendly smile and his chaotic, dark red hair. "Of course, I won't forget you. How are you?" She hugged him a little longer than the others, because he always felt safe. He was just as big as other two men, but he felt harmless.

"Do I get hugged, too, or do I have to know you forever and a day?"

Startled, she turned towards the unknown voice.

Dade laughed. "Well, you knew her about twelve years ago. If you hadn't been running around the planet, you might get hugged."

She studied the large man. He had to be well over six feet, probably by at least two or more inches. He had a build like a bodybuilder—a very nice build. His blond hair was neat, although with it that short, did it have a choice really? When she stopped at the pale blue eyes, she knew exactly who she was looking at. "Well, Owen Grey, it has been a long time." She offered a hand.

He smiled at her and took her hand. "I haven't seen you since you started high school." He studied her. "How have you been, Aileena?"

She wasn't sure she was comfortable with the way he was looking at her and tried twice to pull her hand free. "I've been good. Get tired of the rest of the world? Did Dade drag you here?" She offered a slight smile.

"Oh, he didn't drag me. I all but begged to come with him. I'm doing some research for a new book, and this is where I need to be."

He unknowingly found her weakness. Books. "Really? I've read most of your work, Owen. It always surprises me what comes out of your mind. What are you researching here?" She knew his work was mainly fantasy fiction, but she was uncomfortable knowing that he would be looking for ideas in one of the few places she felt safe.

"I've been toying with the idea of adding some mythology into a book or two. Dade is the one that convinced me that mythology and the many practices of the occult are very misunderstood... so I'm hoping to mix fact with fantasy and come up with a good story." He watched her relax.

"Well, I'm sure you'll make it work." Giving him a polite smile, she turned back to Steven. "See you at the opening circle?" At his nod, she started to walk away.

"Leena." Dade put a hand on her arm to stop her. He lowered his head and voice. "He won't expose anyone."

She stopped and sighed. "No, I guess he wouldn't, having been friends with you and your family for so long." She felt guilty at her first impression. "I'll see you later, Dade."

Owen stood with his hands in his pockets and looked at the woman walking away as Dade stepped back over to him. "You didn't tell me she went from cute to mysteriously sexy, Dade."

Dade laughed. "You didn't ask, bro." Dade slapped him on the back, "but I'll tell you, there's no chance with that one. No one gets close enough to get a chance. She went through a bad marriage and has never been the same since."

Owen grinned. "Good thing I came back then. A woman like that shouldn't be alone."

Steven and Chris started laughing from behind them.

Chris, still chuckling, walked over and patted him on the arm. "Good luck to you then, Owen. You'll need it. Even more when she has her women swarming around her. Those four together will boil your blood, in *every* way known to man." He grinned. "This is why we spend as much time with them as possible."

Dade and Steven nodded as they headed back to the van to get the rest of the supplies

ཀྵ Chapter 2 ༄

As dusk started to fall, the drums began to chant. They spoke to the Earth and called to the souls who felt their meaning. At larger events, there would be as many as sixty drummers. Being a smaller gathering, there were a few more than twenty. But their purpose was still to call to the attendants and make ready for the circle. Some call it a ritual, others a celebration.

People responded to the rhythm from all directions. Owen stood to the side of Dade and Chris were drumming, and watched the women's cabin. As they came into sight, his heart stuttered and his breath hissed out. The guys hadn't been joking.

The four women began walking toward the circle.

He was sure it was a trick of the setting sun, but they appeared to glow as they walked. Their brightly colored outfits floated around them, seeming to be part of the quiet breeze, giving them the appearance of floating. Noting each woman in as much detail as memory would allow, he hoped he could use this imagery in his writing.

The short, curvy blonde with shy eyes walked with a confident glide. Atop her helter-skelter blonde spikes was a halo of flowers and ribbons trailing down.

Next to her, a dark-eyed woman with bright flowers contrasted with her midnight black hair. Her smile, he noted would make any male ache.

The woman walking, actually gliding gracefully, beside her had to be close to six feet tall. She was a walking epitome of feminine grace and beauty. Her dark complexion and deep red curls made a man's mind think of things that heated his blood and played with his soul.

His eyes moved to the only one of the women he knew, and his heart tripped once more. Her long, shiny brown hair reached past her waist and flowed around her like a cape. With each step the ribbons from her halo twisted and played in the tresses. Oh how he wanted to be those ribbons Leena's smile made him wish he knew what she was thinking. She was obviously very happy and content with the company, and he imagined the event about to take place pleased her as well.

Steven patted him on the back. "Tried to warn you." He pushed him toward the drummers. "Stick with the drummers, and you'll be close to them. The drums call to them more than most."

Nodding, Owen looked over to the drummers and met Dade's eyes. His friend's grin was saying, "Told ya so."

As the women reached the circle, Dade caught Leena's attention and motioned for her to come to him. She did, smiling as she worked her way through the drummers. Owen watched her lean down to Dade, noting that his friend didn't miss a beat on his drum.

She lifted her head and looked quickly over to Owen, staring at him for a moment, and then nodded down to Dade. Reaching up she pulled a flower from her halo and stuck it in the cords of Dade's drum, much to his friend's pleasure judging by the smile on his face, and then she walked back over to her friends. Owen watched for a moment more as she spoke quietly to the other women and they turned and started toward where he and Steven were standing.

His blue eyes jerked to Dade, a devious grin on his face. He'd never been a nervous man, but watching those four women with the swaying hips glide toward him, he felt a nervous buzz in his veins.

"Steven!" Kasey shrieked as she launched herself into his arms. She grinned at Owen while she hugged Steven. "I'm Kasey."

He couldn't help grinning down at the blonde woman pulling herself out of the other man's arms. "Owen Grey." He started to extend a hand then was surprised when the woman he thought had shy eyes hugged him tightly.

"The author?" She stepped back and looked up at him. "Yes."

She grinned again, "You just became my new best friend!"

The dark-haired woman pulled her back. "You will have to ignore my silly friend. She broke out the mead earlier than normal." She studied him for a minute. "I'm Rachel." She hugged him and grinned again, it made his blood flow faster. Then she stepped back and leaned closer to Steven. "How's life, Doc?" He received a brief hug.

Steven winked at her, not minding the nickname. He was, in fact, a doctor of pediatrics. "Great, Rach."

Owen wasn't sure whether to smile or faint when the tall, dark woman wrapped her arms around him. "I'm Cora. Nice you could be here."

"Thanks. Although I have no idea what's going on, or going to happen."

Leena laughed. "Yes, we know. Dade asked if we'd keep an eye on you and keep you out of trouble while he's busy. Of course we can probably answer any questions you can come up with."

He smiled. "Awesome. Okay, first question?" No one spoke. "Why don't you four have very large, protective males guarding you?"

Cora laughed a husky laugh. "Oh, I like this one." She gave him a warm smile, "I have a question for you, Mr. Grey." She waited until she had his full attention. "You've known Dade a long time... so do you believe in magic? Real magic?"

Everyone, including Steven, turned and waited for his answer.

Owen cleared his throat. "I've been friends with Dade since we were about six, and, yes, I believe anything is possible." Not one responded, and he grinned. "Having been at his family home more than my own growing up, I've seen more than I could ever explain. Does that help?"

Smiles flashed at him from the women. Leena stepped beside him. "It does. We're very careful with whom we trust. Our beliefs and magic are very guarded. We will trust you, because Dade has asked it of us. Don't abuse that."

He felt his nerves settle. "Fair enough. I give you an open mind to fill, ladies." He grinned and put his arm casually around Leena's shoulder, noticing that she tensed at the contact. "Now, how about giving me a wee preview on what to expect? I feel like the only person here that doesn't know what's going on."

Leena was tense, he could see the emotions flash through her eyes and was about to release her when she relaxed and smiled up at him.

"I guess that makes you today's sacrifice then." When he tensed, she laughed. "I'm kidding, Owen. We're going to begin the rite for May Eve, or Beltane. Tonight we dance and celebrate the coming fertile season, and the men will set up the maypole for the morning." She grinned. "You've heard of dancing around the maypole, haven't you?"

He shrugged, "Always thought it was just a saying. It is real?"

She nodded. "It is. I'm sure you'll have more questions, but why don't you just relax, observe, and enjoy?" She moved to take her place in the center of the circle, waiting for the drumming to escalate again.

Owen tried to listen to everyone around him, but wasn't able to focus on any one conversation as the drums grew louder and faster. He could feel the beat inside his chest, and it made him light-headed, but he enjoyed it all the same. He felt Steven step beside him.

"Most circles will call on this deity and that, making big speeches. This group is more of a do rather than say, kind. The women will dance shortly after everyone is centered. Then, we'll go outside the circle and help bring in the pole." He paused to listen to the drums a moment himself. "The pole represents the masculine, and the ribbons the women will put on represent the feminine."

He grinned up at Owen. "In years gone by, this night was a night for 'a-maying' and couples spent it alone in the woods. Married couples could even take off their rings for the night..." Steven noted that he had Owen's full attention now. "But those were the days before AIDS and all that, we don't practice that now. But if a woman places her wreath upon your head this night, then you'll have a female to dance the pole with in the morning, at least." He grinned at the disappointment on Owen's face. "I always hope to be lucky enough for a few kisses. You never know."

Realizing that was all the insight Steven was sharing, Owen turned back to the circle. The drums were nearly frantic now, in speed and volume. He glanced at Dade and realized the drummers seemed to be in a trance.

They stopped on the same beat, and the silence was suddenly deafening. Everyone in the circle stood motionless, breathing deeply. No one spoke. No one moved. Relaxing his shoulders, Owen took a deep breath and let it out slowly. He tried to feel as relaxed as everyone else appeared to be.

A few moments later the drums started with a quiet, gentle rhythm. He watched the women walk slowly in the center of the circle. With slow, gentle movements they started to sway with the drumbeats as they walked around the circle, arms pulling up from the ground and pushing skyward. He'd never seen anything so graceful and lovely in his life.

All of the women had wreaths of flowers on their heads. Owen noticed that none of them came close to the glowing beauty of Leena and her friends. Maybe he was biased, for he only knew those four out of the many. As the drums grew louder, the women changed their movement to match the volume, but their mist-like speed didn't change at all.

Steven tapped his arm, motioning him to follow away from the circle to a group of men a few yards away. He wanted to object, afraid to miss any of this mystical dance, but he followed, questions bubbling to the top.

He heard Steven say something about a newbie. Owen found himself being placed at the front of a twenty-foot log. Steven stood opposite him, grinning. "Best seat in the house. Just walk beside me into the circle and help hold this up as the women put their ribbons on." He winked and grinned before turning back toward the circle.

The log wasn't heavy, not with more than twenty men carrying it. He didn't really have to lead, the men just pushed the leading males toward the goal.

The drums were still playing. The women opened their dancing circle as the men carried the pole into the center. He realized each woman had a ball of ribbon in her hand as she danced past, and he just noticed the hole at the center of the circle.

So caught up in the beat of the drums and the fluid movement of the women, when an older woman appeared in front of him and placed her ribbon over the end of the pole on a nail, he was shocked to find her there. After securing the ribbon, she began walking along the side Steven was on, running the ribbon from her hand down the pole. And in turn, each male was gently touched when her hand went past him.

He would have turned his head to see what she did at the end, but another woman was standing in front of him and smiling. She secured her ribbon then gently touched his shoulder and walked past him to the man behind him.

Owen chanced a glance at Dade, and found his friend drumming slowly and smiling at him. Dade winked and went back to watching the woman dance slowly around the pole.

After the fifth or sixth woman had secured her ribbon and walked down his side, Owen wasn't sure whether he should feel as excited as he did or not, but he certainly wasn't going to fight it. Cora was next in line, and she gave him a look that set a buzz in his system, then attached her ribbon and went down Steven's side. Steven flashed him a grin that said he wasn't at all sorry she chose his side.

Kasey was next, and he knew she would walk down his side. She ran a gentle hand up his arm and across his shoulder before moving past, and he was quite pleased with the buzzing feeling she left behind.

He again watched Steven grin as Rachel was next and she ran her hand along Steven's arm, similar to what Kasey had done to him. He did hope though he didn't have the same dazed look on his face the Doc did.

Turning back to face the next woman, he realized it was Leena. His heart picked up immediately. He smiled and was shocked at the one she gave him in return. He watched her secure the ribbon. As her hand traveled up the length of his arm with a whisper-light touch that burned a trail in its wake. When her hand caressed his cheek, as soft as a gentle breeze, his smile widened and he could honestly say if he dropped his hold on the log, no man there would blame him.

He felt her pass behind him, her body brushing gently against his back as she continued moving along the pole with her ribbon. Catching Dade's eye, he knew it was more than obvious how damn pleased he looked at this moment. His friend was grinning and shaking his head.

Owen didn't know all that much about rites and circles, or even Beltane, but he vowed he would volunteer to hold the log every year, single-handedly if need be, to see that this season was always celebrated. His whole body was buzzing. He couldn't recall how many women went after Leena, but instinctively he knew how many would go past before she would dance by again.

After all the ribbons were placed and the pole lowered into the hole, the drums changed to a loud, flighty, faster rhythm. He watched several of the males join the dancing, as a few females came and went. He noticed almost immediately Leena wasn't in the dancing circle. Turning to the drummers, he saw that she and Cora were walking among the drummers, bringing drinks. Dade winked at him and turned his head back to the women.

He saw his friend watch Cora, almost daring her to bring a drink. He also saw that Cora moved to the drummers away from where Dade sat. Leena walked up and squatted down beside Dade and spoke in his ear. Dade laughed and shook his head. Owen watched as Leena pulled a bottle of water out of the bag and offered it.

He recognized the playful dare in the man's eyes as he spoke, and was surprised when she smiled, uncapped the water and placed it to Dade's lips. She literally was giving him the drink. Swallowing, Dade grinned again and said something. That something was enough to make her lean down and place a kiss on his cheek. Owen made a note to have a private conversation with his lifelong friend and find out how the hell he did that.

Not wanting to see Dade gloating, Owen turned back to watch the dancers and wait for Leena to return to the circle. He noticed Kasey and Rachel were sharing a bottle of wine, and headed that way. He didn't want to leave the circle to get a beer, so maybe he could beg a sip from the ladies.

The drumming remained steady, which surprised him when Dade walked up beside him. He knew it wasn't just his friend drumming, but he seemed shocked they continued without him. "Do your arms get tired?"

Dade shrugged. "Sometimes. I just take a short break now and then. Most often I'm too caught up in what's going on to notice. So, what do you think so far?" They slowly moved around the outside of the circle toward where the women were standing.

"I am going to need a little time to digest this. I feel like I'm on a high and I haven't had a bloody thing to drink, or anything else." He grinned at him, "I do know I will hold that pole every year for the rest of my life, though."

Dade threw his head back and laughed. "You haven't seen anything yet, my friend. The best is yet to come."

"Any better and the showers here better be good, because I'll need one. Long and cold!"

Chris caught up to them and grabbed the bottle of water from Dade. "Did I offend one of the ladies, or all of them? I didn't get a drink brought to me. Or a kiss. How did you manage that, Jones?"

Dade winked at Owen as he answered, "I'll never tell, my friend."

Chris laughed and turned to Owen. "I think if you're planning on attending on a regular basis, we need to teach you to drum. You enjoyed that pole far too much for a newbie."

Owen nodded. "I will hold that pole every year until I'm so old someone has to hold me up."

Cora noticed the three men walking toward them and elbowed Steven, who had moved up to stand beside her. "Owen's all right, isn't he? I haven't sensed anything off with him."

Steven grinned, "He's fine. He just doesn't know what he already knows. Yet."

"Well, let's hope we don't scare him into never wanting to know." She smiled as Chris walked over. "Hello there, Mr. Lawyer Man. Sorry I didn't bring you a drink. These two," she motioned toward Kasey and Rachel, "were partaking of our ritual mead a little too healthily, and I don't want to have to carry anyone back to the cabin tonight."

Chris shrugged, "I'm always happy to take drunken women where they need to go, Cora."

Dade put his arm around Kasey. "I'm sure they're going to be able to walk back just fine, Coralee." She glared back at him as he watched Leena glide over to the small group and said, "Are you ladies up for a bit of fun after the festivities?"

Kasey smiled sweetly up at him and snuggled more into his chest. "What kind of fun are you looking for, Dade Jones?"

Dade smiled down at the tiny woman under his arm. "Oh, nothing that isn't acceptable. I just thought maybe we could bring some light into Owen's world. You know, rather than break it to him gently..." He grinned at his wary looking friend. "We'll just lay it all out for him. Well, not *all*, but enough."

Leena laughed softly and then frowned at Dade. "You're not very nice sometimes, Dade." She turned to Owen and smiled. "I assure you, it's all harmless, just a way to bring you into our little circle, Owen."

Owen cleared his throat, not sure whether to laugh or whimper. "I'm game."

Chris, who had been looking around the rest of the crowd, frowned at Dade as he liberated Kasey from under Dade's arm and swung her into his arms. "Great. Now ladies, how about you get back out there and dance so we have motivation to drum this night?" Setting Kasey down, he grabbed her face gently between large hands and kissed her lips, hard.

Kasey, grinning wide, nodded and headed back into the circle.

"Come on, Owen, sit with the drummers, and we'll give you a silent beater."

Owen looked at Chris as he walked past. "A what?"

"A drum that's muffled so you can get the rhythm but no one will hear a sound from your drum."

Owen laughed. "Sounds like my kind of drum. Lead the way."

Owen found himself between Dade and Chris, caught up in learning the rhythm and watching either Chris' or Dade's hands to pick up the beat. This was a good place to be, as the dancers stopped often to dance right in front of them, or bring them drinks.

After an hour, his arms were tired and he had new admiration for the men who were still going strong, moving effortlessly from one rhythm to the next.

During a slower beat, he noticed several of the women moving through those at the edge of the circle. He watched as they took their wreaths off and placed them onto a head. He was sure the men didn't realize how silly they looked wearing flowers and ribbons, although when the women gave them a kiss, he was sure they didn't care.

Kasey paused in front of the drummers and began to weave her way toward them, slowly taking off her wreath. She smiled in a shy, nervous kind of way at the drummers. Neither Dade nor Chris paused, but Owen could feel them both waiting to see who she was going to place her wreath on. When she passed Dade and went to Chris, Owen enjoyed the grin on his new friend's face.

Chris actually missed a few beats as he raised a hand to place it behind her head to receive the kiss. Owen didn't see steam, but he felt warmer just witnessing their kiss.

He was wishing some woman would make him look like an idiot and place her wreath on his head. He turned to watch the scene repeated with Doc and Rachel. He was sure Steven was blushing after, or maybe it was just from the heat.

At the point when Cora began seductively dancing her way into the drummers, his heart stopped. She was far too exotic for him to handle, but if she placed her wreath on his head, he would certainly try. He felt like a schoolboy wanting to jump up and say, "pick me," but he dug deep and found his dignity somewhere.

She passed him by and held the eyes of the man beside him. When she placed the wreath on Dade's head and leaned her mouth down to his, Owen was sure the sparks that flew burned him. In his own amazement, he realized it was a kiss out of a movie that made your heart speed up. Dade didn't miss a single beat, though the kiss seemed to last more than just a few moments.

He found himself wishing for mistletoe, a cute puppy, anything that would bring one of the women to him. His heart tripped when he noticed Leena dancing toward the drummers. He fought the urge to look around and make sure he was the only one in the area without a wreath, but held onto what composure he had left.

When she stopped in front of him, it was all he could do to not stand and meet her halfway, he held the drum in front of him tightly and stayed seated. As the wreath touched his head, her smile made his insides burn. He reached up to gently guide her head down to his.

As Leena lowered her head toward him, she still wasn't sure why she felt compelled to pick Owen. Maybe it was from those years in school wishing he'd notice her, hoping her first kiss would be from him. He was older, and that made her invisible then. Now she was long out of school and if a woman didn't allow herself a few luxuries, then life held no meaning at all.

When he palmed her neck, she felt the heat and couldn't stop herself from looking into his blue eyes. They had darkened to the color of steel, and the little voice in her head tried to tell her "mistake," but she didn't care.

Feeling the heat sear through her, she had to stop from moaning into his mouth, and slowly pulled back before it was too late. His passion-filled steel eyes captured hers as he loosened his hold and let her straighten.

Owen forgot where they were. Her lips were soft and warm as they touched his as heat coiled in his stomach. Turning his head, he deepened their kiss, knowing this may be the only chance he would get to taste what she offered. She tasted of dark passion and hunger. He didn't know where he was going to find the strength to keep this brief, but he really didn't care if it never ended.

As she danced back to the circle, he felt Chris lean over, and heard him whisper. "Boil a man's blood... welcome to our world." Chris smiled a lopsided grin at him and then lowered his head back to his drumming.

❧ Chapter 3 ☙

He could still hear the drumming and wondered if it would stop before dawn. It wasn't that late, but he was certain midnight had passed and it was heading into morning. "What are we doing again?" he asked, to no one in particular.

Steven grinned, "We'll let the diehards do their thing at the circle and go challenge fate with the ladies whose flowers we're wearing..."

Every man grinned. Owen touched the wreath on his head. "Good enough reason for me." He tried not to notice how odd they looked with the ribbons, and hoped he looked better at least. "How long do we wear these?"

Dade smiled, "Until the woman that put it on takes it off in the morning and puts it around the pole."

"Do we get a kiss again?"

"Feeling juvenile, Owen?" Chris asked, amused.

"Maybe... a bit... don't you? I haven't felt this good, without drinking, since, well, ever."

Chris nodded. "Yep, and it feels great. If we're lucky, we'll get a kiss. If the gods are happy, we'll get more."

Steven laughed. "When you figure out which god gets you that Chris, please share with the rest of the class."

They kept walking away from the circle. The only light was from the flashlights two of them held. Owen looked back toward the camp. "Where are we going exactly?"

"To meet the ladies by an old picnic shelter, away from prying eyes." Dade motioned to the left, "and they're already here."

Kasey hopped off the picnic table. "Good thing we have this shelter; it's going to really rain soon." She offered Chris the bottle of mead.

He took it and looked at the sky. "Tell me it's not going to rain the whole weekend, Kase." He lifted the bottle to his mouth.

"Would like to, but I'd be lying." She reached up and took the wreath off his head. "I think you guys could take these off until morning. Seeing you with them outside the circle is a bit distracting." She grinned at Chris, "wouldn't want to be distracted and scare Owen."

Those nerves, the ones Owen never had before, returned. He really was beginning to wonder what everyone was hinting at. He put his hand out for the bottle Chris held. "I don't scare too easily, Kasey, but you do have me wondering." He accepted the bottle and took a swallow. "You guys make this? It's good."

Leena nodded as she took his wreath off and set it on the table. "We prefer it to the stuff you buy. You never know what's in that." She settled against the side of the table. "So, Owen, back to a question asked of you earlier. Do you believe in magic?"

He nodded, "I believe all things are possible. Are you going to show me magic, Leena?" He held her eyes with his, wishing everyone else would disappear.

She grinned, "If your mind is open, you might see some." She glanced at the barbeque pit in the middle of the shelter. "Do you suppose that's safe to light? I don't want to burn down the shelter."

Steven kicked some sticks into it. "It should be safe. Rach, want to give me a hand?" She shrugged and stepped up.

Rachel smiled and faced Steven across the pit. Owen watched as they both raised their hands a few feet in the air over the sticks, and he blinked when it started to smoke. When flames licked at the wood, he looked around at the smiles and lifted the bottle for another drink.

Leena reached over and took the bottle out of his hand. "I don't think this will help you believe."

He opened his mouth, shut it, and thought a moment more. "Are you trying to tell me you all can do that?" He looked at Dade.

Dade shook his head. "I would give anything to do that, pal. All of us here have different talents, and some more than one."

"Does everyone gathered at this event all have... talents?" He tried to process what that could mean.

Leena stood up and walked over to the fire. "A small number do." She looked down at the fire for a moment, "but they don't realize it. Most don't, but it's enough that they believe in the spiritual and pagan rituals" She held her hands over the fire, and the smoke began to swirl and rise, then drift into circles that twirled around the shelter.

Turning, Leena sent the smoke to dance in front of Owen. "I believe every person alive has some gift. It's whether they believe enough to discover what it is." She dropped her hands, and the smoke fell.

Owen sat down, shocked and processing. "I'll have questions—later, when my brain kicks back in."

Chris grinned at him, "Of course." He turned to the two men still wearing their wreaths and lifted his hands. His mouth moved in a silent incantation as the wreaths lifted off their heads and went to gently rest on the table.

"Talk about being outdone." Kasey walked over to the fire and put her hands on her hips. She stared down at the fire, then clapped her hands once. The flames went purple. Grinning over at Chris, she lifted her hands and flicked her fingers at him. His hair ruffled up for a moment, then laid back down.

"Ah…" Owen swallowed and glanced at Dade. "Tell me you haven't been hiding these *talents* all these years, man."

Dade grinned again and then laughed. "I wish I could do this cool stuff." He winked at Cora, "and it *is* cool. We don't hide it; and as far as I know we don't get them until we're older, which is a good thing. Could you see the playground at school if everyone could do this? As for me, I do some things that are very serious and better left alone most of the time."

"Like the things your mother did?"

Dade looked back at him. "Yeah, like those things that used to keep us awake all night afraid something was going to come and get us. My talent lies in the instruments. I can call all sorts of spirits. Occasionally, I can get a lady to dance my way with the right sound and instrument, but other than that, I leave the magic to this bunch."

Owen thought for a moment then turned to Cora. "And you?"

She grinned and walked over to him. Placing her hands on his arms, she closed her eyes. She stood like that for a moment. "I see things, sense things, and know things." Cora stepped away from him. "You, Mr. Grey, have a talent of your own. I wonder if you are aware of it," the others turned to look at her.

"Elemental?" Kasey inquired.

Cora shook her head. "No, he can't play in fires and winds." She smiled down at him. "I've always wanted to also. No, his is something else. Almost on the same level as mine… but not quite."

"Interesting." Leena walked over and placed her hand on his shoulder. "Can you sense anything, Owen, or see what I'm thinking?"

Owen sat silently for a moment. "I wish I could get inside your head, Leena. Nope, nothing different."

"Well, don't push it. Just stay open and it will come to you," she suggested.

Cora turned and looked into the darkness as the rain started to sprinkle. "Speaking of feelings, has anyone else picked up something wrong in the circle and this area? It reeks of negative and dark energy, then it's gone. I felt it several times tonight at dinner, then dancing."

Dade went over and stood behind her, resting his hands on her shoulders. "And you didn't say something sooner?"

She shrugged under his hands. "I didn't want to spoil the dance of May eve. It was fine again until a few minutes ago. It weighs very heavy, though, right now. Almost painful."

Leena glanced at Chris who was looking out in all directions.

Owen walked over to Cora and took her arm gently. "Is there something we should do?" He had no idea why he was offering to help with something he totally didn't understand, but he could feel the tension coming off her in waves and didn't want anything to spoil this oddly wonderful night for everyone.

Cora looked down at his hand for a few moments then back to his face. "Let go for a moment, please."

Feeling as if he had done something wrong, he dropped his hand and put it in his pocket. "Sorry."

She smiled and shook her head. "Don't apologize. Take my arm again."

Bewildered, he did as asked.

She chuckled, "I think we have found Owen's talent. He absorbed the negative feelings I was feeling, just by touching me. Of course, it floods right back when he's not, which worries me. The energy is that strong out there, but at least we know Owen is a very strongly grounded empathic."

Owen looked down at his hand. "I did what? I'm what?"

Rachel smiled up at him. "You can take the negative and, I'm willing to bet, the pain from others. I'm guessing it doesn't affect you in any way, or you would have known before now. *That* is cool, Owen." She grinned over at Leena, "We could really use him at the factory."

Leena laughed. "Yes, a resident empath would be easy to explain to the boss."

Dade was still staring at Owen. "It figures you'd have something cool. I wonder..." He walked over to his pack and pulled out his pocketknife. Dade grinned at Owen as he held up his hands with a startled look on his face. "Relax, it's for me." He opened the blade and pulled it over an inch on the back of his arm. "Can you fix stuff, too?" He held his arm out to him.

Owen was thinking he was stuck in a seriously weird dream, but still walked over and placed his hand over the small cut on Dade's arm. "Is this all I do?" Dade shrugged and looked at his hand. He lifted it to look at the cut. "It's still there."

Dade ran his hand over it. "It's not throbbing now and it's not bleeding either. So, you can stop the pain but not completely heal." He shrugged and dropped the knife back in the pack. "Well, it's still cool." He slapped Owen on the back, "welcome to our little circle."

They both turned to watch Cora walk to the fire and place her hands over it. "It's really damp now that it's raining."

Kasey handed her the bottle of mead. "It's going to get a lot damper." As she dropped her hand, the rain increased even more. "Did anyone bring umbrellas? We're going to drown getting back to the cabins."

Leena walked over and rubbed her hand up Cora's arm. "It's really bad isn't it?" Cora nodded. "Should we try to see where it's coming from?" She glanced around at the others, then back at Cora.

Cora let out a breath. "It could make it worse."

Chris walked over and took her hand. "There are eight of us here, we can shield anything together. Do you have what you need with you?" He glanced around at the others who nodded. "Let's give it a try then, shall we? Maybe we'll have a breakthrough that will let us know what to expect."

Owen watched as everyone reached for their backpacks and bags, and within moments there were candles, rattles, dishes, herbs, and more things he couldn't name. He watched them light herbs and candles. "What should I do?" He knew nothing of this.

Dade looked around. "Well, this wasn't what we intended to welcome you, but it needs to be done." He glanced at Cora then back to him. "If it gets to be too much for her, it will cause her a lot of pain. *If* that happens, I'd like you to go stand behind her and place your hands on her shoulders and see if you can ease it for her." Cora stopped what she was doing and looked over at Dade. She offered a quiet smile to him then went back to what she was doing.

Owen let out a slow breath, "okay." Everyone looked so serious. "Just... if you could try not to scare the shit out of me, I'd really appreciate it." Chris tapped him on the back, and the Doc grinned at him.

Kasey walked over and reached up to kiss him lightly on the cheek. "Just stay in the circle until we're done, and you'll be fine." She turned to Leena and Steven. "You ready?"

They nodded.

The eight stood in a circle around the small fire pit. Outside the shelter, the rain poured so hard it was a steady, deafening sound. Cora stepped closer to the fire and stared into it. She glanced up and nodded to Leena. Taking Dade's hand, she whispered, "Let's hope the ancestors are available tonight."

Dade lifted her hand and kissed it before he let go. "I'll make sure they are." He picked up the instrument in front of him and gently began to shake it from side to side. His lips moved in a silent chant, and he closed his eyes.

Owen watched as Leena and Steven both turned their backs to the circle, facing the pouring rain. Raising their hands, they lowered their heads in concentration. If he hadn't seen it with his own eyes, he'd never have believed. As their heads came up, the wind circled the shelter and blocked out the pouring rain. He could no longer see, or hear, the heavy downpour. Not knowing what to expect, he looked at the others. Chris, Kasey, and Rachel were standing with their hands clasped and staring into the fire as the flames rose, flames that were nearly white now. He blinked just to make sure he wasn't seeing things.

Dade's motion with the shaker became faster and louder as he moved to stand beside Cora. Her head was thrown back and her eyes closed, she seemed to be shaking with the rhythm of the rattle. Her eyes flew open as she stopped moving and looked into the fire. He could see the sweat beading down her face, and her hands trembled. The look on her face told him she was afraid, but she said nothing. She reached empty hands toward the fire, and the flames flew higher. Not knowing what else to do, Owen went to stand behind her in case he was needed, hoping he would know if he was at some point.

She stepped back and cried out in fear. He caught by the biceps and held her, as Dade instructed. Glancing over her shoulder and into the fire he saw, he blinked again, images. They blurred together and he couldn't understand them.

Cora cried out again and sagged back against him. He caught her tight against his waist and held her to his chest. His own chest began to burn. He didn't know what was going on, but he felt compelled to stop it. "Stop now!" He said roughly.

At once, Dade stopped shaking the rattle and the three controlling the fire dropped their hands and gasped when they looked at him holding the slumped woman in his arms.

Leena and Steven settled the wind and turned around to see the others crowding around Owen. He looked at Leena. "I have to set her down, or my legs are going to give out."

Dade set his instrument on the ground and scooped Cora into his arms. She was still shaking and breathing hard, as if she'd been running. He walked over to the table and sat with her held in his arms.

Leena and Chris helped Owen to sit at the table. "Hell of an initiation." He put his head down on the table for a moment and then looked over at Dade. "Is she okay?"

Dade looked down at her as her eyes opened. "Yeah, but she didn't quite share the strength of this with us." He glanced back at Owen. "If you hadn't discovered your gift tonight, it would have been a lot worse."

Owen looked over at Leena, who was looking worried. "Can I drink now?" He let out a long breath and accepted the bottle she handed him. After taking two long swallows, he looked back at Cora. "I dunno what just happened, and I don't know what I saw, but as soon as I touched Cora, the fire had images in it... images I'm not sure I even want explained."

Cora sat up slowly in Dade's arms. "I'm okay now, Dade. Thank you." She pushed against his arm. "Well, you can just sit here for a moment or two longer. You scared the shit out of me! If Owen hadn't told us to stop, I don't know what would have happened. Jesus, Cora, why didn't you tell us it was that strong?" Dade asked.

She touched his cheek lightly, then rested her head against his shoulder. "I had no idea it was that strong, Dade, or I wouldn't have exposed all of us." She took a deep breath, then climbed off Dade's lap and looked over at Owen. "I owe many thanks to you, Owen Grey. I couldn't pull back completely, but I felt when you took the burden. You're going to come in handy when I have seeing to do."

Owen took another drink, before offering her the bottle. "You're welcome, and I'll get back to you on whether I want to help again or not." He rubbed his chest. "My chest still burns like hell."

Everyone glanced at Cora then back to Owen as Leena sat beside him and grasped the hem of his sweater. "May I?"

He shrugged as she lifted his sweater. He heard gasps then looked down to see a burn in the shape of a cross on his chest. It covered the skin from his collarbone to the bottom of his rib cage. She touched it lightly. "It's not hot; does it hurt?"

"It burned like hell when I told you to stop, but it's fading pretty quickly. Is it permanent? No offense, but I don't want a cross burned into my chest."

Everyone looked at Cora. She was running her hand down the outside of her sweater. "I felt the burn, but only briefly." She pulled her sweater out a bit and looked down it to see if she was marked. She sighed and shook her head. There were no marks.

Owen looked around at everyone as Leena dug around in her backpack. "So, would someone please explain to me what the *hell* just happened?" He reached for the bottle once again, and then changed his mind. It would not make it any clearer.

Leena was back on the bench in front of him and lifting up his sweater again. He didn't know what she was rubbing into his chest, but it felt heavenly after the burning, so he didn't complain. It crossed his mind briefly that it was just the feel of her hands on his chest making him feel better. "That is really helping. Keep slathering it on." He hesitantly stroked a hand lightly down her long hair. It felt like satin.

Chris dropped onto the bench across from him. "Apparently, during the ritual, your abilities are stronger, and in turn you saved Cora from having a cross burned into her chest. What did you see in the fire, Owen?"

He continued to run his hand down Leena's hair, encouraging her to continue touching him. "I have no idea. It was like a blurry dream. Were you able to see anything?" He looked up at Cora hopefully.

Cora took an unsteady breath. "I was only able to make out two deaths and blood. That's when the burning started in my chest, and the next thing I knew you were handing me to Dade." She walked over and leaned down and kissed his cheek. "Thank you for pulling me out, Owen."

He smiled up at her as Steven laughed. "Great. The guy finds his gifts and has women kissing and stroking him, all in one night. Talk about luck."

Leena straightened and took her hand off his chest as everyone burst out laughing. "We'll talk this through tomorrow. Someone cleanse this area so I can go to the cabin and get some sleep."

Rachel sobered, "I'm on it."

They silently gathered up their stuff. The men grabbed the wreaths and stood at the edge watching the rainfall. "We need a canoe," Steven suggested as he checked his flashlight.

Kasey chuckled and pulled out plastic sheets and handed one to each woman. "I guess we'll have to walk you back to your cabin, as none of you brought anything to keep you dry." Chris grabbed the sheet from her hand and held it over her head. Laughing, they walked out into the rain together. "See you at the cabin." He shone the flashlight ahead.

Dade pulled the still-shaky Cora to his side and took the plastic sheet from her hand. He handed her his flashlight. "Let's get you back and some tea into you." She nodded and stepping out into the rain, stayed close to his side.

"Ready to go, Rach?" Steven held out his hand for the sheet when she nodded.

Owen stood in the silence with Leena watching the progress of the others on the slippery ground, except Steven and Rachel, who apparently weren't using any sort of light.

He turned his flashlight towards Leena and grinned as she handed him the sheet. "A golf cart would be great right about now." He touched her arm lightly. "Thanks. My chest feels better than it did. Do you think it will disappear?"

"It should. If not, you'll appear to be a very devout Christian for the rest of your life." She stepped out of the shelter with him and had to laugh at how loud the rain sounded against the plastic. "That's going to make quiet conversation hard."

He laughed and pulled her closer to cover them better. "Sometimes words aren't needed."

Leena looked up into his eyes, then quickly back down at the flashlight-lit ground again. The echo of the others from the group laughing could be heard over the rain.

As they neared the cabin area, Owen paused. "I'll take you to yours, then give you back the sheet tomorrow." She nodded and looked up at him for a moment.

He slowly backed her under the shelter of the eaves on the back of one of the larger sheds. Letting go of the sheet with one hand, he leaned against the shed and caged her in. "This has been one hell of a night."

"You're dealing with it pretty well."

"Can I ask you something?" He ran his hand down her arm. "If I kiss you again, will you bring a tree down on my head, or something equally as painful?"

She paused to think about it before answering, he hoped that was a good thing. "Well, it is May Eve. I think you're safe from injury." She placed her hand lightly on his chest and lifted her face.

Owen leaned down slowly, searching her eyes. She watched him back just as carefully. When he brushed his mouth against hers, he forgot he intended a light, caressing kiss and reached his hand around her to pull her tight against him, deepening the kiss.

When her mouth opened against his, Owen dipped his tongue and tasted the heat of her passion. He felt her body go soft, her every curve fit against his hard outline perfectly. Needing more, he broke the kiss only to pull her head closer and plunder again. Her soft moan sent heat coiling straight through him and settling in his groin. He'd never gotten so hard so quickly in his life.

Leena grasped at his shoulders, wanting to climb him like a tree. His mouth was torturing her with things she hadn't felt in a long time, and she wasn't sure she'd felt this hot, ever. His mouth offered a path straight to pleasure that her body wanted to take. His hard body pressing her against the wall was more than she could handle, and she moaned into his mouth as his hand gripped the back of her head, exploring.

She was sure her legs were going to give out when he softened the kiss and loosened his hold, but didn't release her. His lips brushed lightly against her a few more times before resting his forehead against hers.

"We better get you back before they come looking." He continued to nuzzle into her hair.

"Yes, they'll worry," was her barely audible response. Dropping her hands, she waited for him to step back.

Letting out a ragged breath, he picked up the plastic sheet, holding it open, waiting for her to get under it.

Walking the rest of the way to the cabin was harder than she thought it would be. The silence was strained, as if they were both trying to forget that electrifying kiss.

When they reached her cabin he quickly kissed her so hard and fast it felt like a wave crashing over her. She handed him his wreath and flashlight, then ran the last few steps to the cabin door, not looking back until she was on the other side of the door looking out.

Owen waited until she closed the door, then turned and headed down the line of cabins toward his own.

He *could hear the drums as he reached to the bottom of his bag. Closing his hand around a case, he pulled it out slowly.*

They *had come right to him, their souls screaming to be saved.*

He *caressed the case open, and gently picked the knife up from its resting place.*

They *had come to him knowing they had sinned, knowing he could cleanse them.*

He *would not let them down.*

ॐ **Chapter 4** ॐ

Owen sat in the shelter at the center of the camp, scowling at his notebook. He'd made several notes regarding Beltane and the ritual. He stumbled over details of the pole ritual and the odd, but interesting events of the day before.

The men had humored him, sitting up for most of the remainder of the night answering at least a hundred of his questions. His problem? Each question they answered, he thought of two more.

When he woke, even though he should have been exhausted, he charged out of the cabin with renewed energy. Then he ran back to grab a rain cape, notebook, and cell phone, and then once again to get his wreath.

He stared at the phone and wondered who he would have called. He was compelled to call and say, "Guess what I can do?" or "I'm a... what?" What was he exactly? A witch? A wizard? He didn't know, and that was just one more question he needed answered.

Glancing up, he waved at the older woman making her way toward the kitchen building. Gwen was a blast from the past. She projected a carefree attitude and her dress made him think she could be a sixties love child. A wonderful lady.

He noticed her husband, Justin, stood in the pouring rain looking at the dripping ribbons on the maypole. Beside him stood the events handyman, as Dade called him. He'd seen him set up chairs at dinner and collect wood. An odd older man Charlie was. Mumbled a lot to himself, and though he smiled, Owen never saw those smiles reach his eyes. He'd make a perfect character for one of his books. A dour butler, more pagan than British though.

Everyone here would make a great character, as he now thought they all fell into the slightly odd, yet intriguing, category.

"Rather deep thoughts so early in the morning."

He jerked his head around to see Leena standing at the edge of the shelter. "I've had nothing but deep thoughts since I arrived. Not even sure if I slept longer than a few moments."

She smiled and wandered to the table. "I remember when I realized what I could do. I spent days making things dance around, just testing to see what was and wasn't possible. It's invigorating." Leena glanced at his phone. "Were you calling to tell all your friends?"

Owen looked down at the phone again. "I don't know what I was going to do. It doesn't much matter though, there's no signal here."

She leaned on the edge of the table and looked at him thoughtfully. "Sharing what you can do with the wrong people only brings more problems than you know, Owen. Trust me on this." She ran a hand over the wreath on the table. "How is your burn this morning?"

"Barely there, but it gets itchy when I think of it."

Leena frowned as she reached into her pocket. "I wondered about that. I made this for you when I woke up." She offered him a small bottle.

He took it, opened it, and then sniffed the pungent concoction. "Out of what?"

She smiled and sat. "I won't bore you with the details, but it will help cleanse leftover negative energy." She turned and reached for his shirt. "We felt bad when this happened. It wasn't intended…but, life rarely happens without little surprises."

Lifting his shirt, she ran her hand gently over the faded marks. She took the bottle from of his hand and began to tenderly rub the oil into them. His breath caught as her hands moved over his skin.

Owen didn't care about the marks. He could feel nothing but her cool fingers gliding over him. Leaning forward, he pushed his face into her hair and inhaled. She smelled of fresh leaves and rain. A smell he'd never found tempting until that moment.

When she lowered his shirt and lifted her head, it brought her face a few inches from his. He could feel her breath against his jaw and his mind went back to the night before.

Leaning away, she capped the bottle and dropped it into his pocket. "Would you like to go for a walk on this wet Beltane morning? I don't think breakfast will be ready for at least another hour or so."

"Yes." He scooped up his notebook and phone, stuffing them in his pockets. Tying the wreath to his belt loop, he pulled the cape over his head. "Maybe you could answer a question or two for me?" He grinned, "After last night, I have several thousand."

She laughed. "I'll see what I can do." Then she turned and started away from the camp.

Little streams of water rushed along the ground, having carved trails after the intense downpour. The morning was a dull gray, but Owen found it more beautiful than he ever had before. He watched the water trail and thought of how he would describe them in words. "So, what am I, Leena?"

"A man, a writer. Nothing's changed from what you were yesterday." Leena watched his brows draw together. "You don't need a label, Owen. The world is already filled with far too many. Among ourselves, we joke and call each other witch and other silly names, but in truth we're all human and really no different than anyone else." His eyebrows shot up in surprise. "Okay, we are a little different in certain ways, but unless we tattoo it on our foreheads, no one knows, or cares, in the outside world. Most are happy with not knowing that different is possible."

He walked a few more steps and then stopped. "You each follow your path in secret, except in the company of each other, and just carry on same old, same old then?"

"Basically, yes. The world, for all its wonders and words, isn't all that accepting of different. If you aren't mainstream, then you're not normal."

"And your path is what?"

"Harder to define with a name or label." She motioned around them. "My beliefs are what you see. I believe in nature and all that she holds. I don't have deities, really, not in the sense that Kasey does. She follows the Goddess path. For details, you will need to speak to her."

He filed this new information for later inquiry. "I think I've already figured out the Doc, Chris, and Rachel have the same beliefs, as Dade and Cora have theirs. That leaves me standing here wondering what I believe. If anything."

Leena touched his arm in reassurance. "You don't have to convert overnight, Owen. Take your time, follow your heart, and you'll find your own path."

She continued walking. "Some never settle on one path, they remain open and revel in all ideas."

Owen sighed, "Well, until I can process everything I saw last night, I think I'm better off hanging back to see what's what." He cleared his throat. "I've decided the underlying message of my next series will tackle religious tolerance, or differences, in some way... in a fictional storytelling way." The fine mist turned into drops again.

She reached out and ran a hand down the bare, slick branch of a tree they were passing. "Quite often, serious research into a subject comes from a passing mention in fiction. It's more fun." She stopped and looked up at him.

"Each faith, or religion, likes to believe they are tolerant." She paused and glanced at the sky. "I would like to believe I am, but I know when wars break out and horrible crimes are done, I will push it onto another faith, or the values of people who practice a specific faith. If you can make just a few deeply think of religion and acceptance, or even accept those that are different, then I'd say you will have performed your own little miracle." Raindrops ran down her face, but she didn't seem to care.

Owen was drowning in her expression. "Someone's belief in a particular faith shouldn't predict what they do. They are still free to make their own choices despite the path they follow. Blaming anything on your particular set of beliefs is simply an excuse for your own failings."

"Exactly." She smiled. "I would love to help you in any way I can with your book, as long as you keep me out of it." She sighed. "As soon as you get home, you're going to digest all that's happened here, and more questions will come."

He shook his head. "I don't know if I'll ever digest all this. If I hadn't been there last night and saw and felt what I did, I'd still say it was a fantastic dream." He reached out and tucked a wet lock back under the hood of her cape. "Including you." He dropped his hand to her shoulder and gently pulled her close. "You send me straight from dream to fantasy, Leena."

She stood there just looking up at him. He recognized the look in her eyes and lowered his head to gently brush his lips across hers. He forgot the dampness, forgot the rain.

When he would have kissed her again, she placed a palm against his chest to stop him.

"Owen..." her voice was a whisper, "please don't take this the wrong way. I know last night was... well, it was... I'm not looking to get into a relationship right now."

Owen studied her eyes for a moment. He could see her fear. What scared her from accepting a few kisses? Even if he admitted he wanted more than that. Last night, he'd wanted a whole lot more.

Her hand was trembling. "I can't..."

He placed a finger over her lips. "I'm not asking for your heart and soul, Leena." He brushed his hand down her damp cheek and stopped at her chin to lift her face again. "A friend, nothing you don't want." He smiled. "Of course, if I can steal the odd kiss from those inviting lips of yours from time to time, I'm going to try."

She relaxed visibly under his hand. Proving his words, he lowered his head and brushed his mouth over hers. He dropped his hand as he straightened. "Someday I'll ask why, but for now, you've got a free pass."

Leena slid her hand down his chest and turned away. "Thank you for not asking." Taking a deep breath, she looked back toward the camp. "I had wanted to see the river, but I think the closer we get, the harder it will be to walk in this mud, so let's go back and get a hot cup of tea."

He nodded and put his arm around her shoulder as they started back toward the camp. The rain came down harder still, and he saw how she shivered from the cold of it. Looking around, Owen spotted the top of some sort of shelter in the trees. "Want to take shelter for a few minutes and shake off some water?" He motioned toward a roof he had seen.

She laughed and nodded. "A hot tub would be welcome right now."

Moving faster, they headed off in the direction of a small picnic shelter. A few moments' reprieve from the pounding rain was welcome. She slipped in the mud, and when he reached to steady her, he also started to slide. They slipped a few feet in a struggling dance, and when they finally righted themselves to stand still, they were both laughing, clasping each other's arms. "Thank you for the dance." She tensed as her head jerked up. "Oh, Owen, look."

He turned toward the shelter and saw the bare feet sticking out from under a small tarp. "Someone had way too much mead last night, from the looks of it."

She dropped her hands and started to walk over. "We can't leave them to catch pneumonia while sleeping off too much fun." She grinned at him. "They're going to be sorry enough as it is."

Shrugging, he walked over then squatted down and patted the leg. "Oh, they're out for the duration. Freezing, too."

Leena smirked, "pour souls." She jerked her head toward the second pair of feet that had appeared when he had moved the sheet. "Well, let's see if we can rouse them enough to stumble back to their cabin at least." She walked to one end and pulled the sheet back. With a gasp, she stumbled back and covered her mouth.

Jumping to catch her before she fell over the wood scattered on the ground, Owen pulled her toward him. "What..." He looked down, following the path of her eyes. The faces she uncovered were covered in blood and deathly gray. Two pairs of sightless eyes looked back at them.

"Shit!" He pushed her away gently and squatted down. He fought the nausea in his gut and touched the neck of the first cold, lifeless woman, then the other. Shaking his head, he looked back to Leena who stood with her eyes closed as a tear rolled down her cheek. He lifted the tarp to uncover them completely, afraid to see what was underneath.

"Fuck!" He dropped the tarp and moved to stand with Leena at the edge of the shelter. He rubbed his hand over his chest. "Leena." He had to clear his throat before finding the words. "There are crosses in blood on their chests." She gasped and hid her face in his chest, holding him as tightly as he held onto her.

Leena was trembling so hard her teeth were chattering. "We have to get Justin."

He grunted an affirmation, looking around to note exactly where they were. "Come on." Not letting her out of his grasp, he began to trudge back over the muddy ground toward the camp. He wasn't sure whether he or Leena was holding them upright, and wasn't about to let go and find out.

As they reached the edge of the camp, they spotted Charlie heading toward the maypole. "Charlie." Owen cleared his throat. "Do you know where Justin is?"

The older man barely paused, pointing toward the entrance gate. "Up there. Bridge is washed out."

Leena looked up at Owen and stammered, "We can't leave."

He pulled her tightly under his shoulder. "I'll carry you if I have to." He pulled her closer to his side and marched her forward.

When they finally fought up the hill on the muddy road to reach the bridge, they found Justin, with the medic, Kevin, and Dade standing together looking at what was left of the bridge.

Dade turned and frowned at them. "What's up?"

At his words, tears started pouring down Leena's face and his heart stopped. "Owen?"

Owen turned and gently pushed Leena down on a nearby boulder. "Sit." Then he turned back to the three and tried to find the words to tell them what they found. He knew his voice was shaking as he watched the faces blanch.

Justin let out a long breath and stared at the bridge again. "I'll go radio for some help, but if the broadcasts are any sign, there's flooding everywhere. I don't know how soon help will get here."

Walking over, Justin squatted down in front of Leena. "Aileena. I want you to go back to the cabin with Owen and Dade." He glanced up at Owen, "we have to keep this under our hats until help comes. The last thing we need is panic." Owen nodded. "Kevin, you go find Jean and Gwen and let them know what's happening, then meet me at the pole. The fewer people who know, the better." Kevin nodded and started the walk back down the hill. Justin glanced back at the shaking woman. "Aileena, go and get dry. We'll come talk to you when we get back."

Dade stepped over and looked down at Leena. "We'll take her back, then get Chris and Steven. They can help with what needs to be done. Then I'll come back here and see if I can't figure out a way to get across. I'll need a truck. A four-by-four, if anyone has one, to pull the logs over." Justin nodded and started to walk down the slope toward the gate.

Owen helped Leena to her feet, pulling her tight against him. He nodded to Dade, and they started walking. They met Chris in the center of the camp as they headed toward the cabin. He looked questioningly at Leena in Owen's arms, but didn't ask as he fell into step with them.

As they reached the cabin, Steven rushed to the door, and pulled it open.

"Cora." Owen stepped inside with Leena.
Rachel, who was just pulling a sweater over her head, jumped in surprise and then saw Leena. "What happened?"

Cora sat up on the bunk at the sound of Rachel's voice. Cora rushed to Leena and ran her hands over her as Owen was pulling the cape off her. "Oh, no!"

Leena pulled back from Owen and spun for the door.

When Owen got through everyone to get outside, Leena was on her knees beside a tree, leaning her head against it. He didn't have to ask if she'd been sick. He could feel her suffering before he reached her. Pulling her wet hair from her face, he brushed it over her shoulder and picked her up, cradling her in his arms. She wrapped her arms around his neck and buried her face in his chest. The sounds of grief as she let the tears fall, tore his heart from his chest.

As he held her, he glanced back to the cabin to see everyone standing helplessly in the rain. He didn't need to ask if Dade told them. He could see the women were white with shock as they clung together, unaware of the soaking rain. "We need to get her warm and dry." His voice croaked out as he carried her back to the cabin.

Once inside, he fought the urge to hold her until she stopped shaking, but the women were pushing him away to wrap her in blankets. Dade pulled him back, turning toward the door.

As the three men filed through the door, Chris stopped. "None of you leave this cabin until we get back and find out what the hell is going on!" It wasn't a request, and each woman nodded in agreement.

"Lock it," he called as they stepped out the door.

More than two hours had passed before they returned to knock on the cabin's door. "Cora, open up." The women sighed with relief when Dade's voice boomed through the door.

Leena watched as the four men came through the door. They were dripping wet, pulling rain ponchos over their heads, hanging them on the pegs by the door. She watched Owen as he walked toward her, seated on the top bunk wrapped in a dry blanket. Taking it off, she wrapped it around his shoulders and offered a small, helpless smile. "You look frozen."

He held her hand and relaxed into the warmth of the blanket. "I may never be warm again."

Cora offered a blanket to Dade. "What's happening?"

Dade took the blanket and threw it around his shoulders. "We aren't able to get out of the valley, and rescue services are up to their asses with flooding and emergencies." He glanced over at Steven. "We've done as requested, and wrapped the bodies and stored them until we can get out or they can get in. After we warm up a bit, I'm going to see what I can do about the bridge."

Rachel looked up from her clasped hands. "Who were they?"

Chris shook his head. "No one we know. A couple of newbies that came together and stayed pretty much to themselves. Gwen is looking up their contact information so they can decide what to do from there."

Kasey gave a blanket to Steven. "How did they die, Doc?"

Steven took the blanket and sighed. "Immediately."

Leena let out a long-held breath. "That's good at least. I've been sitting here thinking they'd suffered in the cold, unable to get help." She accepted the comfort that Owen's nearness gave her. "How's your chest?" She looked in his eyes. "It was like the burn on your chest, wasn't it?"

Owen nodded and dropped her hand, lifting up his shirt to show her. There wasn't a mark. His voice was shaking again. "Either that smelly oil you put on this morning took care of it or..."

"The vision is complete," Cora said softly.

Dade sat on the edge of the lower bunk and looked at Cora. "There's more," he said softly. She shook her head and stepped back, reaching for the small cloth gris-gris bag around her neck. "There was a note," he said.

Leena sat straighter. "Left by the killer?" He nodded at her.

Cora took a deep breath and looked at Dade again. "What did it say?"

Dade looked at the men. "Two for your Beltane sins. Fifty-two days until you sin again."

Leena gasped as Cora blanched. "This wasn't a... random?" Leena looked at Dade. "Someone planned this, this..." She lowered her face into her hands and took a deep yet shaky breath.

"Where's the note, Dade?" Cora asked.

Dade stood up and reached out toward her, only to see her step back. "Justin has it." He looked at Owen. "We told him what happened last night."

"I'll want to touch that note." Cora raised her head with determination.

He stepped closer to her again. "I don't think that's a good idea." He'd lowered his voice and glared at her. "You took on too much last night, and hurting yourself again isn't going to help."

She shook her head and stepped past him. "If I can catch a glimpse of the killer, then it will be worth it, to have them stopped. Won't it?" She glanced around the room.

"How are they handling this?" Kasey asked, nodding toward the door, to no one in particular.

Steven pulled the blanket she had given him off in frustration, tossing it onto the bunk. "They can't tell people. As it stands, we can't get out of this valley. The only communication we have is an old CB radio." He glanced up at Leena. "We have to keep it between ourselves. Outside of this cabin, the only people that know are Justin, Gwen, Jean, Kevin, and old Charlie."

"And the killer himself," Rachel added in quietly.

Chris walked over and hugged her. "We're going to meet Gwen and Justin at the admissions building. Gwen saved you ladies some breakfast, then we'll decide from there." He glanced around at the men. "Until we get out of this valley, none of us go anywhere alone." His voice shook with anger and worry. "If you ladies need to go anywhere in the camp, make sure one of us is with you, at all times. The more of us together, the better."

"Solstice." Leena whispered and looked down at a confused Owen. "Summer Solstice is in fifty-two days."

Owen let out a breath. "I don't care what is in fifty-two days. Chris is right; none of us go anywhere alone until we're out of this valley." He glanced over at Chris. "Even once we're out of it."

Cora reached past Dade and picked up her poncho. "First I want to go talk to Justin and see this note." She paused. "They're not still planning to dance the maypole, are they?"

Dade stuffed his hands in his pockets and looked down at his feet. "They are."

After she had pulled it over her head, she reached for Leena's and held it out to her. "Fine, then we have some charms to work after the dance... together."

Nodding, Leena jumped off the bunk. "Bathroom first." She glared at Chris. "You guys left us here for two hours, and none of us risked leaving!"

Chris winked at her. "I'll guard over you in the shower, Leena."

She smirked, knowing he was trying to lighten the mood. Owen brushed past him and stood in front of Leena with his arms crossed.

"She had enough water on her head this morning."

Chuckling, Chris acknowledged the warning tone and held open the cabin door. "Fair enough."

✦ Chapter 5 ✦

Owen sank further back into the shadows of the bunk. He watched the women moving around the room, speaking quietly to ask one another about a certain herb or stone.

Chris sat in the corner, also silent. Although he appeared relaxed, Owen knew he was tense and ready to strike at any given moment. Doc sat still, his slowly flexing hands the only indication of the tension within. Dade was leaning against the wall, impatience clearly stamped on his face.

The quiet meeting at the admissions building was tense and upsetting to all. Old Charlie actually looked ill, so Gwen finally persuaded him to go lie down in his cabin and rest. With great reluctance, he finally agreed and left the building. Kevin sat silently with his head down, listening. Jean sat there with a tear-stained face, not making eye contact with anyone.

Cora was more upset with the fact Justin would not let her see the note. He had a reason for that. None of the women, Gwen included, had been allowed. The words had been written in the victims' blood. Written with the tip of a knife, a fact that the men agreed would not be revealed to the women. Owen was sure not one of the men wanted to know, but agreed it would be better to shelter the women from the additional brutality.

He watched Leena as she selected herbs from a seemingly endless supply, in a small black case. He had to admit these four women seemed to be prepared for anything. Then again, this was only his second day at a gathering, and they had been at it much longer.

Owen glanced at the ribbon in his hand. He'd taken it off the wreath Leena gave him. She'd watched him take it and told him to keep it as a reminder of the parts he chose to remember. He'd remember it all, good and bad.

Earlier, he'd moved throughout the maypole dance cautiously, scrutinizing every face in the small group of celebrants. The others that were aware of the horrific discovery did the same. If it hadn't been for the anguish weighing him down, Owen was sure he would have been awestruck as the men and women wove the ribbons around the pole.

For a bystander, it would have been something to see. The single people from the crowd danced around the inner circle of couples. The very few drummers left, beat quietly in time to the dancers' steps. The couples across from each other, with their ribbons in hand, moved in opposite directions as the ribbons went up and over one another until they were only a few feet from the pole. The wreaths were tied to the end of the ribbons, so they hung to the ground in a circle of color.

Owen looked up from his hand when he heard a quiet conversation.

"Protection from crime or danger?" Kasey asked Chris softly.

"Do you have any fire opal in that bag, sweetheart?" Chris asked her quietly. "It will cover all aspects."

She nodded, "of course. It will cover the emotional turmoil as well." She turned back to what she'd been doing.

He noted from time to time, how each of the men regarded the different women. Although Chris glanced around the room as often as Owen did, Chris' eyes always stopped at quiet little Kasey.

He turned slowly to see once again that Dade's impatient stare hadn't yet strayed from the exotic figure of Cora as she knelt and chanted quietly, passing small cloth bags through some sort of smoke he wasn't able to identify by smell.

The Doc was either looking at his own hands or watching the dark-haired Rachel as she silently bent her head over some burning candles.

Owen's mind drifted to the ribbon in his hand and the maypole dance again. Of course, if the earlier tragedy hadn't robbed him of all good humor, he would have laughed when he'd realized that he'd been so distracted by the women and pole ritual the night before, he hadn't noticed they had each placed two ribbons on the pole. Well, he thought with a sigh, at least the rain had eased into a drizzle for the maypole dance and they'd been somewhat dry during it.

He was disappointed that the morning ritual hadn't enthralled him, as the night before. The shadow of the two deaths hung over the little group. When Leena reached up to kiss him as she removed his wreath, he saw the pain in her eyes and knew the kiss was for show, she wasn't able to forget the heartache.

Dade sighed loudly, pushing himself away from the wall.

Owen sat up, tense and waiting.

Cora lifted her head and glared at Dade, lifting her hand in a gesture that, told him to stay put and stay quiet.

Pouting a little, Dade flopped down onto the bunk beside Owen shaking his head. Glancing down at the ribbon Owen was running through his hands, Dade offered him a helpless, defeated smile and leaned back with a loud sigh.

Cora brought the small cloth bags to Kasey, who placed a pebble-sized stone in each. He would have to ask her why she'd run them through the smoking dish later. Actually, he'd lost track of all the questions for later.

Cora nodded and went to Rachel with the dish of small bags. Rachel took the dish and placed it on the floor beside her candles. Dropping some dust onto the candles, she watched as they flickered. Then she picked up the black candle and dripped a drop of hot wax into each bag. She then did the same with the white and then blue, until she'd repeated the sequence for each bag. As Cora picked up the dish and walked to Leena, Rachel carried the candles, one by one, placing them on the little table beside the door to let them burn.

Leena accepted the bowl from Cora and placed it on her lap as she sat cross-legged on the floor. In front of her, Owen noted were four small dishes, three with herbs and a fourth that was smoking.

She picked up a pinch from one of the small dishes and dropped it into a bag, repeating this with each dish of herbs. When complete, she picked up the smoking dish, and blew the smoke over the bags. Nodding to Cora, she handed her back the bowl.

The other men stood, so he did also.

Cora walked with the bowl of little bags to Chris, Leena following with the smoking herb Owen watched as Chris dipped his hands in the smoke, then picked up one of the small red bags from the bowl. Drawing the bag closed with the string, he pulled the cord over his head and tucked the bag inside his shirt. Chris nodded to Cora, so she and Leena moved over to Steven.

Owen waited as the Doc did the same as Chris, followed by Rachel and Kasey. When Cora stepped in front of Dade, she lifted her head to hold his eyes as he too dipped his hands through the smoke and reached for the bag. All of this added to his list of questions.

When they stepped in front of him, he was glad they waited until after he'd had a chance to see what to do. Placing the ribbon inside his pocket he ran his hands through the smoke and pulled it toward himself, not taking his eyes off Leena as he did so. Then he took one of the last three bags from the dish and secured it around his own neck.

Cora nodded and turned toward Leena.

Owen reached over to take the smoking dish from Leena and hold it in front of her. Smiling, she ran her hands through the smoke and up over her head, then reached for her bag.

Cora watched as Owen turned toward her and she then did the same as the seven before her.

When the little smoking dish was finally placed on the table with the candles, Dade headed toward the door. "Now, can I go see if we can get the damn bridge back together?"

He paused with his hand on the raingear hanging near the door and looked to Cora. She nodded and silently clasped her hands together. He paused a moment and looked at her. "Stay together." She nodded again.

Owen followed behind Chris and the Doc and called over his shoulder. "Lock it."

Once outside, he caught up to Dade and kept stride.

"Put the ribbon in your gris-gris bag."

"What?" He glanced over at Dade.

Dade grinned. "Take the little memento she gave you and put it in the gris-gris bag. A personal token will extend the protection to her, through you." He shrugged, "just don't tell her that."

Owen reached into his pocket and pulled it out. "You don't tell them everything, do you?"

Dade laughed as he reached in his own pocket and pulled out a shell, one Owen thought he'd seen hanging from Cora's hair the night before. "Not if I can get away with it."

After two hours of sitting and trying to read Leena tossed the book onto the bunk. "I'm going to the kitchen to make some tea to take to them."

Cora tossed the pillow on the bunk. "Took you long enough!"

Kasey was already pulling a cape over her head. "They could have asked for help."

"No, they treat us like helpless little women. We could use a touch of magic to help them somehow. You'd think the he-men would think of *that*." Rachel snorted as she extinguished the candles.

They headed across the mud-drenched site, thankful the rain was now just drizzle. Justin stood outside the dining hall with Gwen, their heads close together.

He straightened up when the four women reached them. Looking from one woman to the next, he shook his head. "An uphill battle. We've almost got a post solid enough in place to get the logs across." He glanced up at the sky, "it will probably get dark before we can get it finished."

The silence that fell was an admission, no one wanted to spend another night in the isolated campground. Leena fought back a tremor. "Why don't you go warm up a bit, Justin? We were just coming to get some tea to take to the guys."

Gwen smiled at her. "I just put the kettle on, I'll go find a Thermos or two."

"This would be great to slide down on a toboggan," Rachel forced a laugh as she struggled beside the women trying to trudge their way up the hill.

Cora slid to a stop. "You do that, Rach. We'll watch."

As they got closer to the bridge, each woman walked faster. They weren't prepared for what they saw. The four men were struggling to push a log up onto the other embankment. Mud soaked shirts topped hip waders, from who knows where. Still the four were soaked and bedraggled.

Dade was halfway up the embankment on the other side, pulling a rope that was around a tree. Owen stood at the bottom in the rushing water with a rope in his hand. He was pulling as hard as he could.

Both men had lines tied around their waists, and Steven sat, holding both ropes, leaning back with all his weight and pulling them. The only thing stopping both men from being washed away in the fast-moving current was the ropes. The river was angry, if they slipped, it could be fatal.

Chris slowly slid toward the edge as he tried to keep the log from dropping onto the heads of the men in the river.

Leena handed the Thermos to Cora and stepped to the edge. "Morons." She closed her eyes briefly, and then she opened them and raised her hands. The log then rose up a foot off the embankment and moved over far enough to land in place on the other side. All four men turned to look at her. "Maybe your muscles needed to be flexed, but your brains need the exercise *far* more."

Dade waded through the rushing water and started to climb back up, "Probably. We had help until a few minutes ago, and Justin warned us off anything other than physical labor." He grinned lopsided at Cora, "and this way our muscles get bigger."

Leena sighed. "Oh. I didn't realize. Justin didn't say who was here." She leaned over and watched Owen climb the embankment. "I thought you were using a truck."

Chris accepted the steaming cup from Rachel. "It's being used to find some suitable logs." He took a small sip and closed his eyes as the liquid sent warmth through him. "We won't be getting out of here tonight, ladies."

Owen sat on the ground, not caring how wet it was. "We can still try. I'm willing to give my muscles a rest and let the ladies flex their powers." He grinned at Leena. "You just placed that log, first try, when we dropped it into the river more than once." She handed him a steaming cup. "Thank you, darlin'." He winked and took a small sip.

Cora looked across the river. "Was the old bridge completely gone?"

"Pretty much. The main post on the other side washed out with the rain. We salvaged as many of the logs as we could, but we need new ones for support." Dade dropped to the ground beside Owen.

Kasey offered them a granola bar from the bag she carried. "Can we help?" She looked back on the path to see if anyone followed them.

Steven winked at her. "Sure, if you could just fly on over there and tie off that log to the big one sticking out of the ground, then we'd be on our way."

She stuck her tongue out at him. "Cute. You know we can't fly or we would." She handed him a granola bar and cup and glanced at Leena. "Right?"

Leena smiled and walked over to the edge. "We can't, but that doesn't mean the rope can't." She glanced at Owen. "Let me know if we have company." Owen looked quickly down the path then back to her. She looked at the rope on the ground beside the post on the other side. "Rachel, how are you at knots?"

Rachel grinned, "I was a Girl Scout."

Chris walked back down the path to keep watch while the two women stood at the bank.

Leena raised her hands, and a slight breeze passed over Owen's head and rustled Dade's hair beside him. Rachel was chanting and staring at the rope as the wind lifted it. He wished for a camcorder as the rope began to wind around the log then twist itself around the post.

Chris cleared his throat, and the rope pulled one last time to tighten, and then dropped. Justin and Kevin walked into sight just down the pathway. Justin grinned at Chris and glanced past him at the log then down to the steaming cup in Chris's hand. "Good work." He looked over and smiled at Leena, knowing that the resting men had little to do with the log being in place.

Dade stood up. "Have any luck finding one long enough?"

Justin nodded, "Yeah, they're cutting it down now, and then we'll haul it here." He glanced at the sky. "Doubt we'll get it in place before dark." He turned to look at Leena again. "It's too risky to work in the dark near the river."

Leena lowered her head and accepted they wouldn't be able to lend any further aid to the cause until morning. "So, we finish in the morning. Any word from the rescue?"

"They'll be clearing some fallen trees down the road leading to here in the morning, then if the bridge is ready, we can head home."

Home. A word that meant more to them then it had in a long time. They stood silently looking across the bridge, no one wanting to discuss it any further.

Justin looked at the men. "Why don't you guys head down and get dried out. I'll tell them to drop the log here and we'll resume this in the morning. Early."

Cora gathered up the cups. "I'll go give Kathy a hand in the kitchen getting dinner ready."

Justin turned back toward the gates. "We've got the wood stove going in the admissions office if you guys want to warm up a bit." Then he silently headed back down the path, with Kevin following behind.

Kasey started after Cora. "I'll give you a hand in the kitchen." She turned back and watched the others follow. "Stick together, right?" Not waiting for a reply, she slid down the slope through the mud.

Owen dropped his arm around Leena's shoulder. "We all stick together tonight."

She nodded and kept her head down, watching where she put her feet.

Three hours later, the women stared at the men as they came through the door of their cabin. "What are you doing?" Leena asked.

"Why do you have blankets?" Rachel looked at Steven.

Dade dropped his blanket onto a bunk and grinned. "Stick together, remember?"

Cora laughed. "We are. You are not sleeping in here." She turned around the tiny space, "there isn't enough room."

Chris held up his hand. "Relax, we're not going to stay. We brought blankets because none of us have felt warm since playing in the river, which we get to play in again soon, and we thought you ladies might like to leave your cabin at some point and use the bathroom or kitchen. Or whatever." He dropped down onto the bunk and wrapped his blanket around his shoulders.

"Oh." Cora sat back down and glared at Dade.

Leena grabbed her cape and headed toward the door. "I, for one, am quite happy with the visit. I've been wanting to head to the kitchen to get some tea before bed, well, hot water to make some herbal tea anyways." She looked over at Owen as he pulled his jacket on.

"Let's go."

She took his hand when he offered it to her and flipped her flashlight on.

"So, Leena what do you do?" He gestured around them. "Outside of all this."

Smiling, she realized he really didn't know much about her. "I'm a plant supervisor at a paper recycling plant. The girls all work there, too."

Owen grinned. "Let me know if someone recycles my books, would you? It's not a good sign if they end up in the trash." When she laughed, he felt warm again, finally. "What do the others do there?"

Leena steeped over a branch on the ground. "Cora works in the office, yelling at drivers and other collection plants mostly. Rachel works in the shipping department. Don't ever get in her way. When driving one of the forklifts through the plant, she is like a possessed woman." She grinned at him. "Kasey runs the line, and don't let her shy exterior fool you. She can yell louder than a foghorn if needed, when it's not running according to plan."

"And you run around and try to keep the peace and everything running smoothly?"

"Close enough. Of course, someday I'd like to be doing what I want, like you do."

He walked quietly for a moment. "Oh, there are times when writing is the last thing I want to do, especially when my editor is bullheaded and publishers want something faster. But most of the time, I want to write."

As they walked up the steps to the kitchen, he stopped her and turned her toward him. He smiled, holding her in his gaze. "About one of those stolen kisses I mentioned hours ago."

Leena placed a hand on his shoulder. "I thought you'd forgotten about that."

Owen shook his head and pulled her gently to him. He whispered against her mouth. "I could never forget about that." Gently, he brushed his mouth over hers, once, twice. Feeling no hesitation, he moved closer to taste more. He deepened the kiss and felt her melt into him in return. Keeping to his word wouldn't be easy, but he'd follow that rule until the time came to break it. Leaning away from her lips, he grinned. "Mmm, that's the first time I've been warm all day."

She smiled and brushed a hand down his shoulder. "I have to agree." She turned back toward the door. "Now, to get the water and help everyone else warm up."

He held the door for her. "We could mention that kissing takes off the chill, but that could get weird in translation."

Leena chuckled, "No doubt. No, I think this is better left between you and me."

"If that's the way you'd like it, for now."

She didn't comment on the tone she'd heard in his voice, recognizing the *I've staked my claim* attitude of maleness. "Owen, did you move back to Russle, or are you just visiting Dade?"

Pulling up a stool, Owen watched as she moved around the kitchen. "I'm back for good. Got tired of running here and there, and needed a home base. Bought a house in the same neighborhood as Dade It's newer. Townhouses mostly."

"There's nothing like coming home, is there? Even if no one you know is left, it's just the feeling that gets you."

Owen nodded and took one of the biscuits she set in front of him. "Exactly."

As the men headed to their cabin later that evening, each felt the strain of the day.

"So, I was heading back from the bathroom with Kasey and Cora and happened to glance toward the kitchen." Chris paused for a moment and cleared his throat. "That looked an awful lot like Leena wrapped around you on the steps, Owen."

"Yep." Owen grinned and offered no more.

Dade stopped and looked at him. "How did you manage that? And judging by the dumb look on your face when you got back last night, it wasn't the first time."

"Nope." Owen stuffed his hands in his pockets and wished for a hot bath.

Doc tapped him on the back. "You do know once she gets over that bridge tomorrow she's going to run as fast as she can."

He nodded, "I know. Good thing she can't run faster than I can." He grinned at the redheaded man and unlocked the cabin door.

ॐ **Chapter 6** ॐ

Leena breathed a sigh of relief as she dropped down onto her couch. Opening the cell phone in her hand, she hit a few buttons and sent a text message to the group. *Home safe! Lee* then hit send. They agreed on three things before crossing the bridge that morning.

First; they wouldn't take the gris-gris bags off until they knew they were safe. She hoped for the chance the police would be able to find something from the bodies or the note to lead them toward finding out who did such a horrid thing.

Justin dealt with all that, including providing her and Owen's names and information. She hoped for a day of peace before she had to give the police a statement.

Second: they all programmed everyone's numbers into their cell phones, and set up a group for text messaging. She smiled when she remembered showing Owen that technological advance. If any of them had any ideas or feelings to share, they could do it easily.

Finally, the eight agreed to meet once a week, mostly just to be reassured by sight that everyone was, in fact, fine.

The part they hadn't agreed to was the men following the women until they were back in town, but it happened anyway.

Leena wasn't sure how she felt about anything. She was exhausted and brought nothing from the car except her purse. She was just relieved to be home. Dry and home. The phone beside her buzzed. She opened it.

Lock doors, and take hot bath. Owen

Well, he'd figured out the text messaging. She sighed and headed toward the bathroom. She might just fall asleep in the bathtub tonight, it was going to take hours of soaking to feel warm again.

Leena was standing in the kitchen deciding whether to make herbal tea to knock her into peaceful sleep, or one to ease the heartache. Her cell phone buzzed from across the room, where it rested on the counter. Still perusing her tea cupboard, she flipped the phone open.

Police called. Meeting them at your house in morning at 10. Owen

She was relieved. *Thanks. See you then. Lee*

The kettle hadn't begun to boil when the phone buzzed again.

Where is your place? O

Laughing, she sent him the address. Then she sent the girls a quick message letting them know what was happening in the morning. Setting the phone aside, she grabbed a cup from the cupboard and finally chose a tea blend.

As soon as Leena closed the door behind the two officers who had been asking questions for more than an hour, she turned and glared at Owen.

"How mad are you?"

"Mad enough." She paced out to the kitchen and grabbed her cell phone. "Did you men really think we wouldn't find out about that note? Do you have any idea how I felt when they handed me that sealed bag?" She spun back to see him leaning against the door. "I almost lost it in front of those officers, Owen! It was written in blood! *In* blood! You should have told us the note was written in the victims' blood!" She typed out something on her phone, and then tossed it on the counter again.

No sooner had she spun back to the counter and placed the cups in the sink did his phone vibrate. He reached in his pocket and opened it. *Meeting my house 1 today! L* "Well at least I'll be on time."

Leena whirled back on him and stared at the phone he held, still grinning at her. Realizing she had also sent a message to the man standing in front of her did nothing to improve her mood.

Her phone buzzed, and she picked it up. "Chris will be a half-hour late." She put her hands on her hips and stared at Owen. "If you want to stay close to my good side, Owen, following every little thing Dade and his faithful followers suggest is something you should avoid."

He shrugged. "I'll keep that in mind." He stepped toward her but stopped when she shook her head.

"I think you need to run to the store for me and pick up some stuff before everyone gets here."

"Will you be happier if I'm out of your face for a bit?"

She nodded.

"Write me a list of what you want." He stuffed his hands in his pockets and stared at her as she wrote out a list. When she handed it to him, he tried to look repentant. "I'll be back by one."

Dade sat across from Owen, who stood looking out the window. "Once Chris gets here, they're going to storm out of that kitchen and want flesh." Steven nodded in agreement.

Owen spun from the window. "Well, I already donated earlier, so the three of you can step up."

When the doorbell rang, Leena flew to the door to answer it.

Chris walked into the surprisingly colorful room and glanced around. Leena certainly liked bright colors. The couch and chairs were deep purple, the drapes were a rust shade, and the carpet was cream. Somehow, it worked. "Sorry I'm late, I had to speak with the police." He grinned at the women as they walked into the room. "So, do we offer our heads for the guillotine, or are we to receive lashes only?" He perched on the edge of the couch beside Dade.

Cora walked in and sat down. The look she sent Dade would have peeled paint off wood. "You knew I would see all of it if I'd touched that note, that blood, how they died and who did it..."

Dade stood up and was in front of her, glaring down at her before anyone could blink. "Yes, you would have felt it all, too, their pain, his madness. I wasn't going to stand by and let you go through that, Cora, so be as angry as you wish."

Cora stood up. They stood face to face glaring at each other silently.

Leena stepped forward. "I think we can all agree we wouldn't want to see Cora go through that. What we need to settle here is that you won't hide things, regardless of how insignificant, from us again."

Rachel dropped down in a chair to watch the show. "It's not fair, gentlemen. We're all involved. We were all there when Owen was burned."

Kasey stepped from behind Chris and touched his arm. "Do the police know anything?"

He shook his head. "They'll know more after the autopsy, Kase. They're going to send me a copy." At her puzzled look, he grinned. "Being a legal representative has a few perks. I know some of the right people."

Steven leaned forward, "I wouldn't mind reading that, because I have some questions of my own."

Rachel sat up in the chair and looked at Chris. "Have their families been notified?"

Chris nodded and stuck his hands in his pockets.

Dade let out a deep breath and stepped away from Cora. He looked over at Owen, who was silently watching Leena through it all. Dade sighed and turned toward Leena. "I think I should apologize about the note. When we saw how distraught Leena was when they came back to the cabin after finding those girls... well...." He looked around at everyone before turning back to Leena. "I don't think we've ever seen you anything but strong and steady, Lee." He offered her a weak smile. "I don't think I could ever see you like that again."

Leena looked around at everyone for a moment. "I'm sorry for overreacting. Seeing that note really affected me. It was like seeing them all over again."

Owen walked over and stood behind her, running his hands down her arms. Leena closed her eyes and took a breath. She could feel the tension leaving her body at his gentle touch.

"Oh, do me next, Owen. I need the tension sucked out of me, too," Rachel piped up.

Steven glared at Rachel for a moment, and then looked over at Owen. "Here we go again. Golden boy's getting all the attention."

When everyone laughed, Owen dropped his hands "I'm sure I would not get on anyone's good side if I walked around rubbing you women all the time."

Leena moved away from Owen and cleared her throat. "We have some snacks and drinks in the kitchen if anyone is interested." She turned and led the way into the kitchen.

She watched Chris finish his third plate before he looked around at everyone else, his expression said he knew more than he was saying. "Has anyone had any insights about this whole situation? The killer? Motive? Anything?"

Leena set her plate aside and studied him for a minute. "Well, if we can trust the note, I think we're all okay until

Solstice." She took a sip of water and waited to see if anyone spoke. "I'm going to talk to Gwen in a few days and see if they've decided about another gathering."

Kasey shrugged, "If I were them, I'd never do another event again. It can't be easy to know someone they let in did something like that."

Leena sighed, "People aren't always as they seem, Kasey. No one is going blame Justin or Gwen if they don't host another gathering."

"I agree," Chris said softly, "we can relax a bit until Solstice, but don't let your guard down completely. If anyone senses or feels anything that isn't right, get somewhere safe and contact the rest of us." There were several nods.

"Keep the gris-gris bags somewhere on your person when you're outside of the house at all times," Cora added quietly. "I'd like to wait a few days and try to see if I can feel where the killer is. On a mental level, not physically." Dade started to speak, and she held up her hand. "Nothing like before, just a quick peek-, Dade. I won't try anything alone either." She glanced over at Owen, who winced.

Leena watched Steven stand to look out the window. "I think we should meet after Chris gets the reports so we can all go over them. I second what he said about all of us being aware." He turned and looked at the women. "You four work together so obviously, day-to-day, you'll be fine. Do you ride to and from work together, ever?"

Rachel who had been very quiet up to that point nodded. "Cora picks me up, and Leena gives Kasey a lift most days."

"Good. I'm at the hospital surrounded by people most of the time. Chris is in an office building or the courthouse, so he's fairly safe there." Steven turned to Dade.

"I'm at construction sites most of the time or at the voodoo temple, so I'm always among people. I guess the only one who's alone most of the time is Owen."

Owen grinned, "Essentially, I'm alone in my townhouse, but with a top-notch security system. Don't worry, my laptop is fairly substantial and would knock anyone out."

Kasey groaned at his attempt at humor. "So, it's back to work tomorrow then?" She sighed. "My line better be functioning properly or someone will pay." She grinned at Leena, teasing her.

"Oh! I almost forgot, the new forklift is supposed to be in." Rachel jumped up excitedly and looked around at everyone.

"Great, more accident reports to file," Cora laughed and fell back against the arm of the chair.

"You women are all crazy, you know that?" Steven grinned. "Okay, I'm out of here. I have an early start at the hospital tomorrow, and they'll have me double-booked all day as punishment for taking a few days."

"I'm with you. I have to be in court at nine, and I have no idea what cases I'm pleading at this point." Chris stood and started picking up plates to take back to the kitchen.

"Do you want help with the dishes, Leena?" Kasey inquired as she picked up cups.

"No, it's fine, Kase. You go and get some rest before work tomorrow."

Cora walked over and picked up her jacket. "I'm sorry Beltane didn't work out the way we'd all hoped, but at least Owen found us and we had a few relaxing moments." She smiled at Owen.

Dade walked past her and patted her backside. "Wasn't all bad, my drum finally called your lips to mine." He grinned when she huffed out a breath.

"Will be the last time too, you..."

"Don't start, children," Chris said on his way back out of the kitchen.

They filed out the door, one after the other calling out good-byes until it was just Owen standing by the door. He pushed to close the door partway. "Still mad at me?"

Leena studied him for a moment and then shook her head. "No, you're forgiven... this time."

He grinned, "Forgiven enough to get away with stealing another kiss?"

"Owen, I don't think..."

"Just one kiss, beautiful Leena, nothing more." He touched her cheek in a gentle caress. "Send a man home with warm thoughts."

She felt her knees weaken at his words. Stepping closer, she placed her hand on his shoulder and lifted her face to his. "One kiss."

He didn't waste a second and pulled her tightly against him, sheltering her with his body from anyone seeing through the open door. His arm pulled her in as his hand held the back of her head. Owen wanted to seduce slowly and savor the gift of her kiss, but as soon as his mouth met hers, a fire ignited. Then a greed for more took over, and he kissed her deeply, forcing his way inside her mouth.

The way she responded to his need with a matching passion surprised him. *Where was the cool woman men were afraid to talk to?* Where her body was touching his, it was burning through their clothes.

Leena clung to him, not wanting to give more than one kiss, but wanting that one kiss to never end. His mouth led where her body wanted so much to follow. Her hands found their way to his hair and held on tightly, afraid he'd end it too soon. She moaned into his mouth and felt the shudder run the length of his body.

When a horn blared from outside, she jumped away from him so quickly she almost lost her footing.

Owen closed his eyes for a second, before he sent her a passion-filled look. "I'll see you in a few days. Lock up behind me." He touched her face gently, then stepped through the door.

Stepping down the steps she watched him look over into Dade's van to see Dade throw his head back and laugh as he pulled away.

Leena closed and locked the door, then leaned up against it. Well, that would keep the bad dreams out of her head tonight. She sighed and headed into the kitchen to clean up.

They'd paid for their sins.

He watched them dance long after the others had stopped. They bared their breasts and danced in erotic ways that let every man there know they needed to be punished.

They would have to be cleansed of those sins.

He had seen others dance like that before, but he hadn't been asked to punish them. Those had been pure of heart and led the wrong way, forced to do it to fit in with the sinners' beliefs.

He knew the ones that would find their salvation and redemption on their own, just as he knew the ones that would need his help getting there.

The men were not responsible for reacting those women, they couldn't help their weaknesses.

He knew it was always the women that lead the men into sins. Knew, they could be saved when all the sinners paid.

He wiped the polish down the handle of his knife again, cleansing any tainted blood from it the rain hadn't washed away.

He had done his duty and been a faithful servant, he would be rewarded for his service in the end.

His heart was pure, and his soul was clean.

He could rest for now, for he had been told when he had to cleanse the sinners again.

He had time to rest..

cⅿ€ **Chapter 7** ℈℈

Kasey climbed into the car beside Leena. "I was *almost* looking forward to all of us getting together tonight." She did up her seat belt. "If it wasn't to read an autopsy report, I would definitely look forward to it."

Leena laughed. "You just want to see Chris again. Really, Kase I don't know why you don't just tell the man how you feel."

Kasey sighed, "I've wanted to, and then I remember I'm a factory worker and he's a lawyer. Could you see me schmoozing at social events with him? So, Miss Wright, what line are you in?" She grinned. "Oh, Mister Successful, I'm in recycled paper, quite literally most days, when one of the machines jam."

Leena pulled out into the traffic. "I don't think it would matter to Chris if you worked at the dump, hun."

Kasey sat silent for a few minutes. "Maybe." She grinned, "I wanted to just climb right on top of his drum during the May Eve dance. That man sure can kiss." Then she leaned toward her. "I noticed Mr. Grey held your interest without much effort as well, Ms. Duncan."

Leena grinned at the windshield. "No, he has no problems doing that at all." She laughed. "When I was in school I watched him constantly, but I was five years younger, and didn't have breasts at that point, he never really noticed."

"Well, you should show him them now and see if he notices."

Leena's mouth gaped at the suggestion. "I don't think that's advisable. We're friends."

Kasey looked over at her. "I'm sure he'd rather be a lot more, Lee."

"Probably."

"He's not Tyler. He's not going to bang you around, Leena. I don't think he'd hurt a fly."

Leena looked over at her then back out the windshield again. "I know. I'm just not ready yet."

Kasey put her hands over her face. "Six years is more than long enough. You were a kid then. I was a kid. Tyler wasn't, but he was an asshole. Have you ever heard from him?"

Leena shook her head. "Not since the divorce. I'm hoping he moved to Bermuda and got lost there. Start watching the house numbers. We should almost be there."

She grinned. "At least meeting at Owen's, we'll get a peek at his house. I think the way a bachelor lives says a lot about the type of person he is."

Kasey shrugged, "That would make the Doc a slob then."

Leena leaned forward to look at the numbers. "Steven is so busy at the hospital, I'm sure he only comes home to drop his clothes on the floor, shower, sleep, and wake up to do it all again. We're here."

They all sat around the living room in silence. The pages Chris brought with him were being passed around one by one.

"So..." Leena took a deep breath before continuing. "Basically, these don't tell us much but how they were killed?"

Steven lowered the sheet. "They tell us a lot more than that, Leena. First, they weren't violated in any way. I don't know about you, but I feel better knowing there isn't a rapist running around. They also tell us the type of knife, but as almost everyone there would have some sort of athame or blade, isn't any help. The killer was left-handed, which helps a bit in narrowing down people." He took a drink from his cup and shook his head. "According to the decomposition of cells, we know that they died approximately when all of us were tucked up in our bunks."

"Please," Kasey said as she held up a hand. "I understand what you're saying, Doc, but please try to refrain from using words like decomposition."

Rachel nodded quickly in agreement.

"I say we take a break for a few minutes." Dade suggested as he got up and walked around the room.

Chris reached down to the woman resting her back against his chair. "You okay, Kase? Want a drink of something?" She shook her head, but didn't move away from his hand rubbing across her shoulders.

"Is this all you were sent, Chris?" Leena referred to the reports on the table.

Owen ran his hand over his face, and she scowled at him.

"There's more?"

Chris stopped rubbing Kasey's neck and looked over at her. "There are pictures, but I wasn't going to just drop them on the table. We men know what they looked like. We wrapped them up."

Rachel bolted up from the carpet. "I can't look at those. I can't see them and ever close my eyes again. I can't." She headed out of the room toward the kitchen. Steven was up and going after her before anyone else could move.

Dade stopped across the room from Cora and looked at her. "It won't help you find him by looking at morgue photos, Coralee."

Cora lowered her head. "I know, Dade." She looked over at him with a sad look in her eyes. "I can't look at them either." She glanced over at Leena.

"I'd like to think I could not fall apart, but I can't be certain. I still see them when I close my eyes sometimes." Owen stood up and walked toward Leena. She met his eyes. "But maybe I'll notice something."

Owen stopped in front of her. "Something the trained professionals doing the autopsy wouldn't notice? Come on, Leena." He towered over her. As he looked down, he knew from the sadness in her face he wasn't going to stand a chance against those eyes.

"I want to look, too," Kasey whispered. "Maybe I'll recognize them and remember someone that was hanging around them, or something." Chris's hand tightened on her shoulder for a moment. "Kase..."

"No, Chris, I need to. I'll probably regret it, but I need to." She turned to him and held out her hand.

Swearing under his breath, he reached into his briefcase. As he pulled them out, he looked around the room and hoped someone would stop this.

Kasey stood up and took the pictures from him. She held them against her chest and looked at Chris. He didn't say anything, but she could see in his eyes how much he didn't want her to look.

"Give them back, Kase. Put them away, Chris." Leena stood up and walked toward Kasey. She knew Kasey was trying to prove something to Chris, and she wouldn't be able to live with herself if she allowed Kasey to do it. Chris stood up and reached out slowly, taking the pictures from her hand, then pulled her small body against his and hugged her tightly. He just stood with her head burrowed in his chest, running his hand up and down her back.

With a tear running down her cheek, Leena turned and looked at Owen before quickly walking out of the room and hoping somewhere along the way she'd find a bathroom to hide in for a moment.

When she opened the bathroom door, she wasn't surprised to see Owen leaning against the wall across from it. "I'm fine."

He stepped over to her and pulled her gently to him and wrapped her tightly in his arms. "I know. I'm not, though." Owen lowered his face into her hair and inhaled. She still smelled of fresh leaves and rain. Leena wrapped her arms around him and rested her head against his chest. She knew he was doing better than her, but accepted the small lie because she needed to be held for a moment or two. "Are Kase and Rachel all right?"

Owen nodded and leaned her back to look at her. "They're okay." He brushed the hair back from her face, his palm lingering on her cheek. "I missed you these last few days," he whispered. "I thought about you too much." Her eyes held his.

"There you two are. We're thinking of healing circle."

Owen continued to hold her and turned to look at Dade, who was standing there with his hands in his pockets, giving him a big grin. "We're coming."

Leena pulled her arms from around him and grinned. "We better go."

"You aren't going to run from me forever."

"I'm not running, Owen. I'm just not ready for more."

"Fair enough." He put his arm around her and led her back toward the living room. "What is a healing circle, and am I going to get hurt?" he whispered.

She laughed and patted his cheek. "Don't worry. I'll protect you."

The eight sat in a circle on the living room floor, surrounding a plate, with small candles burning on it. Candles that had appeared from thin air, for as far as Owen knew, he didn't keep any in the house. To his right sat Leena. To his left, Cora, across from him was Chris, who held Rachel's and Kasey's hands.

Leena spoke quietly to Owen. "Hold each hand lightly in a comfortable position, and close your eyes. We'll do the rest."

He dropped his head down, relaxed, and closed his eyes. He could hear a few chanting softly. He startled and almost let go of Cora's hand when he felt heat go through his hand and up his arm to travel all the way through him, then down his other arm into the hand that Leena held. It didn't burn but was more of a warm energetic tingle.

Twice more this happened, each time he felt the same warm buzz spread through his body. He chanced opening his eyes to look at everyone. They all felt the tingle too, he could tell by their expressions. Looking at Leena, he noticed her eyes were open and she watched him, a smile on her face.

"Feel better?"

He grinned. "Much."

Dade looked down at Cora's hand in his own. "Do you need a ride home, Coralee?"

Cora pulled her hand from his and smiled sweetly. "I'm not relaxed enough to climb into that van with you, Dade Jones."

He smiled and leaned over to kiss her cheek. "Can't blame a man for trying."

Rachel burst out laughing, and everyone else followed suit.

"Wow, if you guys could bottle and sell that, you'd be rich!" Owen leaned back on his elbows. "I've never felt a buzz like this before in my life without the help of a mind-altering substance. It's boggling."

Steven grinned over at him as he stood up. "We save *that* for special occasions, and never when we've been drinking." He glanced down at his watch. "I have to go; I'm in serious need of sleep."

"So, what day are we meeting next week?" Rachel asked as she stood up and picked up the plate of candles.

"Wednesday work for everyone?" They all nodded at Steven as he put on his jacket. "Let me know the location." He headed out the door.

Cora stood up and walked to the kitchen with her cup.

Dade scrambled up after her.

Owen smiled up at Leena. It was as though Leena knew the look in his eyes and shook her head. "No."

"Aw, but why not?"

She laughed. "If you kissed me right now, I'd melt into a puddle at your feet." She stood up and walked out toward the kitchen.

Owen stood up and went after her. "I'm not seeing the problem with that, Lee..."

They both stopped in the doorway and looked at Cora wrapped around Dade in front of the dishwasher, their mouths devouring each other. He smirked. "That's easier to use if you open the door."

Leena smacked his arm as Dade and Cora jumped apart.

Dade threw a nasty look his way and then shrugged at Cora. "We'd have figured that out eventually."

Cora let out a deep breath. "No more healing circles around these men, Leena."

Leena grinned, "It's never had quite this effect before."

Walking back out of the kitchen, the four stopped and stared at Kasey and Chris. She lay with her head in his lap just looking at him, and he beamed down at her.

"Comfy?" Dade drawled slowly at them.

"Quite," Chris answered without looking away from Kasey.

"Okay, who spiked the energy with all this?" Cora demanded, waving her hands about at all the couples.

"I blame Leena," Dade whispered.

Leena spun around and looked at him. "I did not! It was one of you men." She smirked. "It is more interesting, though, isn't it?"

Rachel came back from the bathroom and looked around at everyone. "What have I missed now?"

They all burst out laughing.

"Obviously, there has to be an attraction for it to work," Kasey mused as she sat up.

"Attraction to what?" Rachel demanded in a plaintive tone.

Cora picked up her jacket. "I'll explain on the way home."

Chris stood up and picked up his briefcase. "I have to get going, too." He watched Kasey walk out of the room. "See you next week." He sauntered out.

Dade went out the door with no more than a wave.

"He's probably chasing after Cora." Owen turned when he heard the door down the hallway close. Then he turned back to Leena and grinned. "Come here, pretty Lee." He crooked his finger at her. "Come on, you're dying to know how we kiss with the way we're feeling." He pulled on her hand to drag her closer.

"Maybe." She looked down the hall. "But Kasey..."

"Isn't in the room right now." He pulled her up against him and gave her no room to object. Holding her waist tightly, he lowered his mouth to hers, and the heat hit him without warning. Gasping for breath, he reached up and fisted his hand in her hair and pulled her mouth up to his again.

Kissing him back, she moaned and leaned into him and grasped the front of his shirt as she stood on her toes to fit her body closer to his. She sighed when he lifted his mouth.

Owen rested his forehead against hers he smiled. "We need to be alone."

She ran her hands up and down his back, enjoying the feel of the muscle under his shirt. "Not yet."

"But soon," he whispered against her lips.

"I..." His lips brushing hers cut off what she wanted to say, and then he was stepping back as she heard Kasey walking down the hallway.

"Meet me this weekend, Leena?"

She started to shake her head.

"For research... I have pages and pages of questions, and I've got about twenty books of information, but I'm still lost." He gave her a coy smile. "Please?"

He looked like a little boy, with his hands in his pockets and a smile aimed at her. She glanced at Kasey, who stood silently in the doorway grinning.

"Come out on Sunday morning, and wear old clothes. I want to start on some yard work." She smiled. "We can help sort you out while my flower beds get their spring cleaning."

"I'll be there."

Kasey stepped into the room. "You should come to the factory sometime, Owen, and have a tour. Maybe you could help convince your publishers to use more recycled paper."

He laughed. "Convincing them my stories are worth printing, can be hard enough at times. But I'll see what I can do." He paused for a moment. "As long as you keep me clear of any path Rachel might be driving on."

Kasey laughed as she picked up her jacket. "She's been enjoying that new toy a little too much this week. I almost lost my foot a few times."

Leena paused to look at her. "I've been watching and *thought* she was behaving herself with it."

"Of course you would. She put a bit of a buzz on the contraption, and it slows when you look at it."

Leena's mouth dropped open. "Really? And what happened to our agreement to keep magic and work separate?"

Kasey grinned. "Oh, I don't know, *Miz Innocent*. I was pretty sure that frightfully windy day had a touch of magic. You know, the one that prevented the big boss from being able to hang out around the shipping docks to see how efficient the system was."

"Doc's right, you ladies are crazy." Owen stated.

Leena burst out laughing. "Well, the boss wouldn't know an efficient system if it bit him on the butt. I was saving him from Rachel covering him in some sort of rash. He grates on her nerves."

Owen sobered. "I really need to watch my step around you four."

"You're doing quite well." She waved a hand. "Accepting all of this. All of us."

He shrugged. "It's like living in one of my stories."

"Please, I've read your stories. The wizard one scared the breath out of me."

He grinned, "But the time travel one wasn't frightening."

Kasey jumped forward. "You wrote that? Oh, my gosh! I forgot that one. I can't believe it. I wore out two copies of that!" She straightened and clasped his hand. "I really, really need to pick your brain, Owen," she almost purred.

"You do?" He knew he looked puzzled.

"Kasey wants to write, is constantly writing." Leena smiled at Owen looking down at the small woman holding his hand. "She's just never gotten up the nerve to actually try and get published."

"What do you write, Kase?"

She dropped his hand. "Fiction, fluffy fiction compared to your stories. They're not very good, really..."

"E-mail me something, and I'll give it a read."

Kasey clasped her hand over her mouth. "Really?"

Owen grinned. "Really." He winked at Leena. "Maybe if I discover a bright new star, my publisher will get off my back. They want more from me, but I need time between books."

Kasey launched herself into his arms and almost climbed him.

He caught her and looked helplessly at Leena.

"Kase, get off Owen and say thank you."

Kasey jumped off him and blushed. "Sorry." She smiled up at him. "Thank you!"

He wandered over to the table and wrote on a piece of paper. "Just send a few chapters to me, and I'll read it." He handed her the paper. "Getting to that first acceptance is the hardest part."

Kasey moaned. "I know. They want a query, then synopsis, and the guidelines seem to be different for each, it's overwhelming. I don't have an agent, don't know where to even get one of those..."

Owen held up his hand. "Let me read what you're working on, and we'll go from there."

She smiled again and picked up her purse. "Thank you."

Leena shook her head. "Well, this has been an interesting night." She paused beside Owen. "Thank you, and I'll see you on Sunday."

He stuffed his hands in his pockets so he wouldn't touch her again, because he knew he wouldn't be able to stop. "I'll be there."

Chapter 8

"So, let me get this straight." Dade took another drink of his beer. "You're reading a story Kasey is writing. I always wondered what she was scribbling in those notebooks. And in the morning, you're going to play in Leena's flowerbeds?" He winked at Owen. "The ladies have accepted you with open arms, my friend."

Owen picked up his beer and sat back. "Open arms? I wish." He stared at the bottle in his hand. "Leena is going to drive me crazy, Dade. She'll wrap herself around me one moment, then she freezes and looks like a scared rabbit wanting to bolt the other way."

Dade sighed, "She didn't have a good marriage. Hell, she was still a kid when she married Tyler."

"Tyler Black? She married Tyler Black? Shit, he's older than us. What the hell was he doing chasing around someone her age?"

"You didn't see how Leena looked when she finished school, my friend."

"I see how she looks now." He took a long drink. "So, what happened?"

Dade sat looking at his beer for a few moments. "I don't know all the details. I do know you should be talking to her about it." He glanced up at him, "but, word is Tyler treated her much like your old man treated you." He watched Owen's hands tighten around the bottle.

"He bashed her around?"

Dade shrugged. "Don't know any details. They left town shortly after they got married...then, oh, about six years back, Leena came home and took over her parents' house. They're traveling all over now. I saw her a few days after she got back." He took a quick sip. "Her face looked like someone used it as a punching bag." He snarled, "Chris had to sit on me for weeks so I wouldn't go find the bastard."

Owen stood up and paced over to the fridge to grab more beers. "Has anyone seen him?" He threw the cap back toward the sink.

"Nope. When Cora told me she was working at the factory, I asked her to keep an eye out." Dade accepted the bottle and opened it. "Of course, then Cora and the girls hooked up with Leena. And the rest, as they say, is history...but Leena's never told any of us. I'm not even sure she knows what we do." He was silent for a few moments, lost in thought.

"Most of what we do know is little bits the girls have shared with us." He winked at Owen. "You've been accepted though, bro. Any time a man has gotten within a foot of Leena in the past, those three swarm like bees protecting their hive."

Owen paced in silence for a few minutes. "Fuck!" He stopped and looked down at his smirking friend. "You could have warned me that trying to get close to her was going to be as hard as climbing up a cliff."

Dade chuckled deeply. "I figured you'd find out soon enough. Besides, you've gotten closer to her than any man recently."

Owen sighed, "Yeah, close enough to burn." He grinned, "it's frustrating as hell."

Dade stood up and tapped his bottle against the one Owen held. "Welcome to our hell, my friend. The rest of us have been feeling the burn from those women for more years than we care to admit."

Owen laughed. "Well, at least I haven't had to chase her skirt for seven years, like the rest of you poor saps."

Dade dropped back down and scowled at him. "Has it been that long?" He shrugged. "Chris felt like a dirty old man the first time he caught sight of Kasey. I think she was twenty at the time, and looked like a cherub with those big green eyes. She wore her hair longer, and it kind of fell around her face. He got so drunk one time we had to drag his ass home to prevent him from declaring his love from the rooftop." He shook his head, grinning wide. "Funny as hell to see Mr. Perfect Lawyer lose it."

"And you with Cora?"

Dade frowned. "My family knew hers. You should remember the dark little pixie-faced girl running around at Ma's ceremonies." He waited for the look to appear on Owen's face that told him he remembered. "Yep, that was her. Imagine my shock when she came back from college and floated into the room at the temple." He took a suck on the bottle, then swallowed. "Couldn't play my drum worth a damn that night, had the priestess thinking I was sick or something."

Owen sat and shook his head. "What's the story with Doc? That man obviously pines after Rachel."

Dade nodded, "Yeah, those two ever hook up and they'll have three hundred kids. He's a pediatrician, loves his work, loves kids. Too brainy for me, though. He's younger, but he finished school way ahead of us." He waved his hand around. "Anyway, Rach came into the picture while he was away at school, and she's just as kid crazy as he is... spends every free second at the community center running programs." He grinned. "If Doc ever gets up the nerve, he's going to have to hang on tight. I don't think that one knows how to slow down."

Owen sat in silence for a few moments. "When the hell did we get old and pathetic, my friend?"

"Don't know, bro, *but* someday soon I have to get my hands on that voodoo witch. I haven't been able to really appreciate another female since she sauntered back into my world."

Owen set the bottle on the table. "I should go. Have to get my notes together so I know what I'm asking Leena tomorrow." He stood up and looked at the man staring blindly into the bottle in his hand. "I'll see you later."

"Yeah. Have patience, bro. That's the best I can offer."

Owen grinned as he headed to the door. "I've just become the most patient man in the world, *bro*."

Leena stared out the window, watching the rain fall as Owen's Jeep headed up the lane. "Figures." She hadn't wanted to be stuck inside with him, she felt safer outside.

She motioned him into the kitchen. "I was just making tea."

Owen grinned and carried a large bag into the kitchen. "Guess the weather decided your yard work could wait?"

"It would seem so." Setting the kettle on the stove, she turned and watched him pull book after book out of the bag and set them on the table. "You have been reading." She picked up a book and flipped through it. "Candle light spells?" She set it back down and looked at him. "Thinking of trying your hand at spells now, Owen?"

"No, I would just like to know what's going on around me when all of you start levitating objects and lighting flames."

Smiling, she turned to get the cups. "Well, I'm pretty sure you won't find much in those books that really will explain what's happening." She leaned back against the counter and looked at him. "I don't do those kinds of spells, but for questions along those lines, then you could ask Rachel, Kasey, or Chris. That's their sort of spells."

"And you and the Doc? What exactly is the sort of thing you two do?"

She crossed her arms over her chest and thought how to word it best. "Steven and I do elemental spells... of sorts. As long as it uses one of the elements..."

"Air, fire, water, and earth?"

"Yes, those. We can manipulate, or nudge and work with them to make things happen."

"You do know that's a bit amazing, don't you?" He grinned at her.

"I do and always feel a little rush after just from knowing I can do it."

Owen shook his head. "I still don't understand what it is I do..." He shrugged, "anyway, I'd like to get some more information about Beltane, its history, its meaning to you, that sort of thing to start."

She poured the tea. "All business today, aren't you?"

"Absolutely. The characters are starting to form in my head, so I really need to give them purpose and intent. I'm working on another story right now, but starting a few ideas for the next is always a good thing."

He watched her set the cup down carefully. Then he reached out and took her hand. "*And* if I give into this need I have to hold you, I'll never get my mind to focus properly again." He kissed her palm tenderly, then released her hand and flipped open his notebook.

As she held her palm with her other hand, she smirked at him. "Well, we can't have characters with no purpose." She sat down and sipped the hot tea.

He read over his notes for a few moments, then sighed. "Beltane has had many different purposes and meanings through the years. Steven filled me in on what used to take place on May Eve. I found that more than interesting, so I researched it and found out the Puritans made the maypole illegal in Sixteen Forty-Four..."

Leena nodded. "The Puritans were like everyone else, Owen. What they didn't understand, they feared... and, whatever they feared became illegal. Things haven't changed that much through the years, not really."

With his head down he wrote for a few minutes. "Tell me about Beltane, Leena. What does it mean to you?"

Sitting back, Leena smiled calmly. "I guess I don't celebrate the sabbat as most do. I celebrate nature and the stage it's at during that time. Mostly it is nice to just to be a part of a group," she shrugged as she continued, "to me, the spring is a rebirth. I love to watch the new plants break through and blossoms return. To see those bland colors of winter brighten to a hundred shades of green. Do you think any leaf is ever exactly the same color as another? They aren't. It's much the same as two people never having the exact same shade of skin." Pausing, she sipped her tea. "I wait through the blinding winter snow, the howling of the wind, the creaking of the cold branches to watch each spring again when life renews itself, when the sun teases the little plants to stretch and grow."

"That's beautiful, Lee." He grinned at her. "The way you see things. For spring, I've never gotten past the mud and rain, not enough to notice the beauty in it." He quickly jotted down a few things.

Feeling foolishly pleased at his words, she cleared her throat. "I forgot to ask if Kasey ever got up the nerve to send you her work."

He nodded while finishing a thought with his pen. "Yeah. She's got talent. With a bit of tweaking and polishing, I think she'll have something the editors would be happy to read." He lifted his head. "Will you stand in front of me to catch her before she actually climbs me when I tell her?"

She laughed, "I'll protect you." Getting up, she took a large pot from the fridge. "I have homemade soup for lunch." He grinned. "I'll put it on now to simmer until lunch time." She set it on the stove. "It's one of Cora's creations, so I can vouch that you'll love it."

"Cora cooks?"

"Like an angel. Why she works in an office when she should be in a kitchen sharing her talent, I'll never know."

She shrugged, "I guess it always goes back to what we should be doing or want to do, instead of what we do."

"What do you want to do, Leena?"

"What do you mean, Mr. Grey? I'm a great supervisor."

Owen clasped his hands on the table and studied her. "I'm sure you are, but that isn't what you really want to do, is it?"

Leena leaned back against the counter and looked at the floor. She began to shake her head. "No. Chasing people around a factory and soothing grouchy bosses are not at the top of my *To Do* list." She looked up at him. "I want... well, I do make clothes, rather fanciful outfits. I love taking a body and finding out what colors and shapes would look best on it."

Owen set his pen down and pushed back from the table. "Those sensual pieces of cloth the four of you wore on May Eve were made by you, weren't they?" She nodded. "Fanciful is an understatement, Lee. The four of you walking toward the circle looked like goddesses from Greek mythology. You glowed and practically floated across the ground." He grinned like he was remembering it. "You should go into business."

"And do what? The things I make aren't something any woman would just walk down the street wearing."

"So make specialty clothes. Costumes, themed weddings... fantasy." He winked at her.

Pursing her lips together Leena studied him. "It's an idea." She smiled, "thanks."

He stood up and came to stand in front of her, grasping her hands he lifted it to his lips. "You're really a romantic dreamer trapped in the wrong world, aren't you?"

She pulled her hand from his. "Dreams have ways of turning into nightmares very quickly, Owen." She moved away from the counter and collected the cups off the table.

"Tell me about it, Leena," he said quietly.

Leena busied herself by rinsing the cups to keep from having to look at him. "About what?"

Placing a gentle hand on her arm, Owen turned her. "Tell me about the dreams that turn into nightmares. About why you freeze every time I get too close." He reached over and tucked her hair behind her ear. "Trust me with it, pretty Aileena."

Her heart stopped, she stood froze and looked at him. *Did it show that much? Did the emotional scars stand out?* "I can't, Owen. I'm sure you wouldn't understand."

His hand rested lightly on her arm. "I'd like the chance to try." He studied her face for a few seconds. "Trust me." He could see the fear flashing in her eyes and wanted to close his arms around her and hide her from the world.

"Owen..." Her voice was trembling, "I really like you... I do, and I know you want to have sex..."

"Sex?" He placed his arms on the counter on either side of her. "I want to have sex with you? Is that why you think I'm here? To see if I can get you in bed?" His voice didn't raise above a whisper.

She didn't answer him. She just looked shocked at his words.

"Leena..." He had to get a grip on the way he was shaking. "If all I wanted was sex, I'd have had it by now." She clasped her hands nervously together and looked down at them. Gently, he lifted her chin and forced her eyes to meet his. "Yes, I want you. Any breathing man would, but if it were only for sex, you wouldn't keep my mind running in circles when I should be working. If I just wanted your body, thinking of you wouldn't make me want to slay dragons." He smiled. "I want to be your friend, first and foremost. I would cherish you as a lover...but I want inside your heart more than your body." A tear slipped out of the corner of her eye and rolled slowly down her cheek. Not wanting to scare her any more, he slowly leaned down and kissed the tear away; his lips lingered over its path. "Let me in a little, Leena, before I lose my mind," he whispered against her mouth.

Her heart trembled from his words, and her body from his touch. Not trusting her words, she wrapped her arms around his waist and rested her head against his chest lightly. She almost sighed when his big arms tightened around her and held her against him.

Owen just stood there, content to hold her. With his arms sheltering her from the world, she almost thought it possible to trust again. The man holding her wasn't like Tyler, she told herself. He said he'd cherish her, and a small part of her believed he meant it. She spoke against his chest. "I've never told anyone everything, Owen. I don't know if I can."

He gentled his hold on her. "Tell me what you feel comfortable with, Lee. I won't abuse your trust. I won't judge." She remained in his arms and rubbed her face slowly across his chest. He continued to hold her with ease, but every muscle she could feel was tense.

"Let's go in the living room and sit." She pulled back from him, ducked under his arm, and walked out of the room.

Leena was already on the couch with her knees pulled up to her chest and backed into the corner when he walked in.

He went to sit beside her, and she shook her head. "No, if you touch me when I try to tell you, I'll fall apart." She watched him sit in the chair a few feet away. He sprawled more than sat, but she could tell by the twitching muscle in his jaw he wasn't nearly as relaxed as his position indicated. She played with the fabric covering her knees. "Do you remember Tyler Black?"

"Yeah, he was an asshole when I knew him, though."

She put her head down, not sure if she could look in his eyes and tell him. "Well, he was a smooth asshole that knew all the right lines to charm his way into this young girl's heart. We were married just after I finished school." She glanced up and saw he wasn't shocked by her news. "He moved me away to the city, feeding my dreams of him becoming more successful in the city. He was to be a brilliant architect."

Pausing, she looked at her hands. "Things were good for a few months, as he found someone to take him under his wing and the long hours of work began. I was the young, naïve, dutiful wife and looked after our apartment and him." Looking over at Owen, he showed no emotion. "The more worn-out with work he became, his need for success drove him to work longer and harder but he was tired and... the more..." With an aching throat, she swallowed and began picking at the fabric on her knees again. "The rougher he became with me. I was young and didn't understand. He was always sorry afterward and very sweet and attentive for a few days." She hugged her knees tightly. "I was his pretty little showpiece for work, so he never marked me where anyone would see." She chanced a quick glance to see him sitting forward on the chair now with his hands tightly held together. His knuckles were white with restraint.

"He..." Her voice trembled. "When I got a job, you know, to help until he made it big, thinking maybe he wouldn't have to work so hard, he was mad that I wouldn't always be at the apartment waiting for him." Taking a deep breath, she willed herself to continue. "He put me in the hospital that time. He told the doctor some horrid lie about me being mugged and not remembering." She could see Owen's hands trembling where he held them tightly. She couldn't bring herself to look at his eyes. "When I was released, he pampered me, apologizing every day, buying me silly little things. I was scared to leave the apartment, afraid to make him angry again..." The tears rolled down her cheeks, but she continued before she fell completely apart. "He came home one night and was pretty drunk. He'd reached some milestone at the office, and wanted to go out and celebrate. I got dressed, and when I didn't wear what he wanted, he..." The tears wouldn't stop. "He just kept hitting me and hitting me. I was on the floor and could see his hand, but I couldn't stop him." The tears started to fall so hard she had to blink to focus. "I..."

"Oh, baby." Owen moved to her faster than he thought he could, scooping her up in his arms to cradle her against his chest. "It's okay." He rocked her gently and stroked his hand down her back. She was trembling in his arms so hard he didn't think his heart was going to make it. With each sob, he shook harder with rage for a man who would treat her the way Tyler had. "Shhh," he whispered to her, fully aware she was so lost in her pain she wouldn't hear.

"S-sorry," she sniffled into his chest.

"You have nothing to be sorry for, Leena. *Nothing.*" He soothed her with his words. "It wasn't your fault, baby. People like that don't need a reason. They're lost in their own sick minds." He rocked her gently, not wanting to ever let her go.

"I ran home and...and hid." She gasped to catch her breath.

"You did what you had to do to get away. No one can blame you." He forced out a ragged breath. Owen tensed when a thought entered his head, and he didn't know if he wanted to know the answer, but it was a question he had to ask, more for himself than anything. "Baby, did he ever..." How did a man ask the woman shaking in his arms a question like this? "Did he hurt you sexually?" Holding his breath, he waited. She trembled harder and just nodded against his chest, unable to look at him. "Fucking bastard should be strung up by his balls," he uttered quietly under his breath

Leena clung to him, how he held her so gently she didn't know. He was soothing her when she could feel the rage shaking inside him. She wanted him to hold her. No one had ever been there to hold her. To tell her it was going to be all right. She hiccupped and tightened her hold, pushing her face into the warmth of him.

Owen sat there rocking her, uncertain what words he should use, or if he should use any. "Baby, have you ever wondered why I lit out of here the day school let out?" He didn't need her to reply. He just wanted to fill the tense silence with soft-spoken words and continued. "My mom told me to go and go quickly." He stroked a hand down her hair. She had shared her worst with him, so if he told her some of his story, maybe they'd be on even ground. "My old man made me his own personal punching bag for most of my childhood, and I practically lived at Dade's. His mom would rub stinky voodoo magic ointments all over my bruises."

Gasping, she lifted her tear-stained face to his. "You were just a child..."

Owen touched her cheek. "No, I was a victim, just as you were, and I ran and hid, too." He rubbed his thumb over her cheek to remove any tears. "I didn't come back until I knew he was dead. Unfortunately, my mom died shortly after." He swallowed the lump in his throat. "I think she only lived long enough to make sure I was safe from him. *But* you and I, we were both victims, baby... victims who did what they had to do to survive." He stroked his hand down her hair and glanced towards the kitchen before he looked back into her eyes and smiled. "As much as I don't want to let go of you, I really have to. Cora's soup is calling me."

"The soup!" Leena jumped up from his lap so quickly she almost teetered over on her flight to the kitchen.

Throughout the afternoon, Owen picked her brain about ideas for his story and characters; what sounded feasible and what didn't. He had to shake himself more than once to keep his mind on research and off her lips, or from reaching out to touch her.

She had let him in, and he didn't want to crowd her. She seemed more relaxed with him now, and he didn't want to change that either.

It was hard to not rush when she was sitting on the floor with a few books beside her, chewing her bottom lip over something she was reading. He wanted to chew that lip, wanted to suck on it. Sighing, he tossed the notebook onto the couch beside him and sat up.

"What?" Leena looked at his notebook then at him puzzled. "Out of ideas already?"

Owen dropped to his knees on the floor and moved toward her. "Oh, I have lots of ideas." She held the book in front of her chest, eyes wide. "None of which have anything to do with anything but you." She shook her head at him. "You sit there looking all focused and sexy as hell, and my brain is having a meltdown." He pulled the book from her hands and tossed it to the side. She bit her lip again, looking nervous. "I need a taste." His eyes stayed on her mouth. "A small taste to feed a starving man, pretty Lee." He dragged her onto his lap.

She struggled, but was grinning. "Your story."

He lowered his mouth to hers. "To hell with the story."

She leaned back "but your publisher..."

Adjusting his hold, he pulled her closer. "To hell with my publisher."

"But..."

"Kiss me, Lee." She stopped her struggle and looked at him. "Take one step toward me, so to speak, instead of away and kiss me."

The softness of his voice melted her bones. She looked at his mouth. He really had very kissable lips.

"One kiss." He was determined to let her come to him this time.

Placing her hands on his cheeks, Leena slowly raised her mouth to his and gently brushed her lips over his. His hand clenched in her hair, but he didn't try to pull her closer. Wanting more, she brushed his mouth again, and when he opened his lips, she hesitantly dipped her tongue into his mouth and flicked it against his.

Owen moved his hand to gently rest on her waist, but he didn't pull her closer. Running her one hand to his hair, she pulled his mouth closer to hers and turned her head to kiss him completely. He groaned in his throat as his lips joined with hers, and he kissed her back with all the heat she'd come to expect from him.

Without breaking the kiss, he leaned slowly back pulling her head gently so that she followed him down to the floor. Still kissing him with urgency, she lay sprawled on him.

When she started to pull away, he growled huskily in his throat. "I won't touch you baby, won't do anything you don't want, but please don't stop."

His throaty pleading caused her pulse to leap. "I want to kiss you, but it scares me." She could feel him trembling from the exertion of controlling himself. She sat up on him and looked down into his passion-darkened eyes.

"Tell me what to do, Leena," he whispered. "What do you need me to do?"

Leena looked down at him and could see how much he wanted her. She could feel the hardness of him under her. Her own insides were trembling with a need she didn't understand. She reached slowly and pulled his hands from her waist and raised his hands over his head. Slowly leaning over him again she whispered against his mouth. "Just don't touch me yet, don't make me feel trapped."

He flicked his tongue against her lips. "Whatever you need." Lifting his head, he kissed her hard. "Kiss me, Leena. Touch me." His arms were shaking above his head, but he seemed determined to do what she asked.

When her mouth touched his neck, he hissed out a breath. Her lips tasted his skin, and her tongue flicked over it. Her hands traveled down his arms from the wrists she'd held. As her hands moved over his chest she could feel him shaking, but he didn't make a move to touch her.

She could feel the heat through their jeans, where she lightly sat against him. Owen turned his head, and his mouth sought hers again. His tongue explored the dark wetness inside. She moaned into his mouth, and his hands tapped against the floor to keep from touching her.

Leena could feel his muscles bunching as he fought to not touch her. She ran her hands over his chest and back up to hold his head as she kissed him. Her legs began to tremble from holding her weight, or from the weakness his kisses were causing, she wasn't sure. When he lifted his hips to push against her, the breath rushed out of her from the intimate contact.

Feeling encouraged by his responses, she slid over and stretched out beside him, stroking her hand down his chest and over his stomach. His muscles tensed under her exploration, his breath hissed out of his lips. She leaned over and brushed her lips against his neck. When she ran her tongue along his ear, he leaned into her mouth, completely enjoying the contact.

"Hold me, Owen," she whispered next to his ear.

In a slow movement, he was on his side in front of her, his hand gradually moving up to her hip to rest on the small of her back—giving her time to object before he settled it there. He leaned on one elbow and slid his arm under her neck, pulling her face closer for a kiss, he distracted her with his lips moving gently over her neck as he fit her more tightly against him. Her arm grasped his head tightly to her skin.

She gasped as his lips brushed over her neck. Slipping her hand down his back, she explored the muscles there; she could feel him trembling. His hand on her back tightened and pulled her firmly against his length; she relaxed and let herself feel the heat from his body.

His mouth devoured her neck. She couldn't stop the moan from escaping from her lips as she let her head fall back and accepted his passion.

"Leena." He gasped against her neck, then lifted his head and sought her mouth again. He was shaking as he held her. "Baby," he whispered against her lips. "You've got me shaking like a schoolboy." He kissed her again and slid his leg between hers.

He moved his hand around to her waist, ran his hand up her rib cage, then he stopped holding his hand still. She loved that he gave her time to adjust. When she nuzzled into his neck and gently nipped against the skin, he growled and threw his head back.

Running his hand back down her hip, he kneaded her ass in his big hand and rocked her firmly against his thigh. She bit into his neck when he moved her gently against his leg, creating friction between hers. She hissed out a breathed and rolled her head back. Finding her mouth quickly, he kissed her frantically while rocking her into him. Moving her hand, she ran it over his hip of his jeans and for just a moment she wished he didn't have them on.

The phone ringing brought her back to reality in a flash.

She tensed immediately. "Ignore it," he growled into her throat. Her breathing was as ragged as his. Her whole body throbbed from his touch. It rang a third time, then she heard the voice on the machine. "Lee, it's Cora. Pick up... Okay, just wondered how the gardening in the rain with that big, sexy man went and if my soup was okay. Call me later." She dropped her hand from Owen's side and leaned onto her back, fighting to bring her breathing back under control. "Sorry."

Owen continued nuzzling her neck. "Her timing sucks." He let out a slow breath, "but I'll forgive her because she called me a big sexy man and her soup filled my stomach."

He brought her chin up so he could look in her eyes. His heart stopped when he saw how foggy with lust they were. He leaned down to kiss her lips gently and let his mouth linger there. He didn't want to let her get up. He didn't want to stop. But she just lay silently there beside him and looked into his eyes. "Are you okay?"

Leena smiled up into his clouded eyes. "Mmm, yes," she replied with a rough whisper. "Just enjoying how you've made me feel." She licked swollen lips. "It's been a long time since I've had this sensation."

He groaned and dropped his forehead down on hers. "Don't say things like that to me when you're practically under me looking all soft and wanting." He grinned, "I could make you feel more, if given the chance." Tenderly, he nibbled on her bottom lip. She didn't tense, so he let his mouth wander to her neck and nipped it gently with his teeth, then let his tongue take the sting away. She sighed and ran her hand up and down his arm. He kissed his way down her neck to her collarbone, slowly lingering over her skin. "You're taking advantage of how good I feel, Mr. Grey."

Owen smiled against her skin. "I'm certainly trying, Ms. Duncan." He ran his tongue along the edge of her shirt collar, from one side to the other, slowly licking his way along. The hand that had rested against her rib cage began to run down over her stomach to lightly grasp her hip. "I could make you feel so good, Aileena," he whispered against her neck.

Leena ran her hand up his arm to cradle his head into her. "You already have. I don't think I'm ready for more."

Lifting his head, Owen looked down at her quietly for a moment then let out a slow breath. "I should go." He smiled at her, "if I don't, I will want to convince you to change your mind." He kissed her gently, then stood up and pulled her to her feet. Quickly, he gathered up the books and his notes then turned to see her standing there watching him.

"Are you upset, Owen?"

Owen stopped what he was doing and set down the case. Walking over to her, he pulled her into his arms. "No, I'm not upset." He smiled. "I am, however, a man, and right now this man would like to devour you." He looked down as if to show her the spot, "and that would go against everything I said to you earlier." She smiled almost shyly at him. He hugged her to him. "I really have to go clear my head." He groaned and squeezed her. "It's so filled with you right now." He let out a long breath, "Yeah, I have to go now."

She reached up and kissed his mouth. "So, you're still going to steal kisses?"

"As many as I can." To prove it, he grabbed her and kissed her so hard she melted against him. "I'll see you at the meeting."

Chapter 9

Cora shut the door to her office and ran around the corner to Leena's office. She dumped the armful of papers on her desk. "You're sure you don't mind? I can stay and finish."

Leena shook her head. "Go. I know you want to whip up something scrumptious to dazzle us for the meeting."

"I still don't know what possessed me to suggest my apartment. Really, where am I going to put everyone?"

"It's not that small, Cora." She watched her friend wringing her hands together. "Tell you what, go grab Kasey as soon as the line shuts down, then pull Rach off that damn forklift. Get them to help you move some stuff around to make more space." She nodded to the pile on the desk. "I'll put the packs together for the tours tomorrow. How many?"

Cora dropped another sheet on her desk. "Three classes of fifth-grade kids. The head count is there, too." She smiled, "You are a gem, you know that?"

"Sure, sure... just make me something sweet and sinful for later."

"Absolutely, and I'll even stop bugging you for details on your gardening with Owen for this."

"Small sacrifice. Go!" Leena sat down and picked up the neatly separated pages. She loved the tour days, well, the children really. It gave her the chance to astonish them with all the facts she'd learned about the recycling industry to get the job. Sighing, she stapled the first of many packets together.

It didn't take quite as long as she'd anticipated to finish up her paperwork and get the handouts ready for the next day. She still had plenty of time to get to Cora's. Digging in her purse for her keys, she smiled, realizing she hadn't seen Owen since Sunday. He'd sent her several text messages though, each hinting at wanting to come see her. She was looking forward to seeing him, that was new.

When she reached her car, she glanced up. The parking lot was empty except for her car and one other. She was going to wave when she realized everyone was already gone for the night. The person was just a shadow in the parked car. The face wasn't visible. A shiver ran up her spine and her heart was pounding as she opened the door to her car.

She immediately put the key in the ignition and started the car, quickly locking the door and reaching for her purse. As she pulled out of the parking lot, she dug in it for her phone. Glancing back, she saw she was being followed. She hit call. Cora answered. "Cor, someone's following me from the plant."

"Who?"

"I don't know, but I was the last one there. I made sure before I locked up."

"Don't panic, Lee. I'm going to put out an all-call to the group and see who's closest. Ah, keep driving, and don't stop for any reason."

"I won't." Leena's hand was shaking on the steering wheel. Glancing in her mirror, she saw the dark car closing the distance between them. When her phone buzzed in her hand, she almost dropped it as she fumbled to flip it open.

"Leena, it's Dade. I'm five minutes away from the factory. Tell me where you are."

"Dade." His name seemed like a talisman. "Um..." she glanced around, "I just went past that old warehouse where they used to store the railway equipment."

"Got it. I'll be coming up behind you in a few minutes. Just keep going. What's the car look like that's following you?"

"It's a dark.... blue... ah... some sort of Pontiac I think."

"Okay, honey, don't panic. I'll be there soon."

"Dade?"

"Ya."

"Just stay on the phone until I see you."

"I'll put you on speaker so I can hear you if you need to tell me any dark secrets, honey."

"Okay." She gripped the steering wheel so hard her knuckles were white and glanced in her mirror again. "I can see you coming over the hill."

"Well, I'm your white knight today," he laughed. "You're doing fine. I'm going to try to get the plate number, and then I'll pull in behind you."

"Okay, I'm going to hang up and call Cora. She'll be frantic."

"Sounds good, Lee. Just keep heading to her place even if I stop."

"But..."

"Just do it, okay?"

"Yes." She flipped the phone closed then opened it again and dialed Cora.

"Lee?"

"It's me. Dade is pulling in behind me in front of the other car now. Cor, I've never been so scared in my life."

"Just get here. Everyone else is starting to arrive."

"Okay, we're about fifteen minutes away now, maybe less with Dade's driving." Her voice was shaking.

"Why don't you stop and get a ride with him?"

"He told me to keep going even if he stopped."

"What? I'll beat that man upside the brain if he tries something stupid."

"I don't think he will, Cora." She glanced in her mirror to see him following close behind her. "He's right on my bumper now; I'll see you shortly."

"Okay. Be safe."

Leena was still shaking when they pulled up outside Cora's apartment building. She parked and got out, knees shaking, her cell phone still clutched in her hand and leaned against her car to steady herself.

Dade walked up beside her placed a calming hand on her shoulder. "You did fine. Bastard followed us until about two blocks back." He held up his hand with a piece of paper in it. "I got the plate; we'll give it to Chris." He sneered. "The windows were too dark to see who was behind the wheel."

"Thank you." She took a breath and pushed herself away from the car. As they started to walk toward the entrance, Owen flew out the door running toward her as his eyes were looking over every inch. She took two steps and launched herself into his arms. She had never felt safer in her life than she did right now, surrounded by his big arms.

"Are you okay, baby?"

She nodded against his chest. Owen stroked his hand down her hair. "Let's go inside and get you a drink." He sheltered her under his arm and started walking her to the door Dade held open.

Dade raised his eyebrows at Owen and smirked at the woman all but hidden in his arm when they walked past. "Got the plate number."

"Good."

"Smart lady you're holding onto right now, my friend. Most would have panicked, but not Leena. She was driving at one hell of a clip heading straight here when I broke every speed record trying to catch up to her."

Owen kissed the top of her head. "I owe you one. Chris almost had to hold me down so I didn't take off when I got here."

They didn't make it all the way in before Cora was pulling Leena out of his arms and hugging her, then Rachel and Kasey, too. "It's all our fault. We shouldn't have just left you there alone." Cora hugged her again.

"I told you to go. It's no one's fault. Dade got the plate. We're here. Everything is fine." She didn't feel fine though, still shaking, she watched Dade hand Chris a scrap of paper. Chris took his cell phone out of his pocket then walked down the hallway. Raising her hands at everyone surrounding her, Leena took a quick breath, "I just need a minute, please." She walked into the kitchen.

Owen was right behind her. "You want some tea, or something stronger?"

"Stronger."

"I'll go see what Cora has."

He was back in less than a minute with two bottles in his hands. "Wine or vodka?" Leena pointed to the wine. Nodding, he set the bottles down and searched for a glass.

He poured her some and handed it to her with a shaking hand.

Leaning back against the counter, she took a gulp and let the burn distract her. Owen stood there with his hands in his pockets watching her, his eyes roaming over her continuously. Setting the glass down, she stepped over to him and wrapped her arms around his waist. She smiled when his arms went around her immediately.

"My heart stopped when Cora sent that message, baby. I've never been so scared."

She could feel him shaking. "I'm okay now. It really threw me when I looked up and saw him just sitting there looking at me." She leaned back and looked up into Owen's eyes. "Before that, I was pretty excited about seeing you tonight."

He breathed a sigh of relief. "Yeah?" He kissed the tip of her nose. "Miss me a little then?"

She shrugged. "A little."

Owen grinned then leaned down to kiss her long and hard. She needed to feel his body close to hers.

"I really hate to break this up, but everyone else is still out here pacing."

Leena turned in his arms to see Cora standing there with a grin on her face looking very relieved. "We'll come out. I feel fine now."

"I wonder why. Must be my good wine." Cora smirked at Owen.

"Cora, I will be your slave for eternity if you would come and cook for me every day for the rest of our lives." Steven winked at her.

"Not a chance, Doc. With the hours you keep, everything would go to waste." Cora laughed.

Leena cleared her throat. "With my interesting drive, I almost forgot. I spoke to Gwen and Justin last night."

Everyone turned and looked at her.

"What are they planning on doing, Leena?" Rachel mumbled, in between bites.

"They're still planning a Solstice gathering. They are going to keep it smaller than normal, and keep it to those we all know, which will be hard."

Cora sat forward. "How are they dealing with everything from Beltane?"

Leena set her glass down. "Gwen is still pretty upset. The police have encouraged them to have the next one. Apparently, they're going to try to get someone in to keep an eye on things." She paused and looked down at her plate for a moment. "Justin has the idea that if they make up a story to warn attendees of a loose animal, he can encourage everyone to travel around in small groups instead of ones or twos. I told him it might work." Leena looked around the room at each person individually trying to gauge their reactions. "They asked if we would still attend. I told them I would, and was pretty sure the rest of us would support them." She held her breath waiting for their replies.

Chris spoke first. "As long as we stick together like we did at Beltane, I don't see a problem."

"Maybe we could request cabins closer to each other as well," Steven suggested.

Everyone nodded, and Leena smiled. "Good, I'll let them know to expect eight with two cabins side by side. The location is still unknown, but I'll get it as soon as they know it."

Steven stood up and looked around at everyone. "That's settled. I'm looking for volunteers, people."

Dade groaned. "No hospital stuff, please."

Steven grinned. "No. I've been asked to help with a children's charity fair in two weeks. It's only an hour away, and only one day of your time. I need volunteers to run grills and games."

Rachel put up her hand. "I'm in."

Kasey giggled. "Oh, me too."

Leena smiled. "Me too."

Cora put up her hand. "Put me behind a grill."

Dade threw a napkin at Steven. "You know that we now have to go to keep an eye on everyone and keep us all together."

Steven sat down and nodded. "Yep. Hoped it would work out that way. Excellent! Seven volunteers."

"How many kids, Doc?" Rachel asked, bouncing slightly in her chair.

He grinned just for her. "Last count was around a hundred and fifty."

Chris groaned and put his head in his hands just as his phone rang. As he pulled it from his pocket, he was still glaring at Steven. He flipped it open. "Larkin." He nodded. "Let me grab a pen." Cora jumped up and grabbed a pen and paper and handed it to him. "Yeah, okay, where? Did you run that? Can you? Appreciate it." He flipped the phone closed and rubbed his jaw as he looked at what he'd written.

Owen sat up from his sprawled position. "That the car's info?"

Chris nodded. "Yes, but, unfortunately, it's registered to a corporation three hours from here." He handed the paper to Leena. "You ever heard of this place?" She looked at it and shook her head, then handed it to Owen.

When the paper came back around to Chris he tucked it in his pocket. "I'll do some checking on the corporation, and I've got a buddy who's going to look deeper into the records for the car."

Dade got up and strolled over to Cora. Without giving her warning he leaned over and kissed her cheek softly. "Amazing food as always, Coralee." She smiled at him and bowed her head. Then he turned back to everyone else. "No more being caught alone." He looked at each woman there for a moment. "If you need to be somewhere or go somewhere, there are seven others. Call around and see who's doing what." He placed his hand over his chest. "My heart can't take another night like tonight." He glanced at Leena when he said that. Then he looked at Owen, he didn't need to say anything out loud, he understood what he was saying loud and clear.

Cora stood up. "I would really like to see if I can get a look. I haven't felt anything since we left Beltane, but I'd like to try to see. Sometimes I'll get little hints and signs. It might help lead us in the right direction." She glanced at Dade. "Then we could maybe point the police in the right direction. Gwen and Justin could help us with that." He shoved his hands in his pockets and looked at her. "I need to try, Dade, please," she whispered.

Dade let out a slow breath and looked around. "Only if everyone agrees. You'll have more protection than last time."

"Oh, yes!" Rachel jumped up and grabbed her bag from the corner. She started pulling out big candles and setting them beside her.

Chris laughed. "I think we were set up." Kasey walked past him smiling and patted his cheek. "Definitely set up." He watched Leena and Cora drag a round copper table from the corner toward the middle of the room. "So, what's the game plan?"

Kasey smiled at Chris as she came out of the kitchen with bowls. "Could you roll up the carpet and move the chairs back?"

Leena walked by Owen and pulled his sleeve. "I could use your muscle."

He flexed. "My muscle is yours anytime you want it." He followed her to a closet. She filled his arms with three-foot iron candelabra. When his arms were full, he turned to go back into the living room.

Leena rubbed her hand over his butt and grinned at him as he spun back around. "Does that go with the muscle?"

Owen groaned. "You would wait until my arms are full. But, yes, that and every other part goes with it." He leaned over and kissed her quickly, then headed off with his armload of supplies.

Cora came out of her bedroom in a white gown carrying a small drum covered in animal skin. She offered it to Dade.

"Your grandfather's?" Dade asked softly. Cora nodded. He took it and pulled her closer to kiss her gently. "I'm honored."

When Steven pulled the drapes closed, he went to stand beside Leena. "A wall of air?"

Leena thought for a moment and nodded. "Solid one, but not moving. Cora will get grumpy if we blew everything around the apartment." Steven nodded and went to take his place across from her.

Owen watched everyone setting up, and looked at Dade. "Same as last time?" Dade nodded as he rubbed his hand over the top of the drum. He watched Rachel as she placed a white candle on each stand he'd carried. Chris went along behind her and mumbled something until each wick burst into flame.

Dade sat on the floor across from Cora and nodded to Leena. Not wanting to miss his cue if he was needed, Owen went and stood a few feet behind Cora and watched. When

Leena and Steven turned away from everyone, he could have sworn it got brighter inside the circle. The candles seemed to be reflecting off the wall of air that was now surrounding them.

Kasey bent down and lit four candles sitting on the copper table as Dade began to softly drum. When Cora stepped up to the copper table, she began chanting in time to the drumming.

Chris raised his hand over the candles and closed his eyes. The four flames joined together, becoming one large flame. Owen was careful to remain silent and remember everything.

Swaying gently, Cora leaned over the flames and held her hands out to the sides. She spoke so softly he couldn't hear the words. He glanced at Dade, who had his eyes open this time, staring intently at Cora. His lips were moving in a silent chant. Cora's whole body jerked, but she continued to sway.

Not sure if he should touch her, Owen stepped closer and held his hands a few inches from her back, ready if he was needed.

Kasey let go of Chris's hand and stepped up to drop something onto the flames. They rose higher and sparked, broadening the width of the flames' radius by almost a foot.

Cora faltered in the rhythm of her swaying. Catching Dade looking at him, Owen gently placed his hands against her back, careful not to interrupt her movement. He stared into the flames over her shoulder and saw flashes of what looked like metal, a knife. Focusing harder, so he'd remember everything that was visible to him. It had, he thought, a light wood handle with a cross burned into it.

Cora jerked again and leaned heavier against his hands.

He looked over to Dade, who shook his head slightly. They would continue. Owen looked into the flames again. He clearly saw a hand on a Bible as if it were in the room with them. On the hand was a ring with a blue stone. She jerked again, hissing out a breath.

"Enough!" Dade boomed then looked to Owen as he stopped the drumming.

At his words, Cora slumped back against him, but she was taking deep breaths and recovering much faster than the last time he'd had to catch her. As she straightened away from him, Chris moved in to calm the flames and extinguish the candles, never actually touching anything.

As soon as the flames were gone, Steven and Leena brought their hands up toward the ceiling, then slowly lowered them as if they were pushing the something to the floor.

"Stay inside the outer circle of candles and sit," Kasey said quietly.

Owen stepped over to Leena and pulled her down to the floor beside him by her hand.

"What was seen?" Rachel asked when everyone was finally sitting.

Cora put up her hand and then looked at Owen. "How much do you see when you touch me?"

He shook his head. "I don't know. It's all a bunch of pretty flames until I touched you, then it's like a slide show. I don't know how much of it I picked up, though."

Kasey pushed a notebook over to him. "Write it out before it's gone."

Nodding, Owen picked up the pen.

Cora turned back to Dade. "As soon as Owen touches me, it amplifies what I see. If it was jumbled before, it clears when he touches me."

Owen frowned, "so, you saw it, too?"

Dade was running his hand up and down Cora's back. "He probably draws any unnecessary emotion you're feeling at that time away, which clears your mind to accept the vision. Ma used to have a friend that could do the same for her."

"Of course," Cora smiled, "I'd forgotten." She let out a long breath. "Well, we saw a knife. It was clean and shining. The handle was pale or at least light wood, and a cross was..."

She turned to Owen, "would you say burned into it or carved?"

Owen tried to picture it. "Pretty sure it was burned."

"Yes, I thought so, too." She took the cup Chris offered her. "There was a hand on a Bible, Gideon's, if I'm not mistaken, and on the hand was a ring of silver with a blue stone..."

"A sapphire blue or turquoise blue?" Kasey asked.

"It was kind of a swirled blue. Not the ones you mentioned, kind of flat and it was on the left hand, middle finger."

Owen quickly sketched the ring and then slid the notebook over toward her. "That's what I saw."

Cora picked up the book and looked down drawing. "Exactly that." She passed the book to Kasey.

Kasey studied it. "The swirl kind of reminds me of tourmaline, but without color, it's hard to say." She glanced at Owen, then Cora. "I can e-mail you a few pictures of stones similar to this and you can tell us if any match." They both nodded. "I think we can safely put out the candles now," Chris suggested.

"Allow me." Leena smiled and waved her hand in a big, arching circle.

The candles went out one after the other, and then Owen felt a gentle breeze tickle the back of his neck. Grinning, he looked at Leena and she smiled innocently back at him. "Okay then, who lives closest to Leena?"

Kasey stuck up her hand. He shook his head. "That doesn't work if she's giving you a ride home."

Everyone realized where he was going. "Okay then, I'll follow Kasey and Leena tonight. I'm the only one that doesn't have to actually get up and leave the house to work in the morning."

"Yeah," Rachel agreed. "We need to have these meetings on nights when I don't have to get up early or during a day on the weekend."

"A Sunday brunch?" Chris mused.

Kasey laughed. "Yeah, we could all bring something for potluck."

Steven shrugged. "Well, I'll get Cora to bring my contribution then." He winked at her. "All I'm good at is programming the microwave." Then got up to gather up the candles.

Cora grinned. "No problem. When and where?"

Chris raised his hand. "Guess it's my turn next."

Kasey giggled. "We'll be brunching in the *refined* neighborhood of Russle."

Rachel rolled her eyes. "Gee, do new jeans or old jeans go with your tapestries, Chris?"

Chris smirked and tossed up his hands in defeat. "Come dressed in your ritual robes and pointy hat if you must."

"Did he just call me a witch?" Rachel's mouth dropped open.

"Christopher Larkin…you did not." Kasey stood with her hands on her hips and glared at him.

"I'd do it again to get a rise out of you, fierce little thing that you are." Chris laughed at her.

Dade swallowed a grin. "Brave man."

Leena raised a hand. "Enough, children. I have to get going. I'm about ready to drop where I sit."

Cora nodded at Leena's statement.

Kasey dropped her head and closed her eyes, and everyone stared at her until Chris yelped.

"Hey!" Chris was rubbing his stomach. "Sneaky witch punched me in the gut. I think I'm in love." He grinned weakly at her.

"Poor baby," Kasey said. "You could get Owen to rub it better."

He threw his head back and laughed. "I'll take the pain, thanks."

Owen shook his head. "We need to go before this gets worse." He glanced at Leena. "Get your sneaky friend in the car, Lee." She nodded and stood up, looking at Cora. "Do you need a hand putting your place back in order?"

Rachel stood up. "I'll stay and give her a hand."

Chris walked over to kiss Kasey on the cheek. "I'll hang around and give Rach a lift home when you're done." He rubbed a hand over Kasey's spiked head. "I'll see you for brunch, sneaky witch."

Kasey smiled. "I'll be there."

Leena stood at her car as he pulled up behind her. She walked over as he climbed out. She smiled. "I'd ask you in, but I have school tours all day tomorrow..."

"I know. Cora told me why you stayed late." He pulled her into his arms and held her. "If I come in, I doubt I'd leave tonight, and I don't want you drooping tomorrow while you're wrangling kids." He kissed the top of her head and then lifted her chin to look at her. "Call me if you need to."

She nodded. "Are you going to steal a kiss before you go?"

"I think you're beginning to enjoy that." His lips hovered over hers for a moment.

"Maybe." Then she closed the space to touch her lips to his briefly. "I would enjoy some of those good sensations again soon, too."

His mouth crushed hers in a desperate kiss, he could never have enough of her. Owen pulled his mouth away just as quickly. "Get in the house, woman. My restraint is almost nonexistent right now," he growled.

Leena smiled and touched her lips lightly to his. "I'll see you at brunch."

⚬⚮⚭ Chapter 10 ⚭⚮⚬

As Leena came out of her office, she looked up to find Owen leaning against a wall a few feet away.

At her startled look, he grinned. "I've got connections in the administration here. They said I could tag along on the last tour today."

Leena looked down the hall to see Cora looking around the corner and grinning at her. "I see." Then she smiled and handed him her safety glasses. "You'll need these, Mr. Grey, if you're coming out on the floor." He walked beside her down the narrow hallway. "Are you here checking up on me then?"

Owen shrugged, putting on the glasses. "I thought you ladies might feel more comfortable if I hung around until the end of the day."

Stopping, she squeezed his arm. "You're very sweet, Owen."

He grimaced, "I don't want to be sweet, Leena.," he puffed out his chest, "I want you to see me as tough and manly."

She laughed. "A very sweet and tough he-man?"

"If that's what you need."

Owen stood at the back of the group as Leena went over some basic rules for the children. He glanced around at the frazzled-looking parents and teachers. If the expressions were any indication, the bus ride had been very loud and trying.

"We'll start the tour in the shipping department so you can see how that works." Leena began leading the group out toward the loading docks. As they went around the corner of the warehouse, Rachel pulled up on her forklift.

"If you have any troublemakers, Ms. Duncan, I can put them up top out of the way." Rachel motioned to the top of the huge metal shelves.

"Thank you, Miss Winters, I'll keep that in mind." She glanced at the group of children to see if Rachel's threat had worked. "Would you be able to show everyone how we receive the paper we recycle, Miss Winters?"

Owen couldn't help thinking how well she controlled the children. Not that he had a lot of experience, but this many and she still held their complete attention.

Rachel shut off the tow motor and leaned over the side of it. "Absolutely. I'm going to need two helpers first." She grinned as every male child in the group raised their hand. Looking around for a moment, she pointed to the smallest boy and a mousy little girl who also raised her hand. They walked quickly over to her. "Climb up here and take a seat." She glanced back and spotted Owen at the back of the group and winked at him. "There's not enough room on here for you, Mr. Grey, but maybe next time." She seated the kids in front of her on the seat and started the tow motor again.

As Rachel disappeared around a corner, Leena turned back to the group. "As most of you know, the paper we recycle is the paper you put out for collection each week." She paused to be sure she had their attention. A few boys were still looking around at the top shelf Rachel had pointed to. "Before it reaches our plant, it goes to a sorting plant where they sort the metal and plastic from the paper. They separate it and then send it to the right place for processing." She smiled at them and paused. "Does anyone know the amount of paper products one family goes through in a year?" No hands were raised. "Each family here uses six to eight trees worth of paper in a year's time. Paper is one third of your household waste." She glanced at Owen. "Of course, some of us use more than others."

He smirked, knowing she was referring to his books being published. It pleased him that she kept looking at him even though she was running the show for the kids.

When Rachel came back around the opposite corner, she had a huge bale of paper on the forks. The two kids were grinning with excitement. Well, at least they'd never forget their tour with the crazy lady driver. Stopping in front of the group, Rachel placed a hand over the little girl's as she let her think she was lowering the lift.

Leena motioned to the huge cube of paper. "This is the baled paper the sorting plants send to us. We have to sort it again before we can begin processing it into useable paper again." She grinned as Rachel helped the two children down. "Thank you, Miss Winters."

Rachel winked at the little girl. "Sarah has a future in shipping and receiving. You might want to get her information, Ms. Duncan."

Leena laughed. "We'll contact her as soon as she graduates." She turned and led them toward the factory floor. "We take the bales and put them through this next machine you're going to see." She paused and turned. "Does everyone have their safety glasses on?" She always had to curb her laughter when she looked at the little eyes behind the too-big glasses.

Nodding, Leena opened the door and led the way in. "This machine we're about to see is called an air knife." She motioned to the tall cylinder in front of them. "It uses a steady stream of air to send the pieces of paper whirling around. Then big fans blow the lighter sheets to the top, and the heavier ones drop to the bottom. When they come out the other side, it's been sorted for us into three groups.

Anyone want to take a guess at those groups?" She pointed to a small blonde girl.

"Cardboard, newspaper, and..." She looked puzzled.

"And mixed papers," Kasey piped up as she walked up beside the group. She stepped up to the bottom step of the air knife's platform and smiled. "I'm Miss Wright. It's my job to make sure this," she motioned to the machine, "does its job without any problems." She started up the steps and motioned to a larger boy standing closest. "Could you give me a hand for a minute?" He nodded and followed her up the platform.

"This panel here slides open so I can see in, if there are any problems with the sorting. Sometimes the sorting plant doesn't catch everything and a bottle or two might get missed." She grimaced. "It usually gets stuck inside here and causes all sorts of problems."

Kasey motioned to the boy to help her pull the panel open then grinned at the gasps and sounds of awe as the class was able to see the paper being whirled up through the air streams. Kasey grinned at the children. "It seems to be working fine right now." She closed the panel and led him back down the platform.

"Thank you, Miss Wright." Leena motioned to the class to go over to where the groups of workers were checking the paper that came out on the conveyor. "Over there, you can give Miss Wright's team a hand in checking to make sure all the contaminants have been removed."

Leena stopped and let them pass her, waiting until Owen was beside her. "Learning anything new, Mr. Grey?"

Owen grinned down at her. "Yeah, you ladies get to play with all sorts of big toys at work."

Leena laughed and motioned him over to the other end of the conveyor, where Kasey was showing the kids what happened when the paper went through the shredder.

"Cool," he whispered, much like one of the young boys in the group. He followed them through the pulping demonstration and screening.

By the time they got to the end where the dried rolls of newly recycled paper were, he was very impressed with what the four women did on a daily basis and had already decided to find out how much recycled paper his publishers did use.

Sitting in the lunch area with the students, Owen munched on one of the cookies handed out as a small bonus to the tour group.

"I hope all of you enjoyed what you learned today." Leena motioned to where Cora stood. "Ms. Avery has packets for all of you to take home with more facts and information, and a sample of each type of recycled paper you saw made today."

After she walked them all out to the exit, Leena returned to find Owen still eating cookies and reading through the information. "Learn lots?"

Owen grinned up at her. "I had no idea that recycling reduces energy consumption by forty percent and..." He glanced at the sheet and read from it, "reduces water use by sixty-four percent, air pollution by seventy-four percent..."

"I know all the facts, Owen. I wrote up those sheets." She perched on the table beside him.

"Really?" He picked up her hand. "Beautiful, witty, creative, and intelligent. I am one lucky man."

"Are you?"

"Oh, yes, I am. A lucky man to just know you."

"Flattery like that might work better than you know."

The door to the lunchroom opened. "All cleaned up and shut down, Lee." Kasey leaned against the doorframe and smiled at Owen. "You today's white knight?"

He nodded and stood up. "Yep, and it comes in handy to know the dangerous toys you ladies play with every day... good to know not to upset any one of you."

Kasey chuckled. "You might want to share your newfound information with your chest-beating friends." She ran a hand through her hair. "I'm beat and so ready to go home and wash the paper slop off."

Leena nodded. "I'll be ready to go in five." She straightened up from the table and watched Kasey swing out the door. Owen reached out and took her hand again, stopping her from walking past him.

"I'd like to come home with you, Leena." His voice was soft. "Just to spend some quiet time with you, without car chases and bickering witches and chest-beating men..." She smirked at that.

"I'll make us dinner." She put a hand against his chest to stop him from kissing her. "Just dinner, Owen. No promises."

Nodding, he kissed her nose. "That works for me."

Leena kept busy in the kitchen as he wandered around her house at her insistence. Could she do this? Her nerves were singing. It had taken changing into three outfits to decide what to wear when they got home. Finally, she'd given up and put on a long flowing skirt and simple top, so she'd at least feel comfortable. She shook her head and continued to cut up the ingredients for the salad. She loved being near him, had gotten comfortable. That, she mused, was something she never thought she could feel again, comfort in a man's arms. Well, she mused, maybe comfortable wasn't the right word, but she certainly didn't feel any discomfort with the way she felt when he kissed her...

"Quite the eclectic home décor you have here." She jumped when Owen spoke. "Whoa, sorry; thought you heard me come in." She gave him a nervous smile. He put his hand on her shoulder and pulled her under his arm. "Tell me, how do you find your bed in among all those plants? It must feel like you're in a jungle when you open your eyes in the morning."

"I like plants, and my bedroom has the best light with all those windows." She set the knife down on the counter and moved to finish what she'd been doing. "Do you have a problem with plants?"

Owen shook his head. "Nope, just don't give me one to look after. I turn them to dust in no time at all." He glanced at the counter. "Can I do something to help?"

She motioned toward the cupboards. "You could get the dishes down."

Carrying the dishes to the sink, Owen turned and studied her. "You're going to have a meltdown if you don't relax, Leena."

Leena looked up at him. "It shows, huh?"

Owen nodded and reached down to pull her to her feet. "I'm not expecting anything here, you know." He moved her chin gently to look in her eyes. "I just want to be with you. Alone in some sort of peaceful setting for a while." He kissed her gently. "I'll leave as soon as you tell me to."

Looking up at him for a moment, she let out a breath. "I'm being silly. Let's go sit and relax." She took his hand and pulled him into the living room.

Leena sat beside him and placed her legs comfortably across his lap. "Did you and Cora ever identify that stone from the vision?"

Owen nodded, slowly rubbing his hand up and down her leg. "After several e-mails of pictures from Kasey, it turns out we've both agreed on the blue topaz." He grinned at her. "Who knew there was even such a thing?" He began to rub her feet gently. "Chris is running the pattern and information through a few of his contacts to see if it's a special ring in any sort of way." He shrugged. "Who knows, maybe we'll get lucky." He thumbed the instep of her foot.

"I won't comment on Cora e-mailing all day while at work." She sighed. "Mmm, that feels absolutely heavenly. Owen, you have magical hands." She smiled at her own pun.

Owen didn't say anything instead, he just watched her face and continued to rub. When he'd done one foot, he started on the other. He turned and dropped down onto his knees on the floor in front of the couch and placed one of her legs on either side of him. "Let's see if I've perfected my talent." He ran his hands up her calves, over the light material of the skirt, and circled back down to her feet. "Just lean back and relax, pretty Aileena," he whispered to her. His big hands ran up to her knees, and he circled them a moment before slowly sliding them up her thighs. As she leaned back and closed her eyes, he circled to the outer side of her hips and back down the side of her legs. He swallowed as he watched her tongue dart out and moisten her lower lip. Owen's hands moved back down to her ankles, and under the hem of her skirt and slowly slide his palms back up against her skin.

She hissed out a breath when his hands glided slowly up the sensitive insides of her thighs and back out to rest by her hips. "It's not fair." She swallowed and opened her eyes to see his steel blue ones watching her. "That you can seduce with a few touches."

His eyes were heavy. "Myself as well," he whispered and rose up on his knees to lean toward her. "I need your lips." He reached out and ran his tongue over her lips. When he heard her take a ragged breath, he began to kiss her softly. As lightly as he could manage, gently probing her mouth with his tongue. "Touch me, Aileena." His voice was hoarse and shaking. He watched her gasp as his hands stroked down her thighs again. "You are so lovely, I'm afraid to touch you most of the time."

He moved his mouth slowly down her throat as he whispered against her soft skin. When she tugged the waist of his shirt from his jeans and pulled it up to touch his skin, his breath left his body. Her warm hands moved over his chest. Pulling back, he tugged the shirt over his head and tossed it on the floor. She leaned forward and touched her mouth against his chest, and a shudder raced through him. She ran her hands lightly up his chest and touched her tongue lightly against his shoulder. Owen tensed under her touch. He kept his hands just above her knees where her skirt was now bunched up.

Slowly she kissed her way up his neck making him moan deep from how good it felt to have her touch him.

She reached to pull his head down to hers. "Kiss me, Owen."

He lost the control he'd held so long and crushed her mouth down on hers. Gripping her hips, he pulled her to the edge of the couch. When he pressed his body between her legs, she gasped into his mouth and held onto his head with both hands.

Owen pulled his mouth away and ran it roughly down her neck, trying to devour as much of her skin as he could find. Her head dropped back and gave him free access to the sensitive skin across the front of her throat. Groaning against her warm flesh, he pulled her shirt slowly up her body and felt her tremble when his lips brushed against her rib cage. When she leaned back slightly, he pulled the shirt over her head and watched her eyes for any sign of hesitating.

Moving his lips back to hers, he distracted her with a rough kiss as his hands moved down her arms to rest lightly against the lace material of her bra. Running his lips slowly down her neck, he felt her tremble as his tongue ran along the edge of the lace hiding her from him.

He nipped a taut nipple through the lace and felt himself harden when she threw her head back with a moan and clutched at the back of his head to hold him closer to her.

Pulling the clasp free, his legs began to shake at the sight of her breasts falling free into his hands. Pushing her back against the couch he ran his face between the soft orbs and felt a hitch in his own breathing as his large hands molded the soft skin. Taking one hard nipple in his mouth he sucked until he felt her squirm tighter against his own jean-covered body.

Leaning down, he assaulted the other nipple with his teeth, as he put his hand up under her skirt and ran it gently over the wet heat between her legs. She jerked when his knuckles brushed lightly against her.

"We can't..." she gasped, "birth control..." She moaned deep in her throat as his knuckles brushed against sensitive flesh again. "Upstairs." She managed to get out before she moaned again.

Owen moved his mouth up to her throat again crushing her hard nipples against his bare chest. "I can please you, baby." He licked her ear. "Then we'll move upstairs." She was squirming against his hand and his jeans felt like they were going to burst if he didn't get rid of them soon. "Let me." He gasped against her mouth while his fingers brushed aside the wet lace between her legs.

Twice he ran his fingers over the slick moisture before pushing a finger inside her tight heat. He shuddered when the muscles clenched around his finger. "Baby, I have to taste you." He moved down her body and pushed her skirt up with shaking hands. Pulling the lace aside he bent down not giving her time to change her mind. When his tongue stroked slowly over her sensitive slit Leena cried out and grabbed his hands holding her thighs open. Once, twice more he ran his tongue over her before thrusting it inside her making her squirm against him.

Reaching up he clamped her hips in a firm a grip and held her down on the edge of the couch. Sucking on her clit he breathed against her throbbing flesh. "Come for me baby, give yourself to me." Then he plundered and sucked until it took all his strength to hold her down. When her thighs tightened and she groaned between her breathless panting, he felt himself jerk inside his jeans and he lapped harder against her until she cried out and shuddered against him.

Kissing his way up her thighs and rib cage he rested his face in her neck. "Bedroom, I can't wait much longer, babe." He pulled her tight to him and stood in one motion as she tightened her legs around him.

Still trying to breathe Leena attacked his neck as he walked unsteadily to the bedroom. With each step he took, she could feel the hardness of him press against her still sensitive flesh. "Bedside table..." She gasped against his mouth as his legs hit the edge of the bed and they fell onto it.

While he devoured her breasts, she squirmed closer to the edge and pulled the can and applicator from the drawer, dropping them beside her, she grabbed a condom. With unsteady hands she tried to do what the instructions had said to do, giving up when his mouth went down over her stomach she dropped her arms and moaned. "Can't..."

Owen lifted his head and looked at her with clouded eyes.

"Have to do this." She held up the can.

Moving off her he ripped the zipper of his jeans open and shrugged out of them as he watched her fill the applicator. Reaching down he pulled the skirt and lace down her body and off her legs, grasping himself tightly in his hand as he watched her insert the foam. Quickly taking the applicator from her and tossed it aside and picked up the condom beside her. With vibrating hands, he put in on quickly.

Kissing his way up her waist he nuzzled the underside of her breasts. "I'll try to go slow baby."

Leena grabbed his head and jerked him up her body until she could cradle his waist between her thighs. "No slow... Now." She attacked his mouth with hers and reached down to grab his waist as he pushed inside her. They both moaned when he was deep inside her.

Unable to control himself, Owen began plunging into her fast and hard, reaching under her to better position her hips to accept him deeper inside her. She was so tight and hot he didn't think he was going to last more than a minute. Her muscles began to clench around him, and she was gasping.

Grasping her knee, he pulled her leg up higher so he could slam into her. He felt his own muscles tighten as she cried out against his throat meeting his thrusts with as much force as he gave. Her nails dug into his sides as she convulsed around him and he felt himself explode with such force it actually paralyzed him.

With shaking arms, Owen held as much of his weight off her as he could. "I'll try to dazzle you with endurance next time, baby." He panted against her damp hair.

Wrapping her legs around him, she purred against his ear. "I don't need dazzling." She ran her hand up and down his back. "Mmm. I'm buzzing from head to toe, Owen." She licked the sweat on his neck. "I need a quick shower; care to join me?"

"I couldn't carry you if I tried, though. Legs are rubber right now." He kissed her lingeringly. "I haven't felt this good in... well... ever, pretty Aileena."

They lingered in the shower, touching soap-covered bodies and prolonging already long kisses. By the time they reached the bedroom again, both were short of breath and needing the closeness again. "Stay tonight," Leena whispered against his neck when he lowered her to the mattress.

"Nothing could drag me away," he gasped as her hand ran down over his stomach.

Chapter 11

Kasey climbed into the Jeep Sunday morning, smirking at the two occupants in the front seat.

"I think I see why boss lady was so damn happy at work on Friday." Then she settled in with a giggle.

Leena blushed and Owen grinned wide. "Problem?" Owen dared as he pulled out onto the street.

Kasey chewed her lip. "Nope. But I lost a bet with Rachel."

Leena turned shocked eyes toward her. "You bet Rachel I was sleeping with Owen?"

Kasey shook her head. "No, of course not. It was a time bet. Couldn't you have held out another week?"

Leena laughed as Owen reached for her hand. "Not a minute more than I did."

It was better having a meeting during the day. Everyone was rested and there was no rush. They lingered around the large table in the very white dining room, enjoying the company. Leena leaned over closer to Owen and fed him a piece of melon. When he licked the juice off her hand, Dade groaned.

"You two are ruining my appetite." Dade grimaced.

"Don't look then," Owen drawled back at him.

"I think it's wonderful, Dade," Cora piped up. "You're just jealous."

"Damn right I am. He's back in town a few months, and she falls right into his bed."

Leena blushed. "We haven't made it to his bed yet, but, as much as I'd like to sit around and discuss our sex life..."

"Can we? Pleeeease?" Steven mumbled around a mouthful of croissant.

Kasey giggled, "I don't think I could sit here calmly and do that." The look Chris gave her made her blush. "Seriously, they're big people and can look after their own sex lives without our help."

"I would help if they needed it," Dade offered with a grin.

Leena shook her head with a serious look. "Kase is right, we are big, very big..." she paused to look at Owen, "people and can look after ourselves, thank you." She smirked at Owen when his mouth dropped open at her words.

Rachel dipped her napkin in her water and dabbed her forehead. "I can't hear any more. I'm going to swoon." They all burst out laughing.

Chris cleared his throat. "Is there anything serious we can discuss for a moment? Before I have to go have a cold shower?"

Steven sobered. "I have everyone's jobs listed for the children's fair."

Dade groaned and slid lower in his chair. "Anything other than that to discuss?"

Rachel threw a grape at him. "Fine, what fun have you volunteered us for?"

Steven pulled a paper from his pocket. Opening it, he grinned at Cora. "Of course, you're running the snack bar, it has three grills and we already have four volunteers taking orders and filling them." She smiled and nodded at him.

"Dade, you are in the ticket booth. You'll take turns with another volunteer." Steven continued.

Dade sighed but nodded. "Could be worse, I suppose."

"Chris, you and Kasey are going to man the gates for the first part of the day. If you want to help in other areas once your shift is done, that's fine, too."

Kasey grinned, "Am I small enough for the rides?"

Everyone laughed.

"Rach, I thought you could help me by running around and problem-solving." She looked pleased with his choice for her. "And keeping the peace." Steven grinned and then turned to Owen and Leena. He looked at Owen long enough to see him squirm. "I've got you two helping run some of the games. There are several other volunteers for that, so you can rotate around and take breaks when needed."

Owen smirked. "Games work for me."

"They're for the children, Owen." Leena laughed at him.

"Yeah, I know, but it doesn't mean I can't play 'em, too." Owen picked up her hand and kissed her palm.

"Don't start again, you two." Dade groaned at them. "So, what time do we have to be there, and are we going to carpool?"

Chris sat up and nodded to Dade. "We could pile most of us in your van, if you cleaned the sawdust out of it."

Dade shrugged, "It's clean... this week."

Cora nodded. "I think we should try to travel together."

Owen lowered Leena's hand from his mouth. "Four could go in my Jeep and four with Dade."

Steven nodded. "I don't have to be there for set-up or anything, so we could all go together. I made sure all our shifts were in the morning, so we could hang out all afternoon."

"How early are we talking here, Doc?" Rachel moaned.

"If we left here at seven that would give us plenty of time."

"Ugh!" Rachel slumped back in her chair. "You're buying the coffee, Doc."

Steven chuckled. "It's a deal."

Chris stood up and motioned to the deck. "Let's sit outside and then we can discuss what I've found out this week."

"Do you have to sound so lawyer-ish when you say that?" Kasey mused as she walked by him.

"I am a lawyer, Kase, how else am I supposed to sound?"

She shrugged, "I dunno...you could say something like 'come sprawl on my deck while we gab about stuff.'"

Chris smiled down at her. "Or I could say this." He leaned down and whispered in her ear. "Come climb on my lap where I can make you squirm." Her cheeks flushed, and he chuckled as everyone walked by them to the chairs. "Go sit before I'm tempted." She smiled shyly up at him and sat in the nearest chair.

Chris turned to see Leena and Owen doing just what he'd suggested to Kasey. Shaking his head when Owen winked at him, he continued to lean against the railing. "Trying to get more information about who drove the car isn't working out well. We can't force them to tell us without a warrant and can't get a warrant without a good reason, which we don't legally have." He looked down for a minute to allow time for comments.

"That sucks." Rachel sighed.

"Now, I've been doing some hunting around with a few contacts in the city regarding the ring. Cora and Owen have identified the stone, and we think we have it narrowed down to two choices." Chris put his hands in his pockets. "Choice one is a school ring, a Catholic school. To which about seven hundred have been made and sold over the years." He waited until the moans passed. "Choice two is a ring that was sold through a specialty order promotion, for which only one hundred and fifty were ever made." He let out a long breath. "Either one is going to mean getting lists and more than a few hours of going over it looking for something or someone familiar."

"Can we get an attendance list from Gwen for Beltane?" Steven inquired.

"I already called Justin about it, and he's sending me one tomorrow." Chris looked around the group.

"Justin thinks if there's a chance in figuring out who did that to those girls, it's up to us, so he's agreed to keep us informed of anything the police share." He looked around the group and studied their reactions. "I will do what I can to go over the information, but I don't have that much free time and I may not notice something someone else would. So, are there any suggestions on how we're going to pull this off in the five weeks left before Solstice?"

There was a long silence, then Owen looked up from Leena's neck, which he'd been gently caressing. "Could you scan the lists and e-mail everyone a copy? That way, between meetings everyone can take a look when they have time."

Chris nodded. "I can." He turned to Cora for a moment. "With school photos, would you be able to pick anything up?"

Dade stood immediately. "Yeah, she'd pick up every sick thing anyone ever did." He wasn't happy with the suggestion.

Cora stood and placed a calming hand on Dade's arm. "I couldn't handle picture after picture, but if we come across any that seem familiar, I could do those." Dade shook his head but didn't say anything. "We might get lucky."

Dade shook off her hand and stomped forward to glare at the others. "Do any of you realize how much it takes out of her every time she goes reaching blindly?" He jammed his hands in his pockets with a growl, and returned to lean against the railing.

Cora stepped to him and placed her hand gently on his arm again. "It's okay, Dade. I won't do more than I can handle." She rubbed her hand up and down his arm a few times. "And I know as long as you're there, you'll watch out for me." He squeezed her hand against his arm and dropped his head down to look at the ground.

"I think we all will agree we won't let Cora try unless we're all certain there's a reason, Dade," Leena added softly.

He let out a shaky breath and turned, keeping Cora's hand in his. "I have to get going. I'm doing some repairs over at the old retirement complex this afternoon." He avoided looking at anyone but Chris. "Send me any information when you get it. I'll see everyone Wednesday. My house," he added before he turned to Cora. "Walk me out." She nodded and walked behind him.

The drive back to Kasey's was quiet. "Is Dade okay, Owen?" Kasey inquired softly.

He glanced in the mirror at her. "Yeah, he just worries about Cora...about all of you ladies, actually."

Leena squeezed his hand. "Worries? He tries to control her."

"Why is he so mean to her most of the time?" Kasey asked.

Owen shrugged. "I don't know; do I look like a shrink?" He grinned.

Kasey was silent for a minute then mused in a singsong tone. "He likes her."

"Just don't tell her that," Leena suggested, "one of these days the two of them will stop fighting long enough to realize they should be together."

"You knew all this time?" Owen asked.

Leena nodded. "It's pretty obvious."

Uncomfortable with the direction things were going, Owen glanced in the mirror again. "I finished the chapters you sent me, Kase." He could see her tense. "You've got some good stuff there. With a little..." Kasey's arms flew around the seat and squeezed him.

"Driving here!" He chuckled as she let go. "Anyway, I'm going to send you a few suggestions about a few areas you could tweak. If the rest is as good as what I've already read, I'd say you have a story good enough to send to the publishers."

"Oh, my gosh! Stop the car!"

Owen hit the brakes. When he turned to see if she was all right, she all but launched herself into the front seat in his lap.

"Thank you. Thank you. Thank you..." Kasey kissed him quickly then squeezed some more. A car went past and honked a few times. Realizing how it looked when she was all but in his lap while he was still in the driver's seat, she straightened and climbed back into the backseat and buckled her seatbelt again.

Owen turned to see Leena with her hand over her face, quivering with repressed laughter. Shaking his head at the two of them, he pulled back out onto the road heading for Kasey's.

ꙮ **Chapter 12** ꙮ

Leena ran back in for her jacket then out the front door. She couldn't focus this morning because she was too excited. She was not as excited about the fair as she was about spending the day with Owen, she hadn't seen him since Sunday, except at the short Wednesday night meeting. He was knee-deep in his writing, and she was determined to settle for phone calls and text messages when he took a break.

She was almost to the Jeep when he stepped out. She jumped into his arms and devoured his mouth, showing him how much she'd missed him and how happy she was to see him.

Turning his back to the audience in the Jeep, he buried his hands in her hair and held her still so he could taste her deeply. Gasping, he hugged her to him. "I feel missed."

"You are." She squeezed him harder against her.

"You're not mad at me for ignoring you all week?"

Leena shook her head and ran her tongue over his bottom lip. "Are you going to ignore me tonight?" Her eyes sparkled with suggestion.

"Not a chance" He lowered his mouth to hers again.

"As heart-warming as this reunion is, we're going to be late."

"Oh!" Leena pulled back and looked in the Jeep to see Chris and Kasey in the backseat grinning at her. "I didn't realize we weren't alone." She smacked Owen on the arm before she walked around to the passenger side.

"I almost forgot myself for a minute." Owen grinned at her.

When they arrived at the fair site, right on the bumper of Dade's van, everyone hopped out. Owen walked around the front of the Jeep and saw Cora smack Dade and then stomp away.

He sauntered over. "You won, barely; you'd think she'd be happier."

Steven walked around the van and grinned. "She wasn't at all happy with our little race and wouldn't listen when I told her you weren't over the limit by much."

Leena stopped Dade with a look. "Is she all right?"
Dade shrugged. "She was jumpy as hell when Doc and I got to her place this morning. I just thought she wasn't pleased with the time of day." He looked to where she had gone. He didn't get one step before Leena had put her hand on his arm.

"I'll go talk to her, Dade." Leena gave Owen a kiss and walked away.

Dade scowled at Owen. "I need coffee." Steven handed him a Thermos as he walked past. Dade opened it, then closed it again and handed it to Owen. "Shit. I better go make peace." Then he headed over to where the women stood.

Owen followed in case they needed a referee.

When they reached her, Cora was rubbing her hands up and down her arms. "I just feel really off today, Lee. I don't know why." She glanced up as they walked over.

"Coralee, honey?" Dade stopped in front of her with his hands in his pocket. "I'm sorry, if it bothered you, I should have taken that into consideration and slowed down." He looked down at the ground.

Rachel stepped beside him. "Dade..."

"It's all right, Rach." Cora took a deep breath. "I'm really feeling off today; I shouldn't have taken it out on you."

Dade's head jerked up. "What do you mean off?" Dade glanced at Owen with a knowing look on his face.

She shrugged, "I don't know. After I woke up this morning, as I was meditating, it just hit me, and I haven't been able to shake it."

Owen cleared his throat. "Wait, like at Beltane when it hit you?"

Everyone stopped and looked at him then Cora.

Cora shook her head. "No. No, not like that." She sighed. "It's just an off day, I guess." She grinned at Owen when he placed his hand on her shoulder, causing Dade to scowl. "Owen, thanks for the thought, but you can't be walking around rubbing one of us every time we're moody or have PMS."

Owen grinned and stepped closer, his palm held out in front of her stomach. "I'm willing to try..."

Dade smacked his hand down. "Back off."

Owen chuckled and turned to Leena and placed his hand on her stomach. "Are you feeling okay, baby? You need me to rub my hands on you?"

Leena blushed and buried her face in his shoulder. "Ass." Her voice was muffled against him laughing softly.

Steven shook his head. "Okay, folks, now that the clown show is over, I really need to show you all where you should be."

Four hours later, Leena wasn't sure if she ever wanted to see another milk bottle or softball again. She counted the minutes until it was her break time.

"Just ask the pretty lady for a ball, and I'll help you."

Looking across the stand to see Owen squatting down beside a shy little blond boy, she stepped forward and smiled.

"Do you have your ticket, sir?" she asked him. The boy shook his head then held up his hand quickly after Owen pushed a few tickets into his palm. She took the tickets from his hand and gave him a ball.

Leena stood back to watch Owen help the little boy aim. He was more or less throwing the ball for the child. When the milk bottles were knocked down, the little boy jumped up and wrapped his arms around Owen to hug him. Before the tears she felt inside her reached the outside, she clapped. "That's the best throw today. For that," she turned and pulled down the biggest stuffed dog she could reach, "you get the special prize."

She watched as the little boy walked away holding Owen's hand. The stuffed dog was actually bigger than the child.

When Owen sauntered back a few minutes later, he nodded to the teen climbing over the stand wall. "It's your break time, pretty lady." He lifted over the wall and tucked her under his arm. "How are you holding out?"

Leena laughed. "Who knew kids were this tiring, well, this many of them. They never seem to slow down." She motioned toward Rachel, who was leading a group of them to a ride. "I think she's the only adult here that can outlast them." Her eyes followed the sound of cheering, and she spotted Steven in the middle egging the cheers on. "Well, except him."

As Leena walked slowly past the ticket booth, she spotted Dade trading off with the next volunteer and waved.

"I'm going to go sit under that beautiful tree way over there and watch." She pointed to the outskirts of the park.

Owen nodded. "I'll go grab us some drinks and fries and meet you there." He spun her in front of him and kissed her quickly. "Be right back."

Leena wandered slowly toward the tree, having to suddenly stop twice before very excited children ran over her. She glanced back and saw Dade and Owen heading to the concession stand. He'd been so good with the kids. It almost…*almost*, made her think she could do that.

She sat down and leaned against the tree. A family, wouldn't that be something? While she closed her eyes, she dropped her head down and sighed. Today would be a day she'd think of from time to time.

"You are still one hot bitch, Lee."

Leena jolted at the voice and jerked her head up to find herself looking at the man she'd run from years before. "T-Tyler."

His blond hair was combed perfectly back from his face, his eyes covered by dark glasses. She didn't need to see his eyes to recognize the way his jaw clenched. She'd seen that too many times, just before he hurt her. Her heart started pounding. She had to get up. *GET UP*, she willed. She had to get up! With trembling legs, she slid her back up the tree. Her thighs felt so weak she didn't know how long she'd be able to stand. "Why are you here, Tyler?"

He stepped closer and looked her up and down.

"Surprised to see me, Mrs. Black?" He pushed his hand against her throat and held her against the tree. His dark eyes glared at her through the glasses. "You won't run from me this time. I signed your damn papers and gave you time to realize your mistake." He leaned toward her and held her body against the tree with his. "I've been watching you. You're quite the whore now, aren't you? You've been letting Owen Grey climb all over you…"

Leena struggled against his weight. "Leave me alone, Tyler. I am no longer your wife." Her voice was trembling. With shaking hands, she grabbed his wrist to try to take the pressure off her throat. "Please… Tyler."

"Begging? What are you begging for, Leena? You always were pathetic!" He shoved her back into the tree again and gripped her hair in his other hand to jerk her head up and look at him.

Leena felt the tears rolling down her face. Her legs were trembling, she felt like she was gong to collapse when a large arm wrapped around Tyler's neck and jerked him back off her. She watched as Owen spun him around and smashed his fist into Tyler's jaw, sending him sprawling to the ground.

Dade and Chris grabbed Owen before he could reach Tyler again.

"Not here, man, not now," Chris said while trying to hold Owen back. Dade stepped in front of Owen. "Go see to Leena, bro. We've got this."

Owen spun around and watched as she slowly slid down the tree. He was to her before she reached the ground, picking her up into his arms and turning so she couldn't see Tyler. "It's okay, baby. I'm here. I've got you," he whispered. His arms were still shaking with the rage he felt.

Leena could barely see through the tears rolling down her face as she looked over Owen's shoulder to see Chris and Dade backing Tyler across the grass. Tyler stopped to face them, his hair fell out of place, down over his brow, his face red with rage. Dade stepped up to him face to face. "Dade," she whispered to Owen.

"Dade can take care of himself, baby." Owen nuzzled the side of her neck as they walked in the other direction. He heard Cora and Rachel heading toward them and opened his eyes. Moving his head back, he stared at her neck and saw the red finger marks. "Son of a bitch!" he ground out between his teeth. "Baby, the girls will stay here with you. I'll be right back." He set her on her feet and kissed her tenderly twice then turned.

"Owen. Owen, no!" Leena tried to call, but her voice cracked. Turning she saw Cora coming toward her. "Stop him! Cora, you have to stop him!" The tears were running down her face so fast she could barely see him.

Cora turned to see Steven coming toward them from the other side. "Go after him."

Leena watched as Steven ran after Owen.

Dade stood in front of Owen. "Let me through, Dade. He marked her. He fucking marked her!" Owen tried to shove past Dade again as Chris ran up and gripped his arm. "Chris, let go. The fuckin' bastard's time is up." He shook with a rage he didn't know he was capable of.

Dade shoved him back further. Clenching his fist, he started to raise his arm when the image of his father came to his mind. "Fuck!" Owen spun away from his lifelong friend. "Fuck!"

Chris put his hand on his arm. "The police are dealing with him, Owen. He won't get near her again, I'll make sure of it." He gripped his arm harder and started to lead him back toward where the women waited.

Owen stopped and bent over with his hands on his knees. He took a few deep breaths and then looked up at Dade. "I'm sorry, man. I fuckin' lost it for a minute there." He let out a long breath. Chris rested a hand on his shoulder. "Chris, can you find something and make it stick on that bastard? Someone should have pounded him into the ground a long time ago. If I get my hands on him..."

Chris gripped his shoulder. "No worries there, my friend. We've *just* learned the car that followed her and scared the shit out of her... he was driving it. We've got him on harassment, assault, uttering threats, stalking. Give me time, and I'll come up with more."

Owen stood up. "It was him following her that night?"

Chris nodded.

"Fuck!" He took a deep breath then started walking fast away from them. "I need Leena." He almost ran back to where he'd left her. She wasn't there. His breath caught in his chest.

"Owen."

He turned to see Rachel waving at him from behind one of the storage tents. He ran the last few yards to it. As he rounded the side of it, Leena lifted her head and jumped up into his arms. He crushed her to him. "I'm sorry, baby. I lost it. I'm sorry."

Owen pulled back and looked down into her eyes. She was so beautiful it took his breath away.

"Baby," he said breathlessly. His fingers brushed over the red marks on her neck, and he slowly leaned down to kiss them gently, as if he could erase them. "Does it hurt? Has the Doc looked at it?" he whispered against her neck.

"The Doc can't even see her when she's folded up in your tree stumps."

Owen turned to see Steven standing behind him. "He marked her neck, Doc..." His head jerked back toward her. "Did he hurt you anywhere else, baby?" She shook her head.

Steven didn't attempt to get too close to her or move Owen away from her; he leaned forward and ran a thumb lightly over her neck. "Hurt to swallow, Lee?" She shook her head 'no.' "She's going to be fine, Owen. She just needs to settle her nerves."

Owen nodded and folded her back into his arms. "Do you want something to drink, baby? We could get Cora to find you some tea or something." He soothed his hand over her hair and kissed her in between words. She shook her head and clung to him.

Chris watched Cora lean back against Dade and whisper. "That is so beautiful. I'm going to cry in a minute."

Dade's arm wrapped around her, and he pulled her gently against his side. "Is the bad feelingly gone now, honey?"

She nodded.

"Yeah, I thought it might be." He hugged her against him for a moment more and then straightened. "Doc, if we've all done our time, I think we should get Leena home where she can rest."

Steven nodded. "I'll go turn everything over to the next supervisor and meet you at the van."

Rachel and Kasey were standing beside each other shaking from the whole ordeal when Chris walked up between them and wrapped one under each arm. "Let's go, ladies." He glanced over at Owen. "You want me to drive your Jeep until we reach my place?" Owen just nodded without taking his eyes off the woman against his side.

Kasey looked up at Chris and whispered. "If he calls her baby one more time, I'm going to cry," she blinked back tears as she said it.

Rachel nodded on the other side of him. Chris slowed his pace and let Owen and Leena go farther ahead. "He's so gone for her, ladies, that if he falls much farther, he's never going to get up."

Kasey smiled up at him, and his heart jerked. "I think it's wonderful. She deserves to be happy, and he'll look after her." She watched them for a minute, the way Owen spoke softly and caressed her hair, the way he kissed the top of her head every few feet. "It's just so sweet," she whispered. She smiled when Chris bent down and kissed the top of her head.

When Leena woke, they were in her driveway. She opened her eyes and looked up at Owen. "Sorry, I didn't mean to fall asleep on you."

He smiled. "That's fine." Owen motioned to the people standing outside the vehicle. "If you don't get out and hug those women and let them see you're okay, they're going to want to stay all night." He winked at her.

Leena grinned and slid over the seat and got out. Kasey was hugging her before both her feet were on the ground. "Take a hot bath and relax. I'll call you tomorrow." Rachel nodded behind her and squeezed her arm.

Cora glanced past her to Owen. "I expect you to look after her." He nodded.

She watched Dade and Chris speak to Owen quietly and then climb into the van with waves to her. When the van pulled away, she looked over at Owen. "Did I miss something?"

Owen shook his head. "No, just lots of advice and tips."

"I am very sure I don't want to hear those."

He scooped her up in his arms and started toward the house. "I have strict instructions to stick you in a hot bath and feed you calming tea." He kissed her gently as he started in the house. "If you tell me what tea is calming, I'll bring it to you while you soak in the tub."

She nuzzled into his neck. "Chamomile is fine."

Leena was stepping out of the bath when Owen opened the door. "Sorry, had some calls to make."

She took the cup then set it on the sink and accepted the robe he held out. "I don't need calming tea, Owen. I just need you." She wrapped her arms around his neck and pulled his head down to hers. "Make love to me, Owen," she whispered against his lips.

Owen's heart was pounding in his chest by the time he carried her into the bedroom and lowered her to stand again. "Let me show you how much you mean to me, Aileena." He trailed light kisses over her face. "Let me cherish you, baby." In his head he said 'let me love you.' He wasn't ready to say that out-loud yet. "I love your soft skin." His mouth trailed down her throat, his tongue licking at her skin. Pulling her robe open, his mouth followed the exposed skin to the valley between her breasts. "So beautiful." His voice sounded rough. Sliding his hands to her shoulders he pushed the robe off. As it slipped to the floor, he trailed his mouth down to her waist. Kneeling in front of her, he kissed her stomach as his hands caressed her hips. "You're so beautiful, I can't breathe when I look at you."

Leena gripped his head and held him to her. His mouth seduced her, his words touched her heart and made her tremble. She ran her hands over his shoulders and cradled his head to her stomach.

He looked up at her, and her hair fell around his face. Bringing his hand to her hair, he turned his face and let it slide across his cheek.

Standing, he lowered her to the bed gently. The look in his eyes made her heart pound a faster rhythm, and she gasped as he gently kissed each eyelid, slowly across her cheek to her mouth. With kisses this tender, she felt light-headed and sighed against his mouth. The hand against her cheek trembled.

Taking a ragged breath, he stared down into her eyes. They were amber with desire and heavy with lust as she looked back up at him. "I need to touch every inch of you. I need to taste every inch of you. I need to show you what I feel, because I can't find the words that say it." He sat and took his shirt off, and then his jeans, never taking his eyes off hers.

When she looked at his body with a slow appraising gaze, he felt a rush and hardened under her stare. She reached out and ran a hand down over his hip. "I can't believe you're here with me. I waited years ago for you to notice me." She leaned up and kissed his chest.

"I noticed." He closed his eyes as her lips traveled across his chest. Not caring for words, he hugged her against him. He took a hitched breath as her mouth burned down his stomach, and then he stopped her. "Baby, get the foam because I won't be stopping for any reason shortly."

When she moved to the other side of the bed, he stretched out behind her and trailed his lips across her shoulders and over her neck. She moaned softly and leaned back against him dropping the foam and condom onto the bed. Still kissing her neck, he picked up the can and put it back in her hands. He watched her hands shake as he trailed his hand lightly down her side sliding in across her rib cage and down over her hip.

Taking the applicator from her, he set it on the bed and slid his hand down between her thighs, pulling one gently up. As he slipped one hand between her legs he pushed his other hand under her waist and trailed it down her stomach to her other thigh. "You're so wet for me," he whispered against her neck.

Owen pushed his hips against her back as he stroked the inside of her thighs. She threw her head back and held his, arching into his hands. "Let me show you." He whispered as his hands continued to stroke and knead with each movement she pushed against his hand moving in unison with his actions. He inserted two fingers inside her wet heat and continued to rub against her clit gently.

Leena gasped and arched back farther, holding his head against hers. Each time she rocked back against him jolts of pleasure ran through him. He rubbed her harder but continued to just hold his fingers inside her. Her muscles clenched around his fingers each time she rocked against him. He pushed his leg between hers and brought up her knee, opening her wider to his hands. Biting her neck gently, he rubbed faster and began to push his fingers in deeper. "Come for me, baby," he growled against her neck. She began panting and moaning as she pushed herself into his hand. When the muscles squeezed around his fingers, she cried out and shook against his hand. Stroking his hand gently over her sensitive clit, he dropped her leg and rolled her onto her back, kissing his way down her.

When his mouth touched her thigh, she moaned. "Again, baby." He blew against her clit and dipped his tongue inside her. Her head thrashed back and forth on the pillow when he gripped her hips and plunged his tongue inside her. She was gasping and gripping his hands tightly. He stroked his tongue over her sensitive, slick flesh gently a few times then plunged it inside and out a few times then sucked hard on her.

Leena bucked up against him and cried out, moaning deeply and pulling at his hands. Not letting her go, he continued to lick her lightly until she stopped squirming under his tongue.

Owen rubbed his face across her stomach as he kneeled between her legs and picked up the applicator. She hissed out a breath when he inserted it and opened her eyes to watch him. Smiling down at her with his vision blurred from needing her so much, he quickly put the condom on and he lowered his weight on her and whispered. "*Again*." Then he slowly thrust inside her.

Sweat coated his back, and he trembled from the restraint, but he kept his movements slow and teasing until she began to gasp against his shoulder. He pulled out heart-wrenchingly slowly and looked into her eyes then thrust hard into her, watching her eyes cloud when their bodies slapped together.

Unable to hold back any longer, he thrust fast and desperate until he heard her moaning against his shoulder and felt her nails digging into his back. Then he let himself fall over the edge with her.

"That... was me... cherishing you, baby," he panted against her throat, then flipped them to their sides and kissed her softly until she fell asleep.

Chapter 13

As she woke to the smell of coffee, Leena opened her eyes to see Owen standing beside the bed looking down at her with a cup in his hand. She grinned sleepily at him. "Hi."

Owen smiled at her. "I wasn't going to wake you yet, but Chris called and he needs to come over and get some paperwork out of the way."

She slid up, propped herself against the headboard. "Paperwork?" Leena accepted the cup from him and smiled. "Thanks."

He sat down and played with the hair hanging over her shoulders. "To do with yesterday, pressing charges."

She sipped the coffee and was silent for a minute. "Can I?"

Owen nodded. "Chris says so, and the police are encouraging it." He fingered her hair again. "You are so beautiful all soft and sleepy."

"I'm sure you're biased, and my hair will be a nightmare to brush. I rarely sleep with it down."

"I think I wore you out last night."

"I think you did, too, quite wonderfully." She leaned up and kissed him. "Do I have time for a shower?" He nodded. "I'm taking the coffee with me. You make great coffee."

"Every writer needs to make great coffee, it's our main staple when we're on a roll."

Leena set the cup down as she swung out of the bed. Her nakedness didn't even bother her this morning. "How is your writing going?" She picked up the cup and walked toward the bathroom. "And you better say *really* well, after ignoring me most of last week." She showed him a pout.

"Baby, if you brought me coffee looking the way you do now, I'd never ignore you again. You could sit on my lap, just like that, while I work."

"I'm sure you'd get no work done that way."

Owen followed her out into the hallway. "I'm sure I wouldn't care. God, woman, you have the most perfect ass." He walked up behind her and gently cupped her butt.

She leaned back against his hands. "Don't spill my great coffee." Then she walked into the bathroom and closed the door, laughing at his shocked expression as the door was closing in his face.

"I can't believe it was him following me." Leena stared at the cup in her hands and then back to Owen. He wasn't as surprised to hear this, as he should have been.

Owen pulled a chair beside her and sat down, reaching for her hand. "There's more."

She looked up at Chris, who nodded. "What more?"

Chris leaned on the table and studied her briefly. "Mr. Tyler Black ran out on assault charges about two months ago. The car he was driving belongs to the corporation he'd been working for, they have been looking for him and their car for the last few weeks." He sat back and shrugged. "If you add charges to his list, the judge isn't going to think kindly of him in any way."

He set a notepad on the table. "I need to ask you some questions, Lee."

She looked at Owen for a moment, then she stood up and paced across the room. "I need bigger chairs."

Owen looked at Chris for a second trying to understand where that was coming from.

Leena grinned. "Seriously, the two of you look like giants sitting on kiddie chairs or something." Grabbing her cup, she moved to the sink and rinsed it. "I definitely need bigger chairs to accommodate all the hulking men I know." She leaned against the counter for a moment.

"Leena..."

She stopped him with a hand. "So, will the assault and harassment stick, Chris?" Leena jammed her hands in her back pockets and let out a long breath. "Would hospital records help? There's hospital records of the one time. Of course, he lied to the doctors, but my throat was so damaged I couldn't speak for days. There were many times I should have gone to the hospital, but I was afraid. It was a long time ago, but would it help?"

Chris held up a hand. "He put you in the hospital, Leena?" She nodded and his head swung back to Owen.

"I told you to let me get a hold of him yesterday," Owen mumbled.

"Bastard!" Chris spat.

"Chris, it was a long time ago..."

Chris leaned back again. "Sorry, that wasn't very professional of me." He let out a breath. "You give me the information, and I'll get the records."

Owen watched her lean over the table and quickly write on the notepad then step back just as fast.

"We'll do this the legal way." Chris glanced back at Owen. "If he tries to press charges against Owen for breaking his nose..." he smirked, "I'll drag him over the coals."

Chris turned in the chair. "Lee, I need to know if Tyler knew about your gifts."

Leena shook her head vigorously. "No, no. I thought about it a few times. They weren't very strong at that point, but I was never comfortable enough to tell him."

"Okay, good." Chris sat back again. "So, do you want me to go ahead with this Leena? I need to know what you want to do."

She paced around the kitchen and stopped to look out the window at her backyard. The plants were so full with leaves now, so pretty. The lawn was green. "I'm going to do what you say, Chris." She smiled at them both. "Then I'm having a garden party."

Owen looked at Chris and then they back at her.

"Next weekend. Saturday, late in the day we'll have a meal and a few drinks and celebrate that part of my life being over." She put her hands on her hips for a moment. "I'm sure with all the rooms in this house I can fit a few bodies here and there to crash."

Owen looked at her silently, watching the way she flitted around the kitchen with her nerves showing.

"Bring the drums, Chris." She added. "I've almost finished new outfits for the girls, and it will be the perfect time to wear them."

He looked at Chris again, they were thinking the same thing there.

Leena continued. "We'll drum and dance, and I can light the fire bowl, then we'll have our own little circle." With that, she walked out of the kitchen.

Going into the living room, Owen walked up behind Leena and put his arms around her waist to pull her back against him. "Are you okay, baby?" She nodded, but he could feel the hitch in her breath. "Talk to me."

Leena let out a huffed breath and tried to relax. "It's just... I've wondered for years if I'd see him again, and if I did what would happen. It's over. It's finally closed." She turned in his arms and hugged him. "I can start fresh now." She whispered against his chest. Lifting her head, she pulled his mouth down to hers and nibbled on his bottom lip gently. He pulled her against him and slowly kissed her with all the tenderness he was feeling.

Chris cleared his throat behind them. "Sorry, I seem to be interrupting a lot of that with you two." He smirked as they turned. "I can only hope its catching." With that, he walked to the door. "I sent those lists to everyone; when you get time check them over and see if anything at all seems to feel familiar."

Leena walked over and hugged him. "Thank you, Chris. We'll see you Wednesday."

As soon as Chris left, Leena spun back to Owen and smiled at him invitingly. "Do you have to rush back to your keyboard?" She toyed with the end of her hair and bit her bottom lip. "And I warn you now your answer will help me decide whether we discuss your not warning me about what Chris found out. I know he told you." Owen frowned and then shook his head and started walking toward her, his eyes searching hers. When he stepped in front of her, she ran her hands slowly up his chest. "Good." Running her hands down his shoulders and over his arms suggestively, she looked up at him. "I really need you to stay for a bit more."

"I'm all yours, baby." He pulled her into his arms and leaned down to kiss her, but she pulled back and grinned at him.

"Good. We need to move the fire bowl, and I want to get the lawn furniture out of storage. For the party."

He groaned, "That wasn't nice." But he still laughed. "I'll stay and help you, but then I really have to get back before my story goes cold." She nodded and kissed him quickly.

By Wednesday, Leena had exhausted herself trying to get the house ready for Saturday's party. She was almost relieved when Steven sent word he had to work Wednesday night to cover for the doctor who was taking his Saturday shift. So, everyone agreed to not meet.

Instead, they would continue going over the endless lists from Chris on their own. The downside was she wouldn't see Owen. She'd only spoken to him once since he'd left on Sunday, and he sounded so tired she sent him to bed, which he agreed to, saying he'd make it up to her. By Thursday, she was ready to drive over and invade his space, just long enough to hug him. She couldn't believe how much she missed a man she'd hardly known any time at all.

Powering down her computer, she sighed. "You're acting like an infatuated girl." She chastised herself out loud, while silently wondering if he'd have his cell phone nearby. She didn't want to phone and interrupt any brilliant plot events, but if she didn't at least hear from him, she was going to pout. A startling thought considering she'd never pouted over anything a day in her life. Leena searched two rooms and found where she had left her cell phone then sent him a quick message.

Lonely woman seeks sexy man's attentions.

Grinning at her own creativity she went to make herself some tea. When her phone beeped she almost dove on it.

Lonely sexy man in need of pretty lady's attentions.

She smiled and dropped down on the couch while hitting the keys. *Can sexy man stop long enough to call and whisper sinful things to lady?*

Leena knew it was distracting and in fact cheating to send a message like that, possibly interrupting him, but she decided it was worth it to just talk to him for a few minutes.

The phone rang before she reached the kitchen. "Hello."

"Hey pretty lady." Owen's voice was low and quiet.

"I didn't interrupt you, did I?"

"No, I was just doing some proofing, trying to give my mind a bit of a rest." He paused. "So, are you missing me, baby?"

The husky sound of his voice made her flush. "Enough to be whining to myself about it."

"I'm really sorry I haven't called you. It's just moving at a frantic pace, and I don't like to stop when it's going so well."

Leena curled up on the couch. "I understand, really. I'm just lonely and missing you," she was barely whispering.

"When I get this finished, I'll take a break and devote every moment to you. You'll be telling me to go write then."

"I look forward to that opportunity."

"I'm really missing you, too, baby." He sighed, "I almost headed over to see you last night when I burned out and then I realized it was three in the morning."

She felt better having heard that. "You're still coming on Saturday, aren't you?"

"I wouldn't miss it."

"I finished the new outfits."

"Definitely won't miss that. I want you to phone here until I answer on Saturday morning." Owen cleared his throat. "I lose track of day and time when my characters are running, so I take naps at strange hours."

"Okay, just look after yourself, please."

"Will do, baby."

"Owen?" She could hear the keys clicking in the background. "Would you allow me to read the first chapter or something? You've never even mentioned what it's about."

There was a long silence. "I don't usually, but for you, I'll send a few. Just don't comment on them until I've finished the story, okay?"

"Absolutely." She sighed quietly. "I miss your mouth," she whispered.

Owen groaned, "Baby, I miss all of you more than I thought possible."

She smiled to herself.

"I just looked at the time, why aren't you sleeping? You have work in the morning."

"I was restless tonight."

"Well, get rest because I won't be letting you have any Saturday night. I have a week's worth of kissing to do."

"Owen, the others are going to be staying here in the house."

"Baby, I don't care. I'll carry you outside after they're all asleep if I have to. I really miss you."

His anxious words reassured her. "Get back to work then so you can stay and cuddle with me all day Sunday then."

"I'm on it. Get some sleep, pretty Aileena. Dream of me."

"I will. Good night."

"Night, baby."

Setting the phone down, she turned the lights off and went up to her room. She wanted to climb into bed when his voice was so fresh in her mind.

Chapter 14

Everyone except Owen arrived, almost at the same moment. Cora immediately went into the kitchen with last-minute preparations for the meal. Kasey was busy getting dishes set up, and Rachel ordered the men around.

Leena had only looked at the clock once when Owen's arms surrounded her waist from behind. She turned and looked up at him. "I'm sorry, who are you?"

Owen gripped her waist with anxious hands and smiled down at her. "I'm sorry for the long week." He searched her eyes. "I've never had a story flow this well," he kissed her mouth softly, "It must be you, baby. You've inspired me."

She heard a woman's sigh before Dade laughed.

"Leena, you're not going to fall for that line, are you?" Dade rolled his eyes.

Leena looked up at the honesty in Owen's eyes and wrapped her arms around his neck, then pulled his mouth down to hers.

When he felt the urgent heat in her kiss, Owen almost turned and carried her from the room.

Breaking the kiss, she nuzzled her face into his neck and hugged him tightly.

Owen glanced up to raise his eyebrows at Dade before lowering his face into her hair.

"Aw, man. You're one smooth son of a bitch. I have never had a line that sappy work for me."

Cora walked past Dade and gave him a look. "That would be because yours are sappy lines, and he's being honest."

Dade stuffed his hands in his pockets and tried to look chastised.

"And Golden boy wins again," Steven joked as he took a tray Rachel handed him to the back door.

"I can't believe how perfect the weather is today, Leena. Did you do a little magic something to get this?" Kasey inquired with a smile.

Leena pulled out of his arms and grinned at him. "No, just threatened to try it if the weather didn't cooperate."

"Threatened to do what?" Owen asked as they went out the door. Leena grinned and stepped out of his reach. A burst of wind pushed against him hard enough to make him step back. He shook his head a huge smile on his face.

"Baby, remind me to never upset you."

Chris walked by. "Oh, I don't know... it could be fun."

Kasey spun toward him with her hands on her hips. He immediately went down on his knees in front of her then rested his hands on her hips and his face against her ribs. He whimpered. "Don't hurt me. I'll be good"

Bursting out laughing, Kasey hugged his head and gently ruffled his hair through her fingers for a few moments.

Owen stepped out and went over to the table and stood beside Dade. Leena had her own piece of paradise here. Full green trees surrounded the backyard.

The table Cora was placing things on was sheltered nicely under one of them. Flowerbeds of herbs and blossoms were scattered around the yard, giving it a planned but natural balance.

In the center of the yard were several small shrubs that formed a fairly large circle. Inside the circle, a fire bowl of copper sat with wide benches that almost rested against the shrubs.

Dade started to wander toward the fire bowl when Cora walked past him. "You could help carry the food out, Dade," she hissed at him and kept walking.

Sighing, he turned and caught up to her. "I'm your servant, honey; just tell me what you want me to do." She paused and turned to look at him then, smiled and walked in the door.

Steven, with a playful expression on his face, sat in the chair near the table. He rubbed his hands over his face. "This is going to be an interesting night." He winked at Rachel when she smiled at his comment.

"So, what are they doing that is taking so long?" Dade reached for another beer and as he looked to Owen for an answer.

Owen met Chris's knowing look then grinned at Dade.

"Well, I mentioned to Leena that the outfits she made the girls, you do remember those from Beltane, were unbelievable, so she's now toying with the idea of starting an internet business making fantasy and specialty outfits."

Dade paused in mid-drink to raise his eyebrows.

"Exactly. So, she's been working the last few weeks to make some samples... and you can thank me later for this. I told her I would get your honest opinions of them."

Dade grinned. "I'll thank you now and later."

Chris laughed and leaned down on his drum. "More importantly... am I to understand that you haven't seen Leena in a week?"

All three men turned to gape at Owen. He got up and added some wood to the bowl. "It's amazing, the story is going so great. I may even get a small series out of this. I've never been able to work at this pace before."

"Unbelievable," Steven added, "If I were with a woman like Leena, I'd set up a camp on her doorstep."

Owen sighed. "I would much rather be here every night, trust me, but I have to work to get paid. And I don't think I could work with her near me." He smirked at them.

"Okay, now *that* I understand." Dade motioned to the bench. "Park it, my friend, and let's see if we can get a good rhythm out of you on that drum."

Kasey giggled. "The outfits are amazing, Leena. I feel like I've just stepped into some fabulous fairy tale." She studied the pleasing image in the mirror.

Leena had taken light pastels and deep, jewel toned material and combined them to make a short skirted, but flowing, outfit. The top appeared to just be fluffy material hugging Kasey, leaving her abdomen bare and her shiny rhinestone belly ring very visible. All that was missing was the wings, Kasey thought. She adjusted the small crown of silver on her blonde locks.

Rachel laughed. "You look like some sort of fairy princess, Kase. That outfit is awesome on you." She stood beside Kasey and looked at their reflections. Rachel's outfit made her look like a warrior. With the multiple shades of red on her short skirt, she decided she was the sexiest Trojan warrior ever. The skirt was short enough to show the tattoo on her left thigh. She rubbed her hand over the little witch flying on her broom in front of the moon. Rachel adjusted the red halter top and thin headband she wore. Awesome. "Lee, you really have to take pictures of us so you can show your work if you decide to start this seriously."

Leena stepped over to them, and both women turned to her. "I'm way ahead of you." She lifted the camera and took pictures from all angles and then turned to look at her own reflection in the mirror. She looked like a princess bent on seduction. The slits on either side of her deep purple shimmering skirt showed much of her legs; she liked her long legs. The top was cut low; and left her back completely open. She had put sparkles throughout her long hair.

"You glow, Leena," Kasey whispered. "Although I'm not sure if it's the outfit or Owen."

Leena blushed, "He's made me feel so good about myself. I couldn't even begin to explain it."

Cora stepped into the room and smiled. "This is amazing, Lee. The best you've ever made for me." Cora was exotic. The skirt was a shimmering copper cut in strips that hung from her waist to her ankles, and the top fell loosely over her breasts leaving her tummy bare. Around it, Lee had fastened a copper chain, which against her dark skin showed off her tummy beautifully.

"Okay, final touch so we literally shine around that fire tonight." She quickly sprayed a faint sparkling mist over their exposed skin then nodded in satisfaction.

"I'm going to be drunk before they ever come back. That should impress and seduce, falling on my face off the bench," Steven mumbled.

Chris threw his head back and laughed. "Well, any attention is good, right?" His laughing stopped, "Fuck me." He knew his jaw dropped, but he didn't have the ability to prevent it.

They all turned toward Chris then followed to look to at the women slowly coming out the door.

"I think I just bit the end my tongue off," Steven whispered.

"How the hell am I supposed to drum when they're dressed like that?" Dade asked to no one in particular.

"So, Leena's outfits have passed?" Owen asked with a smirk.

Chris gasped. "Passed? I'm going to pass out if I get any harder."

"We need to drum, now. I don't think I could speak sensibly right now if I tried," Steven said quickly as he elbowed Chris.

Chris nodded but didn't take his eyes from the women.

"Fuck," Dade said under his breath and began a slow steady beat. The others followed.

Cora grinned and shot Rachel a knowing look as they stepped into view of the men.

"I'd say your outfits are going to be best-sellers if their reactions are any indication," Rachel whispered.

Laughing softly, they slowly began dancing hypnotically to the drums around the small fire. As Kasey passed by the fire, she lifted her hands over it and made it flicker higher to increase the light. Leena passed in front of the men and lifted her hands, gracefully sending a gentle breeze blowing over each man before she turned to continue around the bowl. Rachel glanced at the fire and spoke a few words under her breath to make it change into a blue flame. Cora chuckled as she danced by, knowing from the looks on their faces no magic was needed to draw their attention to the dancers this night.

Owen watched Leena's every movement. With each flash of leg, he struggled to keep the very simple beat they taught him. He wanted those legs wrapped around him. He wanted to lick his way slowly up each leg. His mouth was so dry he couldn't swallow.

"I need to wipe the drool off my drum," Dade said quietly to anyone who was listening. He quickly ended the drumming with a loud beat.

Steven was already reaching for beer.

Chris just sat there with his hand sitting on his drum and grinning at Kasey.

Owen was smiling at Leena walking toward them. "Baby, you need to dress every woman, with the talent you have." His voice wasn't as steady as he hoped it would be.

Leena smiled a siren's smile at him. "So, you like them?"

"Like doesn't begin to cover it." Owen held out a bottle of water to her.

Moving to stand beside him, Chris studied Kasey as she took a drink. His eyes constantly strayed back to the jewel in her belly button. "Kasey, will you be my fairy princess?" he finally said to her quietly. She paused from taking a drink and smiled shyly at him.

"We're going to need more beer out here... or water or something," Steven croaked as he noticed the small witch on Rachel's thigh.

"I'll go get some drinks," Leena said as she took the last bottle of mead out of the ice and handed it to Rachel.

"I'll help," Owen was up so fast, she hadn't taken a single step toward the house.

Owen stood and watched Leena start to walk towards the house. He grinned at Dade. "Those drinks might take a while."

Dade nodded and smiled at Cora. "You are a vision I will never forget, honey." He gave her a pleading look. "Dance for me, honey. Watching you makes my heart spin," he whispered. He began to play a slow, erotic rhythm on his drum and thanked the ancestors, when she smiled and began to move in time to the sound.

Owen turned and nearly sprinted after Leena

Leena hadn't even stepped inside the door when Owen caged her against the wall. "You have no idea the thoughts I've had watching you dance." He ran his hands inside her skirt up the back of bare legs. His lips moved over her neck with an urgency he didn't think he could control much longer. When his hands came in contact with the bare skin on her firm ass, he moaned against her throat and pulled her tight against his hard need. "I can't wait until later," he whispered against her mouth. Her hands were already under his shirt pushing it up just to touch him. While she fumbled with the button on his jeans, he devoured her mouth. His tongue brutally assaulted hers, and she moaned into his open mouth. "Upstairs..."

Leena pulled her head back and looked up at him. "No, need...went to the doctor this week," She saw that he had understood her, but his response was to devour her throat and cup her breasts in his hands, kneading and stroking. She began to tug his pants down over his hips. When his hard flesh was free, she grasped him lightly in her hand and bit against his neck.

"Now," Owen groaned and dragged his hands under her skirt to grip her hips and pick her up.

She wrapped her legs around his waist, grasped his shoulders, and lowered herself slowly to take him inside her. She could hear the drums outside and began to move in time with them as his mouth moved under her top and over her heated skin.

"So tight," he groaned and leaned her back against the wall. The drumbeat outside became louder, and he thrust up hard to the sound. She gasped and bit her bottom lip, her muscles tightening around him. "Can't wait, baby... now!" He growled against her throat and began to thrust faster. Gripping his neck, she pounded her body down on his, and her breathing came in shallow puffs. When he didn't think he could wait a second more, she dropped her mouth to his shoulder, then groaned and convulsed violently around him. He exploded inside her without warning.

Panting and trying to keep his legs from shaking, he held her tightly as they leaned against the wall. "We'll have to try again later when you haven't been tormenting the hell out of me with your dancing." He grinned against her lips and lowered her to the floor. Struggling, he pulled up his jeans then kissed her tenderly. "Go get cleaned up, and I'll take the drinks out before someone comes looking." She smiled back at him, a very satisfied gleam in her eyes.

Dade took one glance at Owen's easy gait when he walked out with a small cooler, and knew exactly what had the lucky bastard smiling. His eyes went back to Cora, who was driving him out of his mind moving in perfect time to his drum a few feet away from him. It would be so easy to use the drum to call her to him. He needed her to come to him...so easy. He slowed the rhythm and stared at her. He knew she felt it immediately as she moved a bit closer to him.

Then he slowed it and stopped. Cora would come to him on her own and not because of his drum's beckon. She panted out a breath and sat on the bench beside him. He could see the beads of sweat rolling slowly down between her breasts. He lowered his eyes to the ground.

"Dade Jones," she tried to catch her breath. "Were you about to use your talent and call me to you?" She smiled even though she should have been upset.

He looked at her for a moment. Then let out a deep breath. "I didn't mean to, all logical thought melted from my brain watching you dance, Coralee. That outfit... you look..." he grinned, "Wow."

Cora smiled and leaned over to gently brush her mouth over his. "Thank you." She held her hand out towards Kasey, who was sipping mead straight from the bottle.

Motioning to where Doc and Rachel with their heads close talking. "They're probably talking about kids," she mused quietly.

Kasey giggled, then took the bottle back and took another long drink. "I forgot how hot dancing is." She took another small sip, "although this outfit makes it much cooler." She turned to see Owen nuzzling into Leena's neck and holding her enclosed in his arms. "They're so happy," she whispered.

Cora nodded.

"I'm so jealous," Kasey said.

Cora nodded again.

Dade agreed silently.

When Cora went to sit for a few minutes, Chris walked up behind Kasey and slipped an arm around her waist, placing his hand over her belly button. With his lips against her ear, he whispered. "You're filling my head full of fantasies. Ones with my mouth and that sexy-as-hell ring in your belly button... I couldn't keep my mind focused on drumming each time I saw it."

Kasey leaned back against him and laughed. "Then I'd say Lee's outfits are a grand success."

Chris turned her and looked down at her. "I think it was more the woman in the outfit." He grinned at her slowly.

"Then go drum, and I'll show you more."

He studied her face for a moment then kissed her cheek lightly. "I love to suffer for you." He walked back over and sat with his drum.

Leena joined the others, hand in hand with Owen. "Look at them. What is it going to take to make them take that first step?"

Owen looked over and saw Chris and Kasey standing close watching each other. Dade was following Cora with his eyes, her glancing at him more often than anywhere else. Doc and Rach were head to head in deep discussion of something. "You could lock them in a room together, that would work."

"It's tempting." She laughed and pushed him toward the drums. "I want to torment you some more, go drum with them."

He kissed her hard and nodded.

"Play something primal. Urgent," Cora said to the men as she walked toward the fire bowl.

"Give us something we'll feel in our souls, gentlemen," Rachel winked at them as she went to stand beside Cora.

"Something with a driving energy," Kasey whispered as she sauntered slowly by them before flicking her hands over the flames turning them a dark red.

"I want to make your mouth water," Leena said looking at Owen as she stood by her sisters.

The four men looked at each other, then back to the women for a long moment. The red flames cast erotic shadows over their glittering bodies. "I think we can manage it," Dade said to them with a smile and began a complicated beat.

Chris nodded and found a place in the rhythm before adding his part of the sound. Steven took another drink and closed his eyes, waiting for the rhythm to repeat, and joined in.

Owen waited for a few more beats and then came in on the heaviest beat adding a depth to it so he could feel it deep inside his body.

Satisfied, the women began to circle the bowl, one after the other turning, hips grinding to the rhythm, heads down breathing in the beat that vibrated around them and through the earth under their feet.

He circled the date on the calendar.

Not much longer now.

He had a few weeks left before he had to punish again.

They would be easier to find this time. The warmer weather seemed to draw out the ones for selection.

It wouldn't be easy to do it without interference, but he was the one who had been chosen to carry out punishment, and he wouldn't fail those in need of his help.

His commitment was strong.

For a little longer he could rest and build up his strength to carry out his task.

❧ Chapter 15 ☙

Leena was excited to receive the date and place for the Summer Solstice gathering, despite the threat of a killer attending. She looked up the location on the computer and was thrilled to see the wild growth all around the campground. Gwen assured her they would get the large cabin with several rooms with two or more beds in each.

She grinned and wondered if it would be fair for her and Owen to take one room. Her friends could fight about who was sleeping where. She was excited, because she'd never been to a gathering as a couple, with someone to share all those moments, and those private thoughts you needed to express.

Leena shook her head and brought herself back to reality. She shouldn't be doing this at work. She chastised herself and closed the window on the computer, opening the shipping schedule instead. When the phone rang, she kept her eyes focused on the list of dates and picked it up. "Ms. Duncan." "Hey, pretty lady."

Work was forgotten. "Owen."

"I went through Cora to make sure you had a few minutes to talk."

"I would make the time if needed. What is so important you called me here?"

He cleared his throat. "I wanted to let you know I'll be gone for a few days. I'm meeting with my editor tonight."

"Oh. Will you be back for Wednesday?"

"Should be. We're meeting halfway. I have quite a few things to go over with him. Normally, we do this on line or by phone, but I want to lay this all out for them."

"I'm happy things are going so well for you with the book." She smiled at the exasperated sound he made.

"Can't type fast enough anymore, it seems. So, I just wanted to let you know... so you could miss me. I should be back late Wednesday afternoon if all goes well."

"I'll want to hear about everything when you get back. I already miss you, and it's been less than a day."

"Hopefully, we'll have something to celebrate when I get back. I'll miss you, and I'll try to take a few minutes to call you tomorrow."

"Okay."

"I better go, I've got a four-hour drive ahead of me and I want to get there first, so I can get this laid out for him properly."

"Okay. Be safe, you."

"I will, baby. Bye."

When she hung up, it took a few minutes to clear her head before she turned back to the monitor and tried to focus work, grinning.

Why did your mind always wander over every odd thought while driving long distances? Owen glanced at his speed again. Leena was amazing. He still wondered how he ended up with her in his life. He hadn't been looking for anyone, that part he knew. What happened to that promise he made to himself years before? No long-term relationships. Safe. No chance of family or being like his father. When had he begun to think of things with her as lifelong?

His mind hovered on the lifelong part for a second. There was no other option with someone like Leena. Her warmth reflected nothing but home. Family. She was meant to have a family to love and care for. She deserved a loving and understanding man, a man who would be a loving, understanding father to their children.

He pulled the Jeep off the road and sat staring at nothing. He was so completely lost in love with her, and he was pretty sure she felt the same way, even though neither of them had said the words

What the hell was he going to do now? He couldn't be a father. Okay, he could, but he definitely shouldn't take a chance on being one. "Idiot!" he cursed himself. "You better figure out what the hell you're doing, and fast," he muttered as he pulled back onto the road.

First, get this series in a contract with the publishers, and then he'd go back and figure out what he was doing with his life... back where his heart was in the hands of a sexy, loving witch.

Leena paced most of Monday night away and all of Tuesday. She didn't let herself send him any messages. Obviously, he was onto something important with his writing, and she didn't dare take the chance of interrupting negotiations with his editor. She picked up a book only to toss it back on the table. The only way to burn this nervous energy off was magic. Lots and lots of magic.

She went over to stand in the alcove of her herb shelves.

Leena loved this little space. The ceiling-high cupboards were a hunter green with deep-tinted windows holding every size and shape of colored jars. The open shelf under held her mortar and pestles. All six sizes for variety were important.

It was important not to use the same containers to mix lavender or something minty after having used it for fragrant valerian. She wrinkled up her nose, fragrant was not quite the right word. She began to flip open doors at random, seeking with her mind each jar she wanted.

At the flick of fingers a book opened, pages rustling as it stopped on the page she wanted. As good a time as any to mix cleansing herbs. You could never have enough of those.

Leena knew it would only be a matter of time before Cora wanted to go seeking again. She watched the herbs mixing in the large bowl then reached for a bag to place them in. Better mix up some protective ones, too, while she was here. The first jar she needed for this was already settling on the counter as she sealed the bag and set it aside. She lost track of her thoughts once more, her mind was far too distracted. She paused and frowned, looking down she realized even magic wasn't going to distract her for long.

Everyone sat around the room in Kasey's small one-bedroom house. The kitchen and living room were one large area, and there were only three doors in the house other than the way out, a bathroom, a bedroom, and the laundry room-part storage closet. The cozy little house was more like a cottage and seemed to suit her quiet personality, though.

Leena looked at her watch again and sighed. She looked up at Dade, who also wasn't listening to the conversation the others were having about the never-ending list of possible killers.

He winked at her and grinned. "He probably got tied up in negotiations. This is a pretty big deal for him, Lee." He spoke softly. "Owen usually writes a story then moves on to a new one, but you've inspired him to try writing a series this time."

She grinned at his reference to Owen's 'sappy line' as he had called it. "I know. I just wish he'd take a moment to call or something."

"He will when he can." Dade turned back to the bickering over the list of names. "Has anyone felt anything vaguely familiar with these so far?" Everyone shook their heads no. "Are we wasting a whole lot of time then?" A few shrugs.

Chris sighed and leaned back. "It feels like we're just running in place."

Kasey nodded in agreement

Cora set the page down. "I haven't even felt a tingle from these, even when I close my eyes and concentrate separately on each name while meditating." She let out a long-exasperated breath and glanced at Dade.

"Don't even think about it. Without Owen here, I won't listen to pleas for giving seeking a try." Dade gave Core a stern look.

"He's right," Rachel added, "without Owen to pull you out, it's too risky."

Steven threw up his hands. "Well, I say we continue to give these lists a glance when time permits, but, until then, if I don't go home and get some rest, I'm going to wake up on Kasey's carpet in the morning."

Everyone nodded.

Leena looked at her watch again.

Dade sighed. "I'll swing by Owen's on the way home and see if he's just passed out on the couch from the trip. If he's there, I'll hand him the phone. Okay?"

She nodded and looked down at her hands. "I'm just worrying over nothing," she said quietly as she got up and ran a hand down his arm. "I'm going to go home. I stayed up half the night last night reading over those lists, and I need some sleep." She didn't need to add she was just passing time hoping Owen would call.

Dade parked behind the Jeep and shook his head. He probably was passed out on the couch, just as he'd said.

Getting out, he went to the door and walked in bellowing, "Security system won't do you a damn bit of good if the door's unlocked, man." He stopped in midstride when he saw the man sitting in suit pants and a wrinkled dress shirt propped against the wall by the kitchen door with a half-empty bottle of what looked like rye.

"Dade!" Owen tried to get up and tipped over. "Have a drink, man. We're cel... brating the signing of contracts!" He took a long swallow before continuing. "I'm doing six books, man. Publisher's all 'cited about it. Me too."

Dade squatted down in front of him and pulled the bottle out of his hand. "So, why aren't you with Leena spinning her around and celebrating then?"

After pulling the bottle back, Owen squinted. "Long drive. *Lotta* thinking." He raised the bottle to his lips then lowered it again. "I can't keep her, bro. Can't, won't take the chance with her." He sighed, "she's so pretty. Have you ever noticed that? So gentle..." He grinned when his friend pulled him up to his feet. As he teetered upright for a moment he enthused, "I love her, man."

Dade supported Owen as he headed toward the kitchen. "You love her, so you're going to stay away from her? How the hell much have you drunk?"

Owen staggered to lean against the doorframe. "Ya, she's gonna wan' babies, an' weddings. Probably not in that order, but I can't." He tried to put the bottle to his mouth and missed. Chuckling he lowered his hand again. "Can't be a father, Dade, you know that. *You* know!"

"I know you're shit-faced right now." Dade pulled the larger man a few feet and dropped him into a chair. He quickly caught him again before he tipped right off the other side. "Leena's so gone for you, man. What the hell are you doing?" He walked to the cupboards and started looking for coffee. Turning back quickly, he pulled the bottle out of his friend's hand and set it out of reach. "What do you mean you can't be a father; you've had a vasectomy?" Dade's stomach clenched when he said the word. What man would intentionally put himself through that?

"Nooo. No... ouch... fuck, no!" Owen slid off the chair and landed on the floor on his side. With an amused look, he twisted his head and looked up at him. "Man, you tall from down here." The expression on his face hardened again. "*Won't.* I *won't* be a father." He leaned back on both hands, squinting at Dade. "Won't take a chance, might snap... beat 'em sense... less, you know? *You* know, man!" Dade flipped on the coffeemaker before turning back to the idiot sprawling on his own kitchen floor. "So, you're just going to blow Leena off? Ignore her and leave her sitting at home wondering where the hell you are?"

"She does this thing with her tongue..." Owen grinned at the dark eyes glaring down at him. "Can't see her right now, would have to kiss her."

"You couldn't see her right now if you wanted to, bro." He gripped Owen's shoulders from behind. "Sit the fuck up and have some coffee." He dragged him back against the cupboard. "Then you're going to tell me what your fucked-up brain is thinking." Dade squatted down so he was level with the idiot's face. "She sat through the meeting looking at her watch every three seconds, Owen."

"Meeting." Owen grinned. "Signed a contract... six books!"

Dade let out an exasperated breath and dropped his head. It was going to be a long night. Long, *long* night.

Dade listened through the slurred stage, commenting only when Owen tried to make eye contact with him. He listened through the angry stage. Owen was angry that he was forcing coffee into him when he wanted rye. He listened through the moaning stage when his friend's head was on the table. Now a red-eyed, depressed man looked at him in silence. "I think you're being stupid if you really want to know."

Owen's held his head in one hand and his other held his stomach. His eyes were half closed and Dade was pretty sure all he wanted to do was go lie down in some dark corner and sleep for the next few days. With the way he flinched at every movement, he was certain Owen had reached the stage where shooting pains went through his head every time he moved.

"I won't take a chance on turning into my father. I won't take that chance with Leena. She's been through enough."

"So, go talk to her. You don't even know if she wants a family, or you, for the rest of her life." Dade waited for Owen's scowl and knew he was on the right track. "She hasn't said she loves you or ever mentioned anything but the odd day here and there...you might just be temporary to her, bro."

Owen's head snapped up, and then grabbed his head, he snarled at him. "What the fuck are you saying, that she sleeps around? I know fuckin' better than that!" He slammed his fist on the table. "Watch what you're saying when you talk about her, or I'll lay you out flat!"

Dade had to bite back the grin. "Have you talked to her about any of this, Owen?" He pushed the chair back just to be sure he was out of reach of those big hands. "You don't know what she wants...only what you think you don't want. You're an idiot." He stared into the red eyes. His head must be pounding. "I knew your father, Owen, and I know you. There is no way that you would *EVER* raise a hand to a woman or a child."

"Fuck!" Owen gripped the sides of his head again. "I just want her so much, Dade, so fuckin' much. She's in my head every minute of every day." He rubbed a hand over his eyes then tried to focus on him. "I'm scared to death I'll hurt her, I'll disappoint her..."

"Go to bed." When Owen opened his eyes and looked at him as he continued. "Go get some sleep, and when you're feeling human again and have your thoughts all sorted out, go talk to her." Dade stood up and waited, hoping he'd get up, too, so he could go home and get an hour of sleep before he had to get to work.

"I don't think I'd survive it if she turned away." Owen stood up slowly trying to prevent the pain he knew was going to burst into his head. "I don't know how to tell her any of this."

"Send her a message for now, and get some rest. Give yourself a few days to get your head together if you have to, but don't leave her sitting there wondering. It sucks." He pushed his friend out of the kitchen. "And for fuck's sake, stay out of the damn bottle." Dade watched the slow-moving man pick up his coat and search for his phone. After he had made sure Owen got to the couch without collapsing, Dade opened the door and went home.

Looking at the text message for the tenth time, Leena smiled.

Biggest deal of my career signed. Will call you later need sleep.

She'd been worried for nothing. He was home now and sleeping.

Cora was climbing into her car to head to work when her phone rang.

Just sobered up drunken Owen and put him to bed. Will explain later. Keep eye on Lee, but don't tell her. He needs to get his head together. D

She sent back that she would and wondered what was going on now. Tonight might be a good night to have a girl's night, just as soon as she spoke with Dade.

Cora was no further ahead at the end of the day. Leena told her Owen was back and had signed the biggest deal of his career, and she seemed very happy about things. Cora sent Dade a message before she cleared her desk. She told him to call her before she headed out with the girls for dinner.

The phone rang less than a minute later. She answered it and heard his voice on the other end.

"You four are going out for dinner in public alone?"

She grinned. Would he ever relax and let her be an adult? "We'll be together the whole time and won't walk down any dark alleys."

Dade sighed., "Sorry, you're right. I haven't had any sleep. I spent the day trying not to cut off my own hands."

"What happened last night?"

"I went to check on Owen for Lee and found him shit-faced on his floor 'celbrating' a signed contract and mourning his relationship with Leena."

"Mourning? How do you mean? She's not aware of it." Cora frowned.

"No, and keep it that way, Coralee." He dropped his tool belt onto the seat of his van and climbed in. "You know what his prick of a father did to him growing up. You saw it as much as I did. Well, the idiot has it in his head he's going to be just like him and is ready to toss the whole thing with her out the window over it." Dade sighed loudly, "He's so in love with her it's fried any sense he had."

"Well, that part is good, because I know she loves him just as much. But, seriously, I've seen that man with her, and with and those children at the fair. He'd never touch anyone to cause pain."

"I know, I know. Tried to explain that to him while I was picking his sorry ass up off the floor." He opened his eyes before he drifted off sitting there in his van.

"So, what do you want me to do, Dade? Why did you send me the message?"

Dade grinned, he knew Cora would catch on. "Keep her busy tonight and tomorrow night if you can manage it. Get Kase and Rach in on it if you have to. Make him have to chase her for a change."

"Oh, I see where you're going with this." She paused for a moment and thought. "Okay, it shouldn't be too hard to do. If we run out of ideas, you might have to drag Chris and the Doc in, too, but I'll do my best." She smiled. "Dade, you're a sweet man to care this much."

Dade shrugged to no one. "Just don't want to see them do something stupid, honey." He sighed loud, "I better head home before I fall asleep sitting here in my van. Keep me posted."

"You do the same and send me a message so I know you got home in one piece."

He smirked at her concern. "Will do."

Leena was exhausted. She'd tossed and turned the night before worrying over Owen, she hadn't slept the night before that waiting to hear from him, and now tonight the girls decided they wanted her to plan Solstice outfits. She loved that they were excited and asked her. But right now, she just wanted to lie down and rest.

When her cell phone beeped, she groaned and got off the couch to find it.

Can I come see you tomorrow after work?

She groaned. She missed him so much, but the girls talked her into going material shopping for the outfits.

Am out with girls for part of tomorrow night. Will let you know when I get back though. Miss you.

I'll be waiting to hear from you. Miss you too, pretty lady.

She closed the phone and smiled to herself. *I wonder how quickly I can buy material.*

When Owen received the message she was staying at Cora's tonight with the girls, he stomped down to the kitchen for coffee. He wanted to see her yesterday not tomorrow!

He knew exactly what he needed to say to her and hoped she'd understand and accept it. Hoped she'd not turn from him completely and never speak to him again. He couldn't do marriage and family, he just felt it deep down. It would take time to be able to explain this to her, and he sure couldn't do it over the phone or by text message. He had to do it face to face, even if he needed to tie his own hands to keep them off her until he was finished.

Grabbing the cup of coffee, he stomped back into his office space and flipped open his laptop. He'd work on the book until then to keep his mind busy.

Leena smiled to herself as she carried the bags into the house. She'd had so much fun last night. The shopping part was necessary, but spending the night laughing and talking to her closest friends had been something they hadn't done since last fall. She missed it.

Glancing at her phone, she saw the message light blinking. Pressing it, she began emptying the bags onto the dining room table.

"Hey, let me know when you're home," Owen's voice filled the room.

With a smile, she picked up the phone and dialed it.

When she got his answering machine, she told it she was home until four then had to go with Rachel to the community center for a few hours to the kid's art night. She hung up and smiled. He's probably asleep on top of his keyboard at this point.

She was wrong.

Owen sat waiting and waiting and trying to focus on his characters. They weren't cooperating. They weren't distracting him from waiting to hear from Leena.

He saw the flashing light on the answering machine as he passed the phone on the way for more coffee, and he cursed. The ringer was off? He listened to the message and looked at the clock. It was four thirty. Sighing, he left her another message saying he'd missed the call and to call him as soon as she got home.

On his way back up the stairs his cell phone beeped and it was an all call for an important emergency meeting at eight that night. Well, he'd at least be able to see her then. He could follow her home and talk to her.

The second time the phone beeped, it was Steven asking if he could pick him up at the hospital and take him to the meeting. Cursing, Owen said he would. He'd get Dade to take Doc home afterward.

❧ Chapter 16 ❧

Leena sat at Chris's waiting for what seemed like hours for Owen and Steven to arrive. Chris wouldn't tell anyone why this was an emergency meeting and wasn't going to say anything until everyone was there.

She killed time reading through the part of the list she had left off on a few days ago. She smiled as Dade and Cora seemed to be having yet another of their face-to-face discussions. Some day they would open their eyes and see what was in front of them.

Dade glanced over Cora's shoulder to see if Leena was still busy on the other side of the room. "Doc said he'd get someone to page him, and then he can pick up his own car when Owen takes him back to the hospital."

Cora nodded. "I'll fake a headache or something I guess." She looked uncomfortable with the plan. "Then you can take me home."

"This is why I picked all you ladies up tonight." He turned toward Chris and looked at him a moment. "What has he come up with to call this meeting?"

Cora shrugged. "I have no idea. He wouldn't share with me."

Leena was up off the chair and in Owen's arms before he got all the way in the door. He'd said he'd keep his distance. Hadn't he vowed that to himself all the way here? How could he not hold her when she was wrapped around him? Unable to stop his own arms, he pulled her tight against his body and held her. Unable to stop his own mouth, he kissed her deeply, and when her mouth devoured his, he forgot he wasn't going to do this.

His traitorous hand reached and held her head gently, forgetting again he wasn't going to do this before they talked.

Leena pulled back and smiled up at him. "I need to hear everything. You've left me hanging all week about this big deal, Owen." She nibbled his bottom lip. "First, we need to find out what was so important that Chris called us all here, though."

He tucked her under his arm, then walked into the room. Owen ignored the knowing grin Dade gave him and settled down on the couch with her still close to his side. Why did just being near her settle all his fears? Wasn't he the one with the talent that was supposed to do that to others?

Rubbing his hand down her arm, he and smiled into those sexy amber eyes. "I really need some time with you later, Leena," he whispered.

She grinned. "You better, after being absent all week again." She snuggled tight into his shoulder and sighed.

Chris cleared his throat and waited until they all turned to look at him. He was holding a tray with flutes of champagne. "I called this little gathering tonight for a rather important announcement, and I've just found out we actually have two important announcements within the group." He set the tray down. "Owen, why don't you share yours first, then I'll tell everyone about the second."

Owen gave him a startled look but grinned. "Well, I spent half of this week haggling with publishers and editors... and signed a contract for a six-book series." He hugged Leena tight against him. "Of course, I'm not sharing the plot line with anyone right now." He winked down at her. "But it's the biggest deal I've ever signed and I won't have to worry over finances for some time to come. I'm well into writing the second story now."

There were cheers and congratulations from all directions. Hands were extended to shake his, kisses sweetly placed on his cheeks. His heart stopped when he finally looked down at Leena again. She looked back at him with a pride he'd never remembered seeing in anyone's eyes when they'd been looking at him. There it was shining back at him so clearly it almost blinded him.

"I'm so happy for you," she whispered and hugged him tightly to her.

Chris walked over and stood in front of them. "It's obviously all about the two of you tonight. Leena. Tyler's case went before the judge yesterday afternoon." She gave him a startled look. "I helped push a few buttons, and it wasn't that hard when they wanted to get it done before he could take off again."

He sat on the coffee table and looked at her anxious expression. "He will be out of the picture for the next ten, with no chance of parole for seven, and once he is out, he is not allowed to even be in the same city as you."

Leena sat there for a moment as she absorbed what he was telling her. "I can't believe it's over." She looked up to see the tear-filled eyes of her female friends and then turned to look at Owen. "I'm really free from him for good," she whispered, still in shock. She half climbed right into his lap as she hugged him tightly.

Half kneeling, she spun toward Chris and grabbed him, wrapping her arms around his neck. "Thank you, Chris." In one excited leap she was up off the couch, over the table, and into the girls' arms.

The four men each reached for glasses on the table and watched the women. It was one of those moments men tried to avoid but certainly didn't mind seeing from time to time. Cora stopped hugging and walked quickly over to the glasses of champagne. She looked at Leena and lifted the glass. "To the ending." She lifted it toward Owen with a smile, "and the beginnings," she smirked into her glass when Owen almost choked on his drink from her well-placed words.

After several rounds of chatting and some more endless chatting, Owen looked at the clock. If he started now, he might get her out of here in the next hour. He was just starting to rise when he noticed Cora holding her stomach.

"I don't think the champagne agreed with me." When he stepped in her direction, she shook her head. "No, it will be fine, Owen. I'll just get Dade to take me home so I can lie down."

"You're sure?" When she nodded, he turned to see if he could persuade Leena to go. Doc swore in the corner as his pager went off. He cursed silently to himself when he headed over to him.

"Can you run me back to the hospital, Owen?" He watched behind him as Cora was hugging Chris and getting her purse. "I didn't think I'd have to go back tonight or I would have taken my own car. I'd ask Dade, but it looks like he's taking Cora home."

Owen glanced around at everyone else. Why did he have that weird feeling? They seemed to be in deep discussion standing at the door. Chris was off in the corner talking quietly to Leena.

Something wasn't feeling right here, but he couldn't put it in words. "What is going on?" he asked no one in particular rather loudly. Everyone stopped and looked at him. Leena gave him a startled look from the tone he'd used.

Dade swore and stuffed his hands in his pockets and looked down at the floor as Cora looked at hands that were no longer clenching on her stomach. Kasey and Rachel stopped talking and looked at each other. That was all he needed.

Owen spun back to the Doc. "You're in on this, too? Do you really need to get to the hospital?" Steven let out a long breath and looked as guilty as Chris stood there with his attorney face on. "What the hell is going on?"

"Owen." Leena started to walk toward him, but he held up a hand.

"You've been doing this to me all week, haven't you?" He glared at Dade. "You son of a bitch! I have been losing my mind, and you're behind it?" Dade only shrugged in his 'whatever' way and continued to look at him.

"Stomach suddenly better there, Cora, darlin'?" Cora at least looked guilty. He gave a brief glance to Rachel and Kasey, then turned back to Leena. She was clearly shocked and confused. He stomped over and grabbed the bag he knew was hers, grasping it in his hand he went towards her. "To hell with all of this!"

Owen walked over and flipped her up into his arms to carry her tightly against her chest. When she yelped, Dade stepped forward. "We'll take care of this ourselves. Just stay out of it."

"Owen, have you lost your mind?" Leena demanded probably looking as bewildered as she felt.

"Close, baby, but not yet. Later ask everyone how hard they worked this week to keep us away from each other, but right now I'm taking you home where I can bloody well see you and talk to you without playing goddamned phone tag!"

"What?" She demanded as he went through the door with her. She chanced a look over her shoulder to see everyone standing together with the biggest smiles on their faces she'd ever seen. "Well," she pushed against him. "Put me down, and at least let me walk. You look like an idiot carrying me and a purple purse."

Leena went with him without another word and continued to not say anything until she was sitting in his living room. She smiled at him when he finally settled down in the chair across from her. "Now will you explain to me what just happened? I think I've been pretty good about being hauled out of Chris's and tossed into your Jeep."

Owen ran his hand over his hair as if rubbing it would help him find the words. "Sorry, but when I realized I'd been going out of my mind all week trying to get some time to talk to you... I'm pretty sure your friends have kept you really busy this week, busy enough..." He stopped and stared at his phone. "Shit. Dade probably turned the damn thing off on me." He leaned forward and looked down at his clasped hands that rested on his knees. "None of that part matters right now." He looked up at her. "I did a lot of thinking while I was driving back and forth this week, Leena."

"I see."

He didn't like how quietly she had said that. "It's not what you're thinking. I'm not telling you to bug off or anything. I just... just need you to listen to me, please."

"I'm listening, Owen, but I have no idea what you're trying to say."

Nodding more to himself than her. "Right. I've tried to figure out how to explain this, spent all week trying to figure out how to explain this, and I still don't know how to explain it." Owen stood up and paced to the window turning back toward her.

Then he stuffed his hands in his pockets. She looked so soft and lovely as she sat there looking up at him patiently. Letting out a long breath, he tried again. "You know how my father was. Actually, if I think about it long enough, I could blame my success with writing on that man. I lived in my own mind when I was growing up, wrote stories when I needed to escape." He paused for a moment and ran his hands over his face. "I really love being with you, Leena, and I am half in love with you. Well, probably a lot more than half, but I'm not being fair to you." Leena sat forward and studied him silently for what felt like an hour.

"In what way, Owen?"

Her soft, understanding voice almost made him crawl to her and rest his aching head in her lap. "I vowed, years ago, I don't know the exact day or anything, but I vowed I'd never have children. I'd never take that chance...that I'd never take the chance I'd be my father." When she went to speak, he pleaded. "Please, let me finish now or I might never get it out."

She nodded.

"I don't think he was always like that, but I don't remember when it started. It was a gradual thing, I think."

Owen walked over and squatted in front of her and took her hands. "I've never been in the position where that could happen. I wasn't looking to get into it either. I see you with children and a warm, loving home. You do want kids someday, don't you, Leena?" He almost hoped she'd say no so he could hold her and kiss her right now, when he'd never needed to more.

Leena lowered her lashes and looked at their hands. "Someday," she whispered.

"You'd be an amazing mother, Aileena," he told her quietly. "I want so much to be with you, don't misunderstand that, but I can't be a father. I won't take that chance with an innocent child." He gripped her hands tightly for a second then let them go. "Do you understand what I'm trying to say?" He looked into eyes that were glossy with tears that didn't fall.

"No, not completely." Leena swallowed and then cleared her throat quietly. "You basically just said you loved me, but you don't want to be with me."

She looked up at him, her eyes filled with pain. "I do want to be with you, Leena, more than I've ever wanted to be with anyone." He stood up and walked back to the window. "You deserve a husband and children and the happy world you were denied for years. I can't be that man." He couldn't let himself think of her with anyone else just yet. "I can't give you that." He turned to look back at her.

Leena had her arms wrapped around her stomach. "So, what do we do now?" Her voice trembled.

The sound of her voice almost brought him to his knees, his chest tightened so much it hurt to breathe. "I don't know." He turned to see her taking her phone out of her purse. He knew she was calling one of the friends they'd just left to take her home. He didn't want her to go, but he stopped himself from telling her.

She closed her phone and looked up at him. "I think you need some time to figure out what you do want, Owen." Her lips quivered as she spoke. "I can't do that for you."

A moment of weakness hit him. "Leena." He actually reached toward her and then stopped, pulled his hand back, and put it in his pocket. "I didn't plan this, didn't plan beyond the fact that every time I looked at you my heart jumped in my throat and I couldn't think."

She sat there a moment with her purse bunched up in her lap holding it before she looked at him.

"I'm sorry," he whispered. His throat felt raw, and he couldn't find any more words for her.

Leena's phone buzzed in her hand. Dade must be at home. He'd be here in five minutes. She put it in her purse and stood up. "I know you didn't, Owen, and I do understand why you think you couldn't be a father." She walked and stood in front of him and looked up to see the torment in his eyes. The pain she felt, he felt too. "Let me just tell you what I know. I know the man that sheltered me and kissed me when I was all but broken would never raise his hand to a woman. I know the man that led a shy little boy around a fair would never so much as raise a harsh voice at a child, never mind his hand."

She reached up and placed her palm on his cheek. "When you work this out..." her voice was shaking, "when you work this out, let me know what to do." She stretched up and kissed him softly on the lips. She turned and moved quickly to the front door.

He whispered her name once as she went out it.

Dade had just pulled in the driveway when he spotted Leena walking quickly out the door. It only took one look on her face to know that Owen had in fact lost his mind completely.

As she climbed in the van, he glanced back at the house to see his friend standing in the door looking much like Leena did. He would give him a day then tell him what an asshole he was. As he backed out of the driveway, he glanced at the woman who was barely holding it together.

Leena didn't remember the drive home. Dade hadn't spoken, He knew she didn't need his words then. As she walked in the house, she heard the answering machine come on.

"Leena, I'm sorry." His voice was rough with raw pain. "I want so much to beg you to come back, but I know that's just being selfish. I... I wish... I'm sorry, Leena. So sorry."

The machine clicked off.

She let the tears she'd been holding in out as she collapsed onto the couch still hugging her purse.

The next morning, Owen ignored the phone. He would have picked it up if Leena's number had come up, but it didn't. He ignored the doorbell. He ignored the loud knocking. Ignored Dade's cursing on the outside of the door. He threw himself into his writing and vowed he wouldn't stop until he burned out this confusion, until he could sit for five minutes without wanting to drive to Leena's and beg her to forgive him.

On the other side of town, Leena read the tenth message that had been sent to her. She ignored each phone call, ignored messages. She made sure all her doors were locked and turned her stereo on low and forced herself to go over each list Chris sent earlier again. Hoping she'd missed something the first time. She needed time to settle. She needed time to decide what she would do with her broken heart when Owen told her he was walking away for good.

ⸯⴰ⳺ **Chapter 17** ⳺ⴰⸯ

Dade pounded on Owen's door hard enough to shake the windows beside it. When he heard the lock click, he opened the door and walked in without waiting. "I've had three women bitching at me since last night because *you're* an idiot. Tonight, Coralee was almost in tears because Leena didn't go to work today, and Leena *never* calls in. I ended up leaving the site early so I could come here and beat your head against a wall."

He spun around and looked at Owen for the first time since storming through the door. He looked like he already had. "But I can see now you've been beating your own head against the wall. Good." He went and dropped down in the nearest chair, not caring if he brought half the dust from the work site with him.

Owen sat across from him and dropped his face into his hands. "What did you mean with 'Leena never calls in'?"

Dade snorted. "Just what I said, she called in sick today. She won't answer the phone or return messages. The girls have been losing their minds all day worrying about her." He threw his hands up. "Short of breaking into her house and assessing with my own eyes that she is in fact in one piece, I don't know what the hell to do to calm these women down! So, I came here to take it out on you."

Owen sighed, "Pretty sure she won't answer the phone for me either, bro, so what am I supposed to do?"

Dade shook his head. "Well, for starters, you could have not done what you did yesterday. When you carried her out of there, I thought you'd come to your senses about all of this." He stood up. "What the fuck happened?"

"You know what happened. I told you what I'd decided, and none of that has changed."

Dade spun around. "You're so fucking in love with that woman that you ripped out her heart and handed it back to her?" He snorted again and walked over to the phone. As he dialed it, he continued to bark at Owen. "If you had half a brain in your head, you'd crawl there on your hands and knees and beg her forgiveness." When she picked up the phone, he wasn't surprised, it being Owen's number

"Leena, it's Dade. I was just hanging out here when Cora sent me a message. She's worried you didn't go in to work today."

"Dade, oh, I decided to take a day for me, catch up on a few things."

"You all right, honey?" He wanted to smack Owen's head on the wall again, because of her shaky voice.

"Yes, I'll be fine. I'll send the girls a message so they're not bothering you. I just needed to take some time, nothing to worry about."

"It's no bother, Leena. You know I'll always be your white knight." He tried to sound easy going and not as upset as he really was.

"Yes, thank you." There was a long pause. "Is he okay, Dade?" Her voice quivered.

Dade closed his eyes for a moment, trying to find the right words. "You want me to rough him up, honey? Say the words, and I will."

"No! No, just make sure he's okay for me, please." She sniffled, "please, I have to go." She hung up.

Dade hung up the phone and then turned to lean against the wall. He looked at the man who appeared to be in as much pain as Leena had sounded like she was in. "You know you're a fuckin' idiot, don't you?" He pushed away from the wall and went and sat down. "She's a mess. Does that put it into perspective for you? But she's still worried about you. I'm supposed to make sure you're okay."

Owen dropped his face back into his hands. "What do I do?"

Dade sat forward and leaned on his knees and stared at him. "Well, you could have started by *not* doing what you did last night. You could have just played it day-by-day, kind of working it out as you go like the *rest* of the planet does, but, no sir, you felt happiness and panicked then set forth to crush it before it went too far and led to a happy life for the next forty or so years."

Owen looked up at him silently for a moment. He had pretty much summarized the same thoughts that had played havoc with him for the last ten or so hours. The thoughts followed his resolve to work until it didn't hurt. After the thoughts of driving to Leena's and holding her tightly until she told him she loved him no matter how it worked out. He was an idiot; he knew this much on his own. "I didn't mean to hurt her," he said quietly.

"Well, you did, and I'd say from the looks of it, your own heart isn't doing so well right now either." He stood and looked over at him. "What are you going to do, Owen?"

"I don't know. It all sounded so good in my head, really it did. I would explain to her, and she would understand. We'd continue to be friends..."

"What? You expected her to stick around and hold your hand after you told her 'Hey, I can sleep with you, but I'll never marry you and I never want kids'? You're the first man she's ever really looked at, since Tyler, and what did you do..."

Owen stood up. "Stop! I know what I fuckin' did, okay. I was there!" He stomped over to the window. "I explained to her how I felt, and she just sat there all quiet and understanding. Do you know when I was finished crushing her heart, she kissed me and told me I was a gentle man and would be a loving father and that when I figured it out to let her know." He rubbed his hand over his heart as if it were physically aching. Shaking his head, he turned back to the window.

"Well, she should have set your ass on fire or blown you out through a wall or something." Dade crossed his arms and stared at him.

"That would have been easier to deal with." Owen turned back to face him. "Fuck! I didn't ask for her heart, Dade. I wasn't looking to give mine to anyone. Ever!" He stuffed his hands in his pockets. "I just couldn't stop it. I looked at her and wanted...I watched her and ached, and when I held her, I thought to myself 'maybe just once there can be someone for me.'"

Dade stared at him. How was he supposed to help his friend when he couldn't even touch the woman he'd wanted for years? How did he fix this? He didn't know. "I can't help you, my friend. I wish I had the answers you need, but I don't."

Owen shook his head in defeat. "I know." He looked at him again. "I really need to be alone. I have to figure this out."

Dade nodded and headed to the door. "Call me if you feel the need to smack your head on the wall...I'm always there to help a friend."

Owen had been staring at a blank page for more hours then he wanted to count. His characters had abandoned him. They had nothing to say and refused to do anything to help him. He closed the Word document and sat and looked at the keyboard. He wanted to call her, but he didn't know what to say. He hadn't changed his mind, that much he knew, but he couldn't get past wanting to talk to her. He toyed with the idea of sending her an e-mail, but he didn't know how to start or what to say, much less how to finish.

With a sigh he closed the laptop and walked over to look out the window. He wasn't even looking out the window, he realized, just vaguely facing the glass but not seeing. He glanced over at the phone again. What could he say that would stop her pain, and his pain? Nothing that wouldn't be a lie.

When the phone in his pocket buzzed, he literally jumped six inches. Shit! He opened it and stared at the words for several minutes before he moved again.

Are you doing okay? L

No, he thought. I miss you. I want you. I'm sorry I'm an idiot. Then he typed back: *Yeah--you?*

So he was a liar.

The message came back: *Yes. Worried about you though.*

Confirming she was lying tonight, too. At least she was lying to make him feel better. He was just lying to himself. He glanced at the clock and realized how many hours had gone by since Dade had left him.

Don't worry about me--try to get some rest baby.

He had sent it before he realized he'd typed baby at the end. How had she gotten so deep inside him in such a short time? When he read her next message, it was a few minutes before he could reply.

You too. Call if you need me Owen.

He wanted to call her right then... if he needed her? How could he not?

You too. Night. He replied, and then sat there staring at the phone until her reply came back to him.

Night

Owen wanted to throw the phone at the floor and stomp on it. Not because he wanted to call her with it. Not because she'd been the one strong enough to send the first message. He wanted to beat it, because even after what he had done to her, she still wanted to make sure he was fine. He wasn't fine!

He was far from fine! His thoughts churned as he stormed through the house with no real destination in mind.

When he found himself standing in the living room with no idea why he'd gone there, he dropped down on the couch and stared at the ceiling. He'd never hated his father more than he did right at this moment. He hated him for putting this doubt in his mind, for making him hurt the only woman he'd ever really wanted to spend the rest of his life with.

After years of running and avoiding he had come home to his mother's grave, having only ever set eyes on her once in all those years he'd been away. He had come home to begin his life finally, and when he thought he'd left all the rest behind, his father was right there in his way *again*.

Why couldn't he get away from that man? Why did he have to stand in front of everything Owen ever wanted telling him no, telling him it, and he, was a waste of time? He clenched his fists and dropped his arms across his head. He shook from the rage boiling inside him. His father had taken from him the one happiness he'd ever found outside his own self-created fantasies inside his stories.

Leena. Beautiful, patient Aileena.

He sighed. He could see her at Beltane walking toward the circle ...he could see her smiling up at him, he could see her in that purple fantasy she wore at her party, see her laughing.

Leena.

He opened his eyes and sat up. With a shake of his head, he looked down at the couch. He'd been sitting there all but screaming with rage just from the thought of his father, and then he'd thought of her. Then rage was gone, his hands were steady, and his heart ached with wanting her. How could just the thought of her do that?

He sat there smiling to himself when reality came back and he remembered the night before. How was he ever going to get through this?

He jumped up and went back to his office. At this rate he'd be in the mental ward at Doc's hospital if he didn't get his head together.

A few miles away, three women sat looking quietly at each other. "That better not backfire in our face, Cora. Leena would blow us all the way to the Arctic if she finds out." Rachel chewed her own lip as she spoke.

Cora leaned back from the hands she'd been holding. "There's nothing to backfire, we didn't do anything that was wrong... really. Well, okay, so the two involved didn't know about it; but all we did was send them the thought of talking to each other." She closed her eyes to avoid looking at the others.

Kasey began picking up the candles and stones, removing the evidence was how she looked at it. "It's what they needed, right?" She didn't stop from putting things away to look at either of them.

When the knock on the door came, they all jumped and quickly put everything out of sight. "Shit!" Rachel whispered then nodded, as Kasey stood ready to open her door. When she opened it, she giggled to see Dade, Chris, and Steven standing there with questioning looks on their faces.

Chris stepped inside the room. "Ladies." He sniffed the air.. "That's not mullein... and rose I smell, is it?" He watched Dade look under the edge of the table and behind where Cora sat.

"Doing anything interesting tonight?" Steven inquired quietly as Rachel sat farther back in a chair.

Cora shrugged and looked at him. "Just girl talk mostly."

"So, we're too late to help?" Dade asked her.

"With what?" she asked him sweetly.

"Sneaky witches, aren't you?" Chris asked as he sat on the floor beside her. "We went to Cora's first, then Rachel's. We knew you three wouldn't leave things the way they were, so we wanted to help." He pulled out a bag of stones and waved them around.

Everyone burst out laughing.

"We didn't do anything wrong, really. I just sent them both the suggestion to talk," Kasey said, examining her own hands.

"Did it work?" Chris asked her with a serious look on his face.

Cora sighed. "We can't know for sure, but it had good vibes. I've never really tried to push a vision, only accepted visions."

"And if Leena feels the magic?" Chris raised both eyebrows at her.

Dade grinned. "You all better run and hide."

Rachel threw a cushion at him. "You three as well. You may not have actually been here to help, but you were looking for us to do it, and now you know about it."

"Sneaky witches," Chris murmured and dropped on his back.

Dade went over and flopped into a chair. "Let us know next time, okay? We could have helped. I spoke to Lee and saw Owen, and after that I'd help tie them up in a room together if I thought it would help either of them."

Kasey sat forward. "Well, now that you mention it, Rach and I have been working on a rather complicated spell of sorts, one to help us see, to help with the lists, but it's not ready yet. Maybe by the end of the week..."

Chris held up his hand, and she stopped. "Is it dangerous in any way?"

She shook her head. "No, that's just it. This one isn't going to draw anyone in. It's kind of a divination sort of thing, perfectly safe as none of us will be directly connected."

"Count us in then," Steven said as he looked at his watch then to Dade. "I need sleep. It took us two hours to get it together to come looking for the three of you."

Kasey stepped over to Chris and looked up at him. "Can we use your place when we do this? We need a fairly open area, and mine's a little small."

Chris stood up and smiled down at her. "Absolutely." He looked at her a moment more. "Let us know if you find out anything."

Dade winked at them and walked to the door. "I'll see you sneaky witches later."

He set his knife on his Bible and began to pray
silently to himself.
He needed to know which ones to punish.
He couldn't make a mistake and fail.
He began to pray for the sinners' souls.
Calling them to come to him.
To meet him at their heathen summer gathering.
To dance by him and raise their arms to him,
accepting their sins.
Accepting their punishment.
Giving their souls to him to cleanse

cଔ© **Chapter 18** ୬ଙ

Leena kept busy at work. Although after taking a day off, she didn't have to go looking to find things to keep her mind occupied. Her friends accepted she didn't want to talk about any of it, and hadn't pushed her. She was very proud of herself for not breaking down again. She had a few weak moments, and those she forgave herself for.

It was those moments when she found herself alone in her office that were the hardest. She wanted to pick up the phone and call Owen and tell him she didn't care about children and marriage and happily-ever-after, but she just wanted to be with him, just wanted what he could give of himself for as long as he could give it, and that would be all she'd ever ask for.

It would all be a lie that would come back to haunt them both eventually, and that's what stopped her from picking up the phone.

Should she go see him tonight? Did he remember to stop working at all to rest? Why had this happened exactly? Was it something she had done to make him think she was wanted marriage and children? She hadn't even thought it. She'd been so caught up in just being with a man again, just not being so alone.

Leena finally came to realize she was in love with him, but she hadn't even gotten to tell him. She shook her head again. Going by to tell him she loved him would not help him in any way, she knew that much. Sighing she looked at the clock again. She'd better make her final check and get ready to go home. Kasey had been an angel this morning. not mentioning it beyond asking if she wanted to talk. Then she chattered about the spell she was working on, that they were going to try on Friday night.

Leena was actually pretty interested in trying it herself. If it worked well, that would put a killer in jail and their lives back to a less paranoid level.

She glanced at the clock, then got up quickly and headed out to the floor to check on the day's numbers. She'd done it, made it through the day without falling apart.

When Leena pulled into her driveway, she held her breath. Owen sat on her steps. It took her three tries to hit park with her suddenly weak arms. Taking a deep breath, she got out. She watched him come to his feet and walk to the bottom of the steps.

Owen watched her walk across the lawn, his expression wary. She didn't know why he was here, but a part of her was just happy to see him. Another part was saying she should just go in the house so her heart couldn't be broken any further than it was.

When she stopped in front of him, he searched her eyes silently for a moment. She held her breath.

"Is it okay I'm here? Do you want me to go?"

Leena looked at him. She could see he hadn't really slept and was more tired than he realized. "No. It's fine. Let's go inside." Her voice was steadier than she felt.

He followed her into the kitchen and sat down.

"Do you want some tea or something?" When he shook his head, she sat down across from him. "Why are you here, Owen?" She couldn't do small talk right now, so it was better to get it over with.

Owen sat there for a few seconds trying to figure out where to start. "After I heard from you last night, I did a lot of thinking, well, I never really stopped thinking from the moment you walked out the door. Is it okay if I stand?"

He got up when she nodded.

"So, I was having a bit of a fit. Well, more so inside my head than an actual physical tantrum." He took a deep breath and let it out slowly, then thrust his hands in his pockets. "I was thinking about my father, Leena, and everything he'd changed in my world, just by not being a normal father. I think about it more than I'd like really. You probably have those moments, so you'd understand that."

She nodded but didn't speak.

"I have dreams sometimes, and will wake up soaked in sweat and shaking with a fear... the kind of fear you feel when you're a child, that paralyzing fear, but that's not what I want to say right now." He paced to the window and leaned over the sink for a few moments.

Her heart ached to hold him, to comfort him somehow. She didn't need to ask to know he was running on too much coffee and too little sleep, so she'd let him get it out however he needed to.

He began talking quietly still looking into the sink. "So, there I am, from wanting to stomp on the phone to hating my father, not just hating really, I guess I was raging with hatred... for a man that robbed me of everything." He spun back toward her and looked at her for a moment. "I was so mad that he'd even managed to take you, or at least come between us in some way, so angry," he whispered. "Then I thought of you, of you at Beltane and how you all but floated across to the circle... how you look when you smile. When you smile, Leena, you're so breathtaking my mouth dries up, so beautiful."

He stood there and looked at her, and her patient eyes looked back at him. "I just thought about you and... and the rage was gone, the anger faded. There was just you." He smiled at her. "I just thought of you, and it all went away."

Owen stuck his hands in his pockets and took a breath. "I know that doesn't really answer or resolve anything really, but I know I did nothing but think about you these last few days, about calling you, writing you, coming to see you. It was wrong the way I just threw everything at you the other night." When she started to stand up so she could go to him, he shook his head. "Just hear me out. I didn't handle it well when I tried to talk to you the other night, so at least let me try it now." He watched her sit back down again and then smiled as best as he could at that moment. "I don't know if I can make the promises you'll need. I don't know if I'll ever be able to. All I know at this point is I can't *not* have you in my life."

Swallowing the lump in his throat, he looked at her again. "I can't... not have you to talk to, to laugh with, Leena. I can't... not have you to hold." He watched a tear roll down her face, but she did as he asked and sat there silently. "I don't know if I can be what you need, Aileena. I'd like to lie and say I could but..."

Leena got up quickly and put her hand over his mouth. She knew her tears were falling, but when she looked and saw the desperate tears beginning to gather in his eyes, she couldn't stand it another moment.

"Stop." She could feel his trembling, or was it possibly her own? "I don't want promises from you, Owen. I don't want you to be anyone but who you are. I don't need to know today, right now, that I'll have children and happily-ever-after. All I want right now is time with you. One day at a time, Owen, not the rest of our lives. I've only just barely realized I love you, trying to take on any more than that right now is too much for me."

Owen gently pulled her hand from his mouth and rested his hands on her shoulders. "You love me?"

She smiled at him in that sweet, innocent way, and his heart almost burst with the emotion that flooded into it. He gently framed her face. "I love you so much, baby. It's hell being without you."

He stood there letting the warm feeling fill him. "Can we try this again, Leena... just try and see where it takes us?"

She nodded.

Two tears rolled down his cheek as he lowered his mouth to hers and kissed her tenderly. "I love you," he whispered against her lips words he'd never said in his life to anyone.

Leena smiled against his mouth. "I love you, Owen. Now, can I have a hug? I really need to be in your arms."

He let her face go and lifted her a few inches to hold her tightly against his chest as he began kissing her again, gently.

A few minutes later when he was trying to catch his breath, he smiled against her mouth. "I missed you so much, Leena. Next time I start acting like an idiot, just hit me with a blast of wind or something to shut me up."

Leena laughed. "I'll hit you with something all right."

"Oh, god, I missed that laugh." He kissed her hard. "I missed this mouth, baby." Owen held her away from him for a moment and looked into her eyes. Just looking at her made his body harden with need. He kissed her eyelids and cheeks. His hands went slowly through her hair. He lightly nibbled on her bottom lip, which encouraged her to open her mouth, then pulled her tightly against his body and kissed her with all the emotion he was feeling. When she moaned into his mouth, he kissed his way down her neck and back as she sighed and pushed her hips into him.

Leena ran her hands down over his back and gently squeezed his hard butt. Running her hands back up, she lightly touched his arms then across his chest. She pulled his T-shirt out of his pants and pushed it up. Pulling her mouth away from his she slowly kissed her way down his neck to his chest. She nipped one hard nipple lightly and felt him shudder with pleasure. Smiling to herself, she licked the other one then nipped it harder, and he moaned and gently pushed his hips against her, grinding his hardness into her.

As she leaned down, she nibbled her way down his chest to run her tongue along the top of his jeans, and his breath stopped. Slowly, as she smiled up at him, she undid his jeans and ran her tongue along his heated skin lightly. She felt his stomach muscles clench in response.

With her foot she pulled a chair over closer to them and leaned back against it as she tugged his jeans down a bit more. With her face, she nuzzled against the hard length of him and felt her own excitement rise as his breath hissed out quickly. Using her lips, she nibbled along the hot sensitive flesh and felt his hands clench in her hair.

"Baby, I'll collapse if you don't stop." He tried to pull her head up. When she lifted it, he started to pull her back up to his mouth, then found himself turned and sitting in the chair. Before he could do anything, she was down on her knees in front of him, her mouth licking up and down.

He gripped her hair and threw his head back and groaned.

Her lips were so hot. Her tongue was so wet.

She slowly closed her lips around the sensitive tip then pulled her mouth over it, licking the bead of moisture from the very tip. His hips jerked with her movement. With her tongue only, she licked in quick, little strokes up the length, he was close to losing his mind it felt that good.

Tangling one of his hands in her hair, he used his other hand to stroke her head gently, encouraging her to continue.

With gentle teeth, she bit the thickness of him then ran her tongue over it to soothe. He moaned again. He watched her lick her lips before she closed her mouth over the length of him and slowly slid up. A ragged breath caught in his chest and he held it not sure if he remembered how to breathe. She moved her mouth slowly up and down, then whirled her tongue around the tip several times before clamping her lips tighter and sucking every time she just held the tip in her mouth. Without realizing it, his hips were rocking gently into her, and his hand tightened in her hair to hold her head where he wanted it.

She took him as deeply as she could and then moved at a pace to match his thrusts. He swore and groaned when she clamped her mouth down hard and sucked as he exploded into her throat. Slowly, pulling her mouth from him, she continued to lick at him until he was squirming in the chair.

"Take off your pants," Owen gasped. He ripped his shirt over his head and then hers. "Now!" She smiled up at him, and he shuddered. "Take off your pants." He still couldn't breathe right, but he didn't care. When she stood up he undid them with shaking hands and shoved them to the floor.

Barely giving her time to step out of them, he grabbed her hips and pulled her over to straddle him. In one fast motion, he pulled her down on top of his still-hard erection and devoured her throat as she threw her head back and moaned. He guided her hands to his shoulders and continued to lift her, pushing her hard against him.

Leena dropped her head down, which caused her hair to surround them both. He thrust up meeting her faster and harder and was so lost in her he never wanted to stop. She began to pant and moan with her face resting against him. Through her bra he bit a nipple then sucked it hard. She groaned and cried out as he gripped her hips harder and pulled her down onto him.

When her muscles clamped around him and she shook from the strength of the orgasm ripping through her, he began to slow, which caused her to shudder as the aftershocks moved through her. As she gasped against his neck, she tried to untangle her hair from them and sit up. "Can't ever get rid of these chairs now."

He laughed. "I'm going to put one in every room of the house, in case they're needed."

She still straddled him and was in no hurry to move but when she looked at him, she could see how exhausted he was, and now with no tension in her body realized she was, too. "Food." She kissed him softly. "I need food, you need food." She kissed him again. "As soon as I find my legs, I'm going to feed us. Then we're going to bed."

He helped guide her to the standing position. Then he watched her put her pants back on. "I'll be back." He got up and pulled up his pants, not bothering with the button, and then he turned.

"Where are you going?" She straightened her shirt.

"Out to the Jeep. I brought you flowers but was so nervous I forgot about them." He went out the door.

"Owen, you're not all dressed," she called out as he left.

When he got to the Jeep, he looked back at her standing in the doorway. Her hair was a mess. Her shirt all wrinkled. She looked so good thoroughly loved.

Leena smiled at him sweetly when he walked up the steps and handed her the bouquet of wildflowers he'd gotten for her. Roses were too ordinary for her, he'd remembered thinking and almost drove the florist crazy wanting wildflowers.

Owen stopped in the doorway and leaned against the open door, smiling down at her with her face pressed into the flowers. "You are so beautiful," he whispered then pulled her into his arms and shut the door.

They had been so wrapped up in each other that neither of them noticed the van that crept by the driveway and stopped behind the trees.

"Doc, wake up," Rachel prodded him gently. "It worked," she whispered as if they could hear her.

"I'll say it did, and then some," Dade snorted from the driver's seat.

"I can't believe we've been reduced to peeping Toms," Chris complained.

"I wish I'd brought a camera," Rachel frowned.

Cora turned and gave her a startled look. "Being a peeping Tom isn't good enough for you; you want pictures, too?"

Rachel shrugged, "They looked so sweet and in love all wrapped up in each other."

"Wouldn't that be something flipping through the photo album. 'Oh, look, here's the time we worked a spell on our friends and they came running out of the house after sex looking all in love,'" Steven muttered while rubbing his scarcely open eyes.

They all burst out in giggles as Dade decided they should leave.

"So, now we're all a bunch of sneaky witches," Dade whispered as he pulled away.

ଓଓ **Chapter 19** ଓଓ

Kasey ran by Chris to go back out to the car. "Did you leave anything at home, Kase?" he asked with a grin as he watched her struggle to carry in a huge, gong-like, object. "Where did you have all this hidden in your little house?" he asked as he took it from her and walked back toward the house.

"I have this lovely huge storage closet, stand back if you ever open the door." She grabbed the last bag from her car and went to open the door for him.

"You know I'm going to have to peek inside now, don't you?"

"Yep."

As they walked into the room Chris cleared out to make the room Kasey asked for, they found Owen and Leena wrapped around each other dancing to nonexistent music.

"Mind if I cut in?" Chris joked on the way by.

"Not if you value your life, friend," Owen joked and spun her the other way.

Kasey set the bag down and then watched them silently. When Chris walked up to her he spun her into his arms and began following his own silent music. Kasey smiled up at him and let him dance her around the room. He laughed and picked her up so they were face-to-face then continued to move around the room with her feet dangling in the air.

Kasey watched as Rachel and Steven stopped in the doorway and watched for a moment without saying a word. Rachel laughed when Steven extended his hand and she took it and they spun out on the floor, dancing closely.

Chris twirled Kasey around and then swayed in place. Glancing over to the door she saw Dade walk in with Cora carrying the candleholders from her car and they just stopped and stood staring at the three couples. He leaned over toward her and whispered something. Cora shook her head and smiled.

Dade stepped into the room. "Are we having a ritual here tonight or a ball?" All three couples jolted and turned to look at him.

Cora laughed and set down the candle stands. "He was afraid he'd gone deaf and couldn't hear the music."

Chris slowly slid Kasey to the floor, not taking her eyes off his the whole time. He cleared his throat and grinned. "Just filling the space with some good vibes."

Dade laughed. "Keep telling yourself that, man, and you might believe it."

Cora glared at him.

"What? What did I do now?" he asked.

Cora smirked. "Nothing, I just like to put that panicked, guilty look on your face."

Kasey almost laughed when his jaw dropped. It wasn't often she got him, but it was worth it when she did.

"Sneaky witch," Dade said loud enough for everyone to hear. That made all the guilty sneaky witches in the room suddenly sober and start setting up. Throwing his head back, Dade laughed in victory and went to help Chris.

After checking at least four times to see if everything was where it should be, Kasey went over and spoke quietly to Rachel again, who looked around and nodded. Chris leaned back against the wall. He might just leave this room empty and let her come here and flit around whenever she needed to. "Okay, ladies, how about you walk us through this before we all drop from exhaustion watching you run around?"

He grinned when they both stopped and looked at him.

Rachel stepped toward the middle. "Okay, this has been painstakingly planned, for maximum safety." She looked down at the list Kasey gave her. "First time I've had a checklist for the start of a ritual. Did everyone have a spiritually purifying bath before coming over?"

Everyone nodded.

Owen grinned. "I've never been more pure in my life." Leena blushed and buried her face against his shoulder. "Well, she had to show me what to do," he added, and she smacked him for it.

"Right, well, my bath may not have been as pleasantly purifying as Owen's, but I'd say you can check that off your list," Steven grinned at the blushing Leena.

Owen dropped his head forward and sighed. "If we keep talking about it I'm going to need my mind re-purified." He winked at Leena.

Kasey stepped away from the wall. "Leave them alone, love is the purest of all." She shook her head when Rachel held the list out to her. "I don't need it. I have done this at least a hundred times in my mind now." She walked around the room slowly. "The candles on the outside, the white ones, are to keep the energy pure within. Rach is going to use sea salt outside of those to cleanse and keep anything unclean out."

Kasey spoke more for Owen's sake than the rest, because they knew more than the basics. She was nervous. "Leena has worked her usual herbal magic and brought the smudge, the smoke you ran your hands through at Beltane, so we'll smudge every piece involved and everybody."

She walked over to where the scent bowls were, near the four corners. "She's also made up four different incenses for us, for protection and to hopefully strengthen what we're attempting." She glanced at Leena as she spoke in case she mixed something up. "They're bistort, frankincense, elecampane, and althea... If I'm not mistaken. So, we're going to smell awesome after this." She glanced at Chris. "This is kind of why I requested this large space... so no one passes out from the mixed fumes."

Kasey thought for a moment as she nervously walking around. "Oh, Leena also has made some extra protection for us and will place it on the inside of the candles, mullein and pine I think, and it won't be the smoking variety."

She stopped in front of the bowl where gems were placed around the edge. "I have garnet inside the bowl with the water, it will enhance all the energies, and I placed four moonstones around the outside for divination. The lists of names are under the dish, so if the person we're looking for is not on the list, we'll see nothing."

She took a deep breath as she looked around. "Rach is going to work on keeping the water dark so images will come out better. Um, Steven and Leena are going to concentrate on keeping the water in a glasslike state so no energy will move it and we'll be able to see." Chris walked up behind her and began to rub her tense shoulders. "Relax, Kase, you've done an absolutely amazing job here."

Kasey nodded and continued to lean back against him for the comfort. "We'll all place our hands on the outside edges of the dish. I've used copper, as it's the best energy conductor, but no one can touch the water or it will break the spell completely. Everyone will have to sit in a certain place, because I've distributed the different strengths we have around the dish so the energy flows from one to the other to bring the vision out, and we'll get to the chant in a minute."

Dropping her head, she looked at the floor for a moment. Then her chin popped up and she focused on Owen. "Can I get you to walk the smudge around and do all the candles and stuff and everyone when they form the circle? You have the purest energy here because of your gift, so any negative will...be gone."

He grinned at her and nodded.

"Okay." She walked over to the copper bowl that sat on the floor. "We can stand or kneel. I think if we kneel, though, we'll see better. I'll stand here, then clockwise it will be Dade, Steven, Owen, Rachel." Kasey stepped around the dish showing them each place. "Cora, Leena, and Chris. Ah, any questions?"

No one stirred.

"Okay, we'll get Steven lighting candles, after Owen's smudged them. Rach doing the salt... Leena the herbs... Cora will light the incenses, then get yourself smudged and get in place."

She turned to Chris and looked up at him. "Can you just keep doing that? I'm so nervous. This is the biggest thing I've ever done outside the Wiccan circle, and even there I really wasn't running the show. Just helping." He nodded and grinned at her. "Oh, good." She stood there with Chris rubbing her shoulders as she tried to focus her energy as everyone moved around silently doing everything as she'd instructed.

Kasey took deep breaths, and after Owen brought the smudge to her, she knelt down in front of the large copper dish and looked into it. Part of magic, the largest part, was seeing the end result before beginning and all the way through.

Chris knelt beside her silently and waited for the others. He knew he shouldn't touch her right now, but he still moved close enough to her so she'd feel his energy beside her. He wanted to kiss her and tell her he was proud of everything she'd planned here. It wasn't a small task, so many variables to plan for, and she'd covered them all perfectly.

When everyone sat down, Rachel spoke softly. "The only thing I did in the figuring part of this was to find the chant. Kase is getting to be much stronger than I am with most spell work. So, the chant is... earth and air, set our sights free; fire and moon, let us see. We'll say it three times after I set the water and Lee and Doc have turned it."

Everyone nodded.

Kasey spoke in a whisper. "Take deep breaths, get centered, and when I place my hands on the bowl, you do it, then we'll begin the chant." She nodded to Rachel.

Owen watched Rachel hold her hand over the dish and focus on the water. It darkened to almost black with the red stone still sitting in the bottom.

Leena and Steven took a deep breath at the same moment and then moved their hands over the water, and it became a glossed-over black, no longer really looking like water.

Kasey set her hands on the edge of the dish, after everyone else did Owen did the same. He expected the copper to feel cool, but it was warm to the touch, and he could almost feel vibrations moving though the outer edge and into his hands.

"Earth and air, set our sights free. Fire and moon, let us see." When it was said the third time, Kasey opened her eyes and stared at the water. She rose up on her knees above the dish and focused all her thoughts on the knife and the ring, as well as the seemingly endless lists of names.

Focus, Kasey told herself. An image began to float to the top of the reflection less water. A Bible was there. Then the knife the others described. She saw a calendar and noted the date circled. She saw dancers, but they were only women, moving around the fire... they weren't dancing as she'd ever seen them do. They appeared to be squirming, touching themselves, and gyrating more like a stripper would than in the tribal way she knew they all danced. She sensed the others now leaning up on their knees to look deeper into the vision.

Chris's hand gently brushed hers, but it didn't touch the water so the vision continued.

She blinked once and stared into the bowl again. There was a very naked, dark-haired man over a very naked female, his mouth was moving down her ribs, and her head was thrown back in obvious pleasure. Her eyes widened when she saw the hair on the woman. It was her. "Oh!" Quickly she splashed a hand into the water, and the images left immediately.

Kasey dropped back and sat crossed legged with her hands over her very hot face.

"Whoa, Kase, wrong channel," Dade said softly.

Leena and Cora were up and over to her before anyone could move. "It happens to all of us, Kase. Visions don't always stay impersonal," Cora soothed.

Rachel jumped up to put the candles out, then stopped when Kasey grabbed her arm. She picked up the notebook beside her. "Leave them going until we've talked this through."

She handed the notebook to Dade. "Write down what you saw and pass it around, leaving out that end stupidity." He took it without a word.

Steven looked over at her for a moment. "That was amazing, Kasey. Really, I've seen people that have been doing it for years, and they see nothing but foggy blobs." He wished Chris would speak to her. He had a way about him that could calm anyone. But Chris sat there still staring at the bowl, his jaw was set. *Oh*, Steven thought. Oh, well that was funny. Everyone knew... at least he thought everyone realized it was in fact Chris *with* Kasey in the little fantasy flash. How could Chris not know? Oh, he was going to enjoy this.

He glanced at Owen who sat there with a look of awe on his face. He couldn't blame him with everything the man had been shown since meeting this group. He supposed what had just happened was even wilder than with Cora's fire visions, well, right up until that last part at least. Poor guy didn't know what to do or say, so he stuck with sitting there doing and saying nothing.

Leaning back, he watched Owen get up and go over by Kasey. As he knelt down, he touched Chris's shoulder. He pulled his hand back like he'd just been zapped. Scowling he looked around. Steven waited until his eyes met his own and lifted his eyebrows at Chris then looked at the bowl before giving him a glare and looking at Kasey.

Owen's mouth dropped open, then he smirked at him. Giving Chris a wide berth this time he knelt down on the other side of Kasey. He didn't say anything, just placed a hand on her shoulder. Really what could anyone say without sounding like an idiot at this point?

Kasey closed her eyes and accepted Owen's silent help. She'd never been so embarrassed in her life. Chris hadn't said a word to her yet. He just sat there looking at the bowl. Well, could she blame him really? How she went from a killer to projecting her unfulfilled fantasy of Chris climbing all over her, she still didn't understand. She sighed. "I'm okay now," she whispered to the four surrounding her. "Go back to your places in the circle and write down what you saw."

They did silently.

When the book was handed to Chris, he spent a few moments flipping through the pages where everyone added their thoughts then tossed it in front of Kasey without looking at her. "I have nothing to add."

Dade smiled at her. "Can we close the circle, Kase? I need a bit of a break."

Kasey glanced at Chris under her lashes and then nodded at Dade. "Yeah, that's a good idea actually."

Rachel hopped up and put the candles out, muttering a chant as she did. As soon as they were all out, Chris was on his feet and out of the room before anyone had a chance to get up.

Everyone else went to stand by Kasey, who looked like she was in going to cry. "Oh, my gosh! I've embarrassed him so bad."

Steven went over and hugged her, and then pulled back and looked at her for a moment. "Kase, he's not embarrassed, he's pissed." Her eyes widened, and her mouth dropped open obviously confused. "He doesn't realize, um...

well, that that was him we saw, wasn't it?" She blushed. That would be a yes. "He thinks that was someone else that you... another man was... well, he doesn't know it was him."

Her hands flew over her mouth. "Oh, my gosh! That's worse than being embarrassed!" Kasey gasped and looked around at everyone to see them agreeing with Steven. "Oh, no! But, no, I have to go talk to him." She turned to go after him.

Cora grabbed her arm. "Let him stew in it. Trust me," she leaned over and whispered so the males wouldn't hear. "It might be what he needs to finally... *finally* make that first move that every single one of us knows he wants to make."

Kasey stood there for a moment and thought. "What kind of woman does he think I am? I practically cuddle up to him every time he's within ten feet, and he thinks…he thought. Oh!" She walked over to the door and paused, only making eye contact with Owen.

Owen smiled at her. "I think we should call it a night, wait a few days until things calm down before we try to discuss this like adults."

Rachel sighed. "He's right. I'll deal with Kasey. Doc, you go find Dade and Chris."

Steven nodded then took a deep breath.

Kasey turned and fled out the door.

Dade leaned against the railing a few feet from Chris and stared at him. "So, you wanna share what that was in there?"

Chris snarled at him. "That was Kasey letting a man climb all over her, *literally*!" he growled.

"Okay, blunt works for me." Dade leaned over and looked at Chris's face. He honestly had no clue. *Ha!* "Is she supposed to wait for you to declare your undying love forever?" He thought of Coralee briefly. "You've been sniffing around her, my ma's saying by the way, for how long? You tease her with words but never follow through on anything, and now you're pissed because Kasey is human and has needs like the rest of us?"

Chris lifted his head. "Fuck off!"

"Can I use that as a quote, counselor?" Dade teased and hoped Chris wouldn't zap him with lightning or something equally as painful.

Chris ran a hand. over his face and swore under his breath.

"Do you mean to tell me you've never been with another woman, Larkin? I'd love to call you a liar," Dade said.

"Me, too." Steven spoke from a few feet away. "I've seen you go through two different women in a week, Chris... *before* Kasey came along, that is."

"Fuck!" Chris smacked his hand on the rail.

"Yeah, I've heard that defense a lot these past few weeks from Owen." Dade smirked.

Chris took a deep breath. "What is everyone else doing?" He glanced at Steven.

"Well, Kasey stormed out the other door shortly after you. She's embarrassed, disappointed, and presently in the mad-as-hell stage. Owen, Lee, and, I think, Cora, are packing up. We're going to resume discussion at a later, calmer, date. We're here trying to find out what your malfunction is." Steven crossed his arms over his chest and studied the other man. "What, in your own words, counselor, do you think, I repeat *think*, you saw in there tonight?"

Chris leaned back against the rail and crossed his arms much like the Doc had. "I saw Kasey with a man... and very much enjoying herself."

"Hell, Chris, that could have been a scene from a novel she'd read or some leftover fantasy; are you suddenly an amateur? You know visions, especially personal ones, could just be a bunch of what-ifs." He glanced at Dade with his last words then back to Chris.

"Well, fuck!" Chris spat. "I have go talk to Kasey." He turned and walked back in the house.

Dade patted Steven on the back. "Nice wordplay there, Doc. Another minute of Kasey's what-ifs and I would have had a hard-on myself."

Steven chuckled and followed him in. "Good, that makes me feel better."

Chris walked in to see Leena attached to Owen again as he spoke softly to her. He didn't need to see that right now. He looked around. The entire room was empty. All the ritual aids were gone. "Where is everyone?"

Leena turned. "Oh. They left. Cora took Kasey and Rachel home, we didn't know where everyone went, so were waiting to say goodnight."

Chris stuck his hands in his pockets, feeling like a moron. "Oh." He cleared his throat. "I'm sorry about all that earlier. My head wasn't in the right place." He paused when Dade and Steven came back in. "Did we decide on a meeting day to discuss the notes?" he added, still trying to get the other image out of his head.

Owen shook his head. "No. They said to message if anyone had any thoughts."

"Wednesday night? My place?" Dade offered.

"I'll let them know," Leena said quickly.

"Great, I'm out of here," Steven called out, already heading for the door.

Chris just stood there and nodded silently.

After tucking Leena under his shoulder, Owen steered them toward the door. "We'll see you then."

A while later Leena lay in his bed looking around the room. "You know, you men are pretty daft from time to time."

"Yes, dear, we are," Owen agreed quickly. He received a smack for it. "Baby, I want you to hang around here with me tomorrow. I want you to read the first book." She rolled over on him and kissed him. "You do?" He nodded and kissed her back.

"I really want, almost need, your opinion."

"Oh, Owen!" She sat up. "I've been biting my tongue and trying sooo hard not to bug you. Those two chapters you sent me left me dying to read more. Mist people! I mean, really, where does your brain come up with all these fabulous ideas? When I started reading, I was in awe. There have been books on people of the mist, from the mist, blah, blah, blah. But people that actually turn into the mist and try to live in the normal world. Awesome!" She leaned down and ran her tongue over his lips. "So, is the second book mist people also or have you found some other fantastic fantasy for it?"

He chuckled against her mouth. "Oh, you'll have to torture me to get that information."

She grinned back at him and began to do just that, forgetting all about the plot of the next book.

❧ **Chapter 20** ☙

Sleeping late was a rare thing for Leena. They lingered over a cozy breakfast and discussed the upcoming gathering, trying to find a way to share a room without offending everyone. They mulled over what they saw the night before, mostly the important parts, and seemed to be of the same opinion the next gathering wasn't going to be worry-free, and they really didn't want to linger on it too long.

When Owen brought her the folder of pages to the story, she almost ran to the couch to read it. "I'm so excited! I'll be the very first person to read this story. Well, after the people paying you, that is."

Owen stood and watched her get comfortable on the couch. She tucked her feet up under her. She looked so cute in his big shirt and didn't seem to want to get dressed. He could get used to this. "Ah, I was going to go get some work on the next one done. Is that okay?"

Leena looked up from the pages she had resting on her knees. "Oh. Yes, I don't want to distract you from your work. You have a contract to fulfill. Go write." She smiled when he grinned and leaned down to kiss her tenderly.

"Just come shut the laptop when you miss me."

Leena couldn't put the pages down. It was certainly a fast-paced story. A good, fast-paced one. How do authors do this, she wondered when finally she moved to stretch her legs. She glanced at the clock, he'd been working for a few hours now. She'd make him a coffee.

She stood watching the coffee brew, and her mind went back to her earlier thoughts. She would never be able to create all those characters, those scenes, and make it seem so real and so believable. That was something she'd always noticed about Owen's books, even though they were complete fantasy, they always seemed have a realism to them that made you believe anything was possible.

She chuckled as she poured the coffee. She of all people knew almost anything was possible. With the magic she could do most would think her fiction as well.

Walking slowly into the room, she watched Owen for a moment. His large fingers flew over the keyboard, not pausing for thought or correction. She didn't want to startle him or to stop what seemed to be a fast flow and was thinking of backing out silently when his head came up and he turned.

"Is that coffee? You made me coffee?" He rolled toward her in the chair. Stopping only when he was close enough to take the cup, he set it on the table. Then he reached out and pulled his chair closer by holding her hips and pulling himself closer. "Thank you."

"I hope I didn't ruin your train of thought."

"No chance." Owen rubbed his face into her stomach and hugged her. "It's gotta be you, baby. The characters run, the words flow. Before I met you, it would take me months to put a story together and make it work." He rubbed his hands over her lower back and nipped her skin through her shirt. "Now I can't seem to stop." He looked up at her. "I may have to keep you, pretty lady." He smiled as she bent down and kissed him.

"Yeah, well, you're turning out to be a keeper, too." She hugged his head into her. "The other story is beyond fantastic, Owen. Really." She kissed him again quickly and spun his chair back toward his desk. "I'm going to read more. You get back to work so your characters don't quit on you."

He chuckled and watched her leave the room. Coffee, she brought him coffee. And told him to work. He definitely could get used to this.

Owen had no concept of how much time had passed when he paused and reached for his coffee cup. It was empty. Hadn't he just set it down? Flexing his stiff shoulders, he stood up and grabbed the cup again. Maybe he could persuade Leena to make him some more. Hers was better than his own great coffee. Working out the next scene in his head, he wandered toward the kitchen.

When he reached the living room, he just stood there and looked at the couch. His pages were neatly on the floor in front of it, and she was curled up sleeping on the one end of it. She looked so innocent in sleep, yet so soft and sexy he had to grin.

He checked the time. Dinnertime? Where had lunchtime gone?

He looked back at her. His chest ached as he watched her sleep soundlessly. She was so beautiful curled up there in his shirt, with those long legs bent, the slope of her perfectly curved hip. He actually sighed.

Moving over, he knelt down in front of her and ran his hand slowly over her hair that covered her shoulder and fell across her waist. She belonged here, like this, in his life. He bent down and gave her mouth a feather-light kiss. Sleepy, sexy amber eyes opened and looked at him, and then her lips curled into a smile.

"Hi. Guess I fell asleep." Leena rolled onto her back and stretched slowly. "I finished the book. I couldn't put it down, then I tiptoed to see how busy you were and you were muttering away." She smirked at him. "So, I decided not to disturb creative genius at work and stretched out. Owen?"

Owen couldn't bring his voice louder than a whisper. "I look at you, Leena, and I want. When I watch you, I ache, I just ache with so many emotions." He ran his hand down her hair softly. "You look so right curled up there wearing my shirt, you make me want." He swallowed. "Want things I've never been able to want before."

She smiled and reached up to him to wrap her arms around his neck. "Those are such beautiful things to say, Owen." She whispered into his neck

"I mean them." He kissed her until they were breathless. When he pulled his head up, she was watching him.

"Can you write anywhere?"

He nodded. "Pretty much, why?"

She slid to the edge of the couch and swung her legs over. "Bring your laptop and come home with me. I'll make dinner and get some laundry done before I have to go to work tomorrow." She searched his eyes. "Come home with me."

He pulled her to her feet and held her tightly. "Yes," he told her with a lump in his throat.

Kasey paced across the carpet again. "I really am sorry I just appeared here. Thanks for dinner, by the way." She looked at Owen cuddling Leena on the couch for a second. "I'm sure you'd both rather be alone, but I was just so mad. The longer I sat there alone, the worse it got." She dropped down on the chair quickly. "He just made me so mad! Jerk!"

Leena sat forward. "It's fine, Kase. You're always welcome, and you know that, but you need to take a deep breath and tell us again, in logical order, what you were going on and on about all through dinner. I think we lost the plot somewhere with all of this."

"Chris is a jerk!"

Owen grinned. "Yeah, that much we caught."

Kasey puffed out her cheeks for a moment then exhaled. "I left last night, well, you know why. I've never been so embarrassed in my life. Anyway, when I realized why he was so crabby, I left before I slapped him up against a wall or something." She twined her fingers together. "My temper is kind of bad at times. So, Cora takes me home, and I debate on calling him. While I'm debating, he calls me, but of course I'm too embarrassed to answer after what happened, so he leaves this message and it starts off all, Chris like, "Hey, Kase, thought I'd call to say you did good tonight and most my age couldn't have pulled that off. Yada yada' and then..." She had to stand again. "Then he suddenly gets all huffy and goes from telling me how great it was we got to see the calendar and everything to suggesting... suggesting that I not try to take that on again until I'm able to keep my fantasies and sex life out of my head long enough to do a ritual!" She stomped her foot. "He's such a jerk!"

Owen smacked his hand over his face and groaned. "Oh, Chris."

Leena sat there silently for several moments. "How is it *he* is, and I'm not trying to embarrass you again, how is it *he* is the only one that didn't recognize himself in that... vision last night?" She looked at Owen, who threw his hands up and shook his head. "Kasey, do you have any idea how you went from totally focus, I mean, that was the clearest vision I've seen, to Chris so quickly? And it was in a flash more or less, as Dade said, it was kind of like you clicked the remote and changed the channel."

Kasey dropped down and put her face in her hands, taking deep breaths. "His hand touched mine when we had them around the bowl." She looked up at them both for a moment. "How pathetic am I that all it takes is his hand to brush mine and I have thoughts of us naked and, well, like that?" She leaned back and looked at the ceiling. "I can't call him, can't talk to him right now. I'll turn him upside down and shave his head if I see him right now."

Owen jolted and looked at Leena briefly. He looked back to Kasey and took a deep, calming breath. "I'd like to give you words of wisdom on the male mind, but I don't have any.

Sometimes our brains work exceedingly well. Then other times, not so good."

Leena glanced at him, as though astonished he was of so little help. "We're all meeting in a few days' time. How are you going to handle that?"

Kasey sighed again. "I'll be fine by then. I just need to blow off some steam before then." She stood up and stuffed her hands in her back pockets. "I had just always hoped that someday, you know, before I'm too old to walk, Chris and I would... well, that he'd..." She puffed out her cheeks again. "I'm going to take my embarrassment one step further, and I might as well say it to both of you, 'cuz she'll just tell you later."

Kasey looked at the silent man in front of her. "I'm a virgin and I always hoped, dreamed that Chris would be, that it would be him..." She sat down again and looked at her feet.

Leena was up and then knelt by her. "There's no reason to be embarrassed. I often wished I'd never started that part of my life so early." They all knew she was referring to Tyler, so she didn't have to say it out loud. "Just give it some time, Kase. Let Chris cool off, and maybe his mind will realize the truth."

Kasey nodded and hugged her.

Owen sat there, he knew his comments were not required. Which, of course, was good because the only thing he could think was, *"Wow. You're twenty-six and still a virgin?"* Did things like that still happen? Then of course his next male thought was, *"Lucky bastard, Chris."* At least he would be if he got it together. He was, however, old enough to understand he couldn't *ever* repeat a word of today to anyone, most particularly the men... not if he wanted to stay living. If he pissed off the little witch across from him, there would be hell to pay. And of course, he could never say a word if he wanted to be with Leena. But wow, you sure got the good inside secrets when you were part of a couple.

"I've made him speechless," he heard Kasey say and looked over at them and grinned.

"No, not really. Okay, yeah, you did. Half-a-dozen things to say came to mind, but none I could possibly say that wouldn't make me runner-up on your jerk list, so I opted for silence," he offered innocently. When they both laughed at him, he knew he got to live another day.

Together they watched her pull out of the driveway.

"Poor Kasey."

Owen grinned, "poor Chris if he ever pisses her off face to face."

"Do you think you could talk to him?" Leena whispered against his mouth seductively.

Owen blinked down at her. "And say what? 'Chris that was you banging virginal little Kasey in the copper bowl. Maybe you should go kiss her feet and it will come true'?"

He got smacked for that.

"That was crude."

"Crude but true, baby. I think just staying out of things is the best plan for all involved this time." When she sighed in defeat, he almost sighed in relief knowing he wouldn't have to go near the angry male witch.

Leena quickly hopped up and gripped his waist between her legs. "So, are you going to do some work for a while?" She ran her mouth over his throat. "Or do you have some time for a lonely lady?"

Owen squeezed her hips and grinned; work was forgotten. "Oh, I think work can wait an hour or two." He lowered his lips to her neck and nibbled as he started up the stairs. "Baby, I need to do some research for the next book. One scene won't play out for me."

She nipped his ear lightly. "Research how?" she whispered.

"In that large bathtub of yours..."

She wiggled against the hardness in the front of his jeans. "Mmm, I think I can help you there. *Anything* to help you."

Owen sat her on the bathroom counter and devoured her mouth as he reached for the taps on the tub. "I need..." he gasped as she undid his pants and reached inside. "I need images to..." He groaned when her hand began sliding up and down his throbbing erection. "To write a scene..." he said between clenched teeth. Her hot mouth was against his chest as she pushed his shirt to his neck. He palmed the back of her head and gripped her hair to slow her movement.

"Baby, we're not going to make it to the water." Leena stopped and looked up at him with those deep amber eyes, they were so clouded with desire, he lost all interest in the bathtub. "We'll try the water after," he moaned against her mouth as he fumbled to turn the taps off.

She pulled his shirt over his head then her own quickly.

His mouth immediately bit into the soft flesh of one lace covered breast. Groaning, she undid the clasp and let his lips touch her skin.

He lifted her long enough for her to pull her shirt free then set her back against the cool countertop. When his hands slid up her thighs, she gasped into his mouth. His hand paused for a moment when he felt the lace thong she was wearing. With a growl, he ripped it in a quick motion from her body and lifted her to the edge of the counter.

She shoved his jeans farther down over his hips and almost screamed as he thrust into her in one smooth motion.

Leena was so wet he groaned against her throat. Lifting his head, he leaned back and bunched her shirt up higher, so he could watch as he entered her body slowly again. He gritted his teeth to maintain some control and looked up at her leaning back on her hands and opening her legs wider to him. Gripping her thighs roughly, he slid her back on the counter then pulled her forward to meet his thrusts.

Leena's head fell back as she gasped loudly. Her breasts shook with each thrust, and his eyes blurred with the straining need he felt. Moaning, he pulled her forward so he could suck a hard nipple into his mouth as he continued to move frantically. She started panting, and his head flew up to watch her face when she groaned deep in her throat and the muscles clamped around him in spasm. He felt the wetness wash over him, and the feeling sent him flying with her until he shook in her arms and panted to catch his breath.

"You... destroy my entire control, woman," he gasped against her throat. He wasn't sure if he'd be able to walk so he leaned against the counter and reached for the taps again. With his every movement, her muscles clenched in aftershocks so hard it made him shake more.

Finally, she leaned back against the wall and smiled at him. "That's a good thing, that I can get to you, isn't it?"

Owen grinned. "Good, yes. Bad, because I never get to enjoy you for very long."

She licked dry lips. "Quality or quantity... Hmm." Leena closed heavy eyes and smiled. "Which would you prefer?"

He stood there, still inside her, and watched the relaxed breaths and her satisfied expression as her dark eyelashes created little shadows over her skin, and he wanted her all over again. "You are so beautiful." He lowered his lips to brush soft kisses over her face. "I love you, pretty lady."

Her arms circled his neck and she rubbed her face against his chest. "I love you, too, Owen."

He'd never felt love before, but he felt it when she said it. He felt loved. Whole. Complete with her in his life. He scooped her up and lowered himself into the hot water settling her across his lap with her head still on his shoulder.

✑ Chapter 21 ✑

Owen sat at Dade's with his arm around Leena watching as she spoke to Cora about some work-related issue. The last week had been so wonderful. They were together every morning and every night after she returned from work. He kissed the top of her head. He smiled as he realized, other than her going to work, they had been together since the night he'd waited for her on the step.

He couldn't see a day without her in it now, and it didn't scare him this time. He loved to wake up and see her sleepy smile, to be greeted by her when she got home, whether it was his home or hers. He was actually writing with a loose sort of schedule. That was a first, he thought with a grin. He'd always written for ten hours, then stopped for a nap, working for a few more afterward. Now he wrote when she was at work, or after she was asleep, if the characters called to him.

His whole world was so different, and the normal he'd never had. It was all because of the woman leaning against him tucked under his arm. He tipped her face up, which interrupted her conversation with Cora, and kissed her long and hard.

Leena smiled up at him for a moment. "Everything all right?"

"Never been better."

Cora smiled at them.

Owen glanced at Dade, who gave him a grin that said, "Told ya so," once again. Grinning back at him, he tucked Leena tighter under his shoulder in no hurry to go anywhere, so normal, he thought again.

Kasey sat there most of the time with her head down, pen going in a notebook, and ignoring Chris as best as she could. She sat as far from him as she'd been able to manage and disregarded the fact he'd been talking to Rachel most of the time since he'd gotten there.

Steven's arrival broke up the various conversations taking place. "Have I missed anything fun?" he inquired as he came through the door and dropped in the first empty chair he saw.

Chris grinned. "Are you ever on time?"

Steven shrugged and grinned back. "Only if you're having a baby."

Cora sat forward and cleared her throat. "Before you two get going on things I'm sure we don't need to know, I think we'd better go over the notes from the vision. We have only a little over a week left before Solstice."

Dade nodded. "I, for one, keep seeing that calendar from it." He rubbed his jaw. "That's a pretty sure sign that they plan to be at Solstice. That was the date circled."

Chris nodded, "I was wondering more about the neurologist's appointment, or I'm assuming the neurology department meant they were seeing a neurologist. Add that to the fact that they're also on some pretty regular medication, to write on the calendar when they need to get their prescription refilled. Doc?" Chris turned toward him. "Thoughts on any of that?"

Steven ruffled Rachel's hair and winked at her before answering. "I can't tell you much with that little information. Now if we'd seen a name of a drug or something that would narrow it down. Possibilities could be headaches or some sort of neurological condition. Many people with tumors display delusional tendencies, and I think those dancing women we saw were very much part of a delusion."

Rachel sat back and nodded. "No woman I've ever seen dances around a ritual fire like that. I think what we saw was more the way he sees them. I mean, there is always a degree of nudity, whether partial or the whole show, but they never move that way…"

Owen put his hand up. "Where is there nudity? At the ritual fires? I didn't see any at Beltane." He looked at Dade's amused expression.

Kasey shrugged. "We usually go off to play with spells and things before the tops come flying off. Well, I don't think too many would have at Beltane, because it was quite cool and damp. But, yes, Owen, quite often there are naked dancers, men included."

Owen's eyebrows shot up, and he looked at Leena. "You guys dance naked?"

Leena shook her head. "No, I don't see the whole reasoning behind naked ritual dance."

"There was that one time a few years back, Leena," Dade reminded her with a smirk.

"Dade, shut up! She was too drunk to know what she was doing that time." Cora glared at him.

Owen turned back to her and raised his eyebrows. "There will be no more of *that*. You want to dance around naked? By all means, baby, but I'll be the only one there." He pulled her tight against him and kissed her quickly.

"Okay, whole new topic here," Rachel said, trying not to laugh. "Have you gotten Owen a sarong for Solstice yet?"

Leena grinned wide and shook her head. "I don't know what color to get him." She said it while trying to avoid his curious look.

"Oh, definitely mixed blues. To go with his eyes," Kasey added as she grinned at Owen.

"A sarong? What is a sarong, and why do I think I'm not going to like this?" he asked Dade, who just shrugged while grinning at him.

"You've seen Dade in one before, Owen. When he's going to the temple," Cora added quite matter-of-factly.

"A skirt? You want me to wear a skirt?" Owen looked at Leena.

"Hey, don't knock it until you've tried it, bro." Dade scowled at him.

Owen looked down into her amber eyes and shook his head. "We'll talk about this later," he said quickly.

"Wow, he's just all he-man tonight, isn't he?" Rachel said as she sat up and reached for the notebook on the table.

"So, back to the discussion..." she waited until everyone looked at her. "Has anyone told Justin what we've been up to?"

Chris, who had been watching Kasey more than he had anyone else, turned to look at her. "Yes, I spoke to him last night. He's going to give us a heads-up on who the police put inside. He's also hoping they don't stand out like a beacon. He'll let us see a copy of the registrants' names on the Friday night, before the opening circle. Discreetly of course, so we can make a note of who was also at Beltane." He looked around the room. "The women dancing the other night, did anyone recognize a face or anything?"

Kasey shook her head. "To me the faces were kind of blurred. I remember because everything else to that point was crystal-clear."

Dade agreed with her. "Yeah, I noticed that, too. The one dancer kind of rang familiar, so I looked to the face for confirmation and couldn't make it out."

"You recognized a naked body?" Cora turned to him and gave him a look.

"What? No, I recognized the bracelets! One of them had those shell bracelets covering half her arm."

"Very observant, Dade." Steven winked at him.

"Hey, I'm an observant kind of guy." He mumbled.

Leena sat up. "Oh! I know who he's talking about... oh, what was her name?" She closed her eyes for a second then turned to Kasey. "The woman that did the dance workshop a few years ago, she had shell bracelets covering over half her forearm."

Kasey bounced for a moment with her eyes closed. "Oh, I know who you mean. Where's the attendance list from Beltane? She was there. I saw her talking to Gwen at dinner the first night.

Chris grabbed the list from the pile and took it over to Kasey. He perched on the edge of the chair and read over her shoulder.

"Oh! Cassidy..." she looked up at Chris. "How would you say that last name?" she pointed to it.

He leaned down and looked at it then straightened away from the temptation of her neck. "I have no idea, but it doesn't matter. We'll tell Justin the killer focused on her at some point and he can make sure she has company all the time." He dropped a hand to Kasey's shoulder and rubbed it gently. "Well, people we may not have identified the killer yet, but we could have very well just saved a woman's life." He was shocked to see Cora all but crawl onto Dade's lap and hug him.

Cora's mouth brushed against his, and Dade smiled. "I'm sorry for snapping," she said quietly.

Dade smiled again and ran his hand up her back. "That's okay, honey, I don't mind your teeth at all." He brushed his mouth over hers again and looked back to Kasey. "Kase, none of it would have been possible without your hard work. I know exactly who I'm going to if I need a spell worked." He grinned at her. His words rewarded him another little hug from Coralee.

Chris noticed Kasey's face light up from Dade's praise and suddenly felt like a worm. Vibrant, sweet Kasey who looked like she was barely containing the desire to jump up and do a little victory dance. He dropped off the arm of the chair so he was face to face with her. Palming her neck gently, he kissed her lightly and whispered against her ear. "He's right, and I'm sorry." He pulled back to see the look in those huge green eyes and knew she had understood. Smiling, he released her and stood up to glance around at everyone. "So, are we carpooling to Solstice, and what's the word on the lodgings?"

Leena sat forward. "Gwen has given the eight of us this huge dorm-type housing. Well, cabin. I'm sure it won't be grand or anything, but it will put us all under the same roof." She looked around as she spoke. "I, for one, will feel better knowing we're all together."

"How many rooms and beds?" Steven asked.

"I'm not sure on all of that. I do know there are separate rooms, but not how many beds per room, so we'll have to figure that out when we get there."

Everyone nodded, and she relaxed and sat back again.

"We'll figure out who pays what when we get there also," Chris added in, not telling them he'd already paid for all of their Solstice stay. "So, who's riding with whom?"

Owen shrugged. "We can do it like we did for the fair, if you like. I'd feel better knowing we all arrived together and no one was driving alone." He looked at Leena as he said it.

Rachel pulled out a map from her purse and handed it to Dade. "I looked it up, and there are no log bridges at this site. And there is a small village with a few stores about fifteen minutes away."

Dade studied it. "Is everyone able to get away earlier in the day on the Friday? I'd like to get there early enough to check the place out, and see who's there that we know. The drive is going to probably be a little over two hours."

All three women turned and looked at Leena. She held up her hands. "I'll see if I can spring us early. If you're caught up in shipping, *safely* caught up, then I can get someone else to run your line for a few hours, Kase." The women all rushed to her. "So, we can probably meet and leave by two.

Does that work for everyone?" she asked when she was able to lean back against Owen again. No one objected.

Owen grinned over at Dade. "Guess you'll have to bring most of the stuff, and the beer. Jeep doesn't have a lot of room."

Dade smiled. "No problem. You just worry about your sarong and I'll get the rest." He winked at Leena and stood up. "Anyone want coffee, tea, or a beer before we call this meeting done?" Hands went up.

Coralee jumped up. "I'll give you a hand, Dade." And she walked into the kitchen. He grinned and followed.

"Is that everything then?" Kasey looked up from the list she made of everyone's wants for munchies and things for the trip. She was on the floor leaning back between Chris's legs as he sat in the chair. She felt much better. She looked around at him to see if he had anything to add. Smiling innocently, she watched his hair rustle under an invisible hand. He reached out and kneaded her shoulder with a smile. "Okay, then. Leena and I can go after work some night and pick this stuff up."

"No need, Kase. I'll do it while Leena's at work the day before or something," Owen offered and put his hand out for the list. He caught the flashing grins the other women gave Leena.

Groans from the men could be heard. "Man you're killing us here, Owen. The womenfolk always run around and get the stuff." Dade snorted, which earned him a smack from Cora and a few female glares.

Owen leaned over and kissed Leena. "Not in this relationship, bro." She smiled up at him with that love he would always want to see in her eyes. "Ready to go home, baby?" he asked her quietly. Leena just smiled and nodded. "We're out of here, people," he said as he stood and reached for her hand. "Are we meeting at all next week?"

Doc shook his head. "I won't be able to get any time next week, not if I'm going to disappear again for gathering."

Dade nodded. "I've got some repairs and things at the retirement home to catch up on, so I'll be out of sight, too."

Kasey frowned. "So, will we get together the night before we leave, to pack everything up then?"

Chris nodded. "Sounds like a good idea."

"Everyone make sure to keep your gris-gris bags handy, and bring them to the gathering. We'll strengthen them once we're there," Cora added.

Steven shook a few hands and gave a few quick hugs before he hugged Rachel tightly. "I could use a bit of help in the children's wing on the weekend, if you have time."

Rachel hugged him back. "I'll be there. Just text me the times." He grinned at her then released her.

Chris wanted to hug only Kasey, so he did. He more or less picked her up and hugged her gently against him. "Give me a call if you need help finding your stuff in that scary closet." He kissed her on the cheek tenderly then looked at her for a moment. Glancing over at the others he reached in his pocket. "I saw this and it made me think of you, so I hope you don't mind that I got it for you. You don't have to wear it if you don't want to." Since when did he babble? "I didn't know if I'd get the chance to give it to you. You've pretty much ignored me since the weekend, but anyway, it's to say I'm sorry." He opened his hand and in it was a small, glittering fairy belly ring.

"Oh, Chris it's so pretty," she whispered as she took it out of his hand. "Of course I'll wear it. Well, not to work or anything. I'm sure it's not a fake stone. Thank you!" She pulled his head down and kissed him tenderly, taking her time to brush her mouth over his for a few moments. "Thank you."

He stood there resting his hands on her hips, just looking down at her for several moments and she was almost lost in his dark green eyes. Then his head snapped up, as she too realized no one else was talking. They turned to see several smiling faces staring at them. Blushing, she stepped away from him and reached to gather up her stuff.

Leena squeezed Owen tighter and smiled up at him. He winked at her and pulled her toward the door. "We'll see you later," Leena said to everyone as she followed him to the door.

He packed his knife into the case he had made for it.

Taking off his ring, he placed it in a cloth and set it on his Bible.

He didn't like to wear his ring while he went to their heathen gatherings. It made him feel unclean again when he was again at home.

He would bring nothing into his house that had been at the gathering. He made sure it all was left in the shed outside of the walls of his home

He picked up the case and set it next to his Bible. It would be safe there until he had to go.

They had called to him and were waiting for him to clean the stain of sins of their souls.

ை<e0 **Chapter 22** இ<e0

Owen finished carrying all the bags into the house and glanced at the clock. Leena would be home in twenty minutes. He looked around her kitchen trying to find something that looked like a vase.

Where would she keep that?

He turned a few more times and then gave up and set the flowers on the table.

It took him most of the day to run around and get everything from the trip list. He still wasn't sure if he'd gotten it all.

Where did he put the list?

Of course, if he hadn't driven into the city to pick up what he'd spent half of yesterday looking for, he would have had a much shorter outing.

How soon was everyone supposed to be here?

He'd managed to talk Leena into dropping Kasey off after work and her bringing her stuff by when everyone else did. He moved bags and packages while cursing.

Where was his phone? He patted his back pockets and found it.

Ha! He'd never felt this nervous before. Flipping the phone open, he checked messages to get the time. Sighing, he looked around.

Where had he put dinner? The Jeep. It was still in the Jeep. He only had roughly forty-five minutes after she got home before everyone else got here. Tough deadline that would be.

He practically ran back out to the Jeep to grab dinner then saw the small box on the seat. Well, good thing I forgot the dinner. He laughed. As he walked back in the house, he glanced toward the backyard. Perfect, he thought, and ran up the steps to try to get everything ready before she got home.

"Owen?" Leena called at the bottom of the stairs. "Are you busy?" She turned to see him coming from the kitchen. "Oh, I wondered where you were." She stopped and looked at the bags all over her dining room. "Did you buy ten of everything?" She smirked.

He shrugged, "Kase didn't put quantity on most of the things, so I thought with a man's stomach and bought double." He walked over and kissed her softly. "I also bought dinner, so you didn't have to try to rush before everyone got here."

She hugged him. "Oh, you are such a sweet man." She started to walk into the kitchen, she was starving. Owen lightly caught her hand and pulled her toward the back door.

"We're having a picnic?" she asked when she saw the blanket on the ground and a few of her cushions.

"Yes," he grinned, "I have something for you, but I thought I'd feed the hard-working supervisor first." She cuddled against him as they walked across the lawn.

"Something like a present?"

"Something like that." Owen purposely left his cell phone and hers inside the house. He had little time, and if there were interruptions, he'd never get this done.

Owen seated her on the blanket and reached into a small box he'd almost thrown out onto the lawn. Pulling out the bouquet of lilies he handed them to her and then sat down.

"Oh, they're so lovely." She leaned over the bouquet and kissed him tenderly. "Are the flowers the something?"

He shook his head and reached over to pull out a flower; he twisted the stem and broke off the blossom, then tucked it behind her ear. "No." He reached into the box and produced a covered plate. "I went to that little café you told me about and got our dinner there."

Leena reached for the plate. "I love their food. It's like a windfall of delicious finger foods." She looked down to see he'd gotten a very wide assortment and pulled off the cover to taste one. "Mmm. Perfect." When she looked up he handed her a glass of wine. "Wine, too. Mr. Grey, are you trying to seduce me?" She grinned.

Owen laughed. "Would have to be a fast seduction, because the gang will be arriving in about a half-hour." He leaned back on one of the pillows and accepted the food she held in front of his mouth. "I see why you love that café." He grinned, "We'll have to get Cora to go there and sample it so she can make this stuff."

Leena shrugged. "She probably can already, although it would be a challenge to her and we'd be in free food for weeks until she got it out of her system."

"Really? I'll have to remember that for future reference."

She lowered her eyes. "I don't expect you to make dinner every night, Owen. If you don't want to, it's not a problem. I've been coming home and making my dinner myself for years."

He lifted her chin. "I don't have a problem with it, Leena. I actually love this. I get a lot of work done while you're at work, more than I did in the past sitting up all hours puttering away." Owen sat up and leaned a little closer. "I love waking up with you and sending you off to work." He picked up her hand and kissed her palm. "I love making dinner and waiting for you to come home." He kissed her wrist. "I can't see a day now without you in it, Aileena. I know we haven't been together very long, and things were kind of shaky while I had that small crisis, but you make my life feel fuller." He reached behind her head and gently brought her mouth to his. "You belong in my world," he whispered against her lips.

Leena leaned into his kiss and devoured his lips. When he pulled away to look at her, she smiled. "I can't even begin to tell you how you make my life complete, Owen. I've never been this happy before, ever." She kissed him again and slid a little closer to him. "I think you need to steal one of those kisses again."

He didn't wait a second before he pulled her into his lap and kissed her tenderly. She relaxed in his arms, and her mouth opened so he could taste her. He felt a heat flash through him and deepened the kiss roughly. If he didn't stop, she'd be half-undressed when everyone else arrived, so he gentled the kiss before he pulled back a few inches. "Stop distracting the hell out of me. I wanted to talk to you about something." He saw the immediate worry in her eyes. "No, not anything as stupid as the last time I needed to talk to you... this is a good something." He held her face gently between his hands and kissed her again softly.

She smiled and tried not to look as relieved as she felt.

"I thought we were packing tonight," Cora called from the back door. Both heads swung in surprise toward her.

"Cora, we didn't hear you drive in," Leena said as she slipped back off Owen's lap.

"*Obviously,* you were busy," Cora grinned as she stepped out the door.

Owen dropped his head and swore under his breath.

Leena was about to stand up and leave. *Now or never,* he thought. He reached for her hand and held her from standing. "You stay!" He turned toward Cora as she walked across the lawn, and he pointed at her. "You go back in the house! Please... and keep anyone else there, too!" He was on his knees at that point, ready to carry Leena in the other direction if he had to. Cora gave him a startled look until he saw her eyes pass over the flowers and wine glasses. She grinned at him and walked back in the house.

"Owen, are you all right?" Leena turned back to him after watching Cora close the door.

"No. *Yes.*" He let out a breath. "Other than I seem to have really bad timing, yes, everything is fine... at least I hope it will be." He turned and pulled her back into his lap. "Leena, I've done a lot of serious thinking lately. Not like before." He took a calming breath. "I meant what I said a few minutes ago. I need you in my life to make it complete. I can't see not waking up beside you a single morning, not being there beside me all soft and sexy every night." He kissed her lightly. "I want you for myself, for always, and me for you, for always."

He reached into his pocket and held up the ring. "I didn't get you a diamond or something flashy... because you're not. You're a part of this earth we're sitting on that you love so much, no flash, nothing fake about you. I spent two days researching stones and thought this was the one for you... for us." He watched her looking at the ring with such surprise on her face he continued. "It's watermelon tourmaline, and it will always stand for love and tenderness and the friendship we'll always have."

"Owen."

"I want to wake beside you as my wife for every morning for the rest of our lives, pretty Aileena. If you'll take me on, that is."

A tear rolled down her cheek as she nodded. She searched his eyes. "Put it on quick, before you change your mind," she whispered. Her hand trembled as she watched him kiss the ring, then her hand, before he slipped it on her finger. She looked down at her hand with the delicate band of silver and stone then threw her arms around him to hug him tightly against her.

Owen nuzzled into her neck and squeezed her tightly. "I almost lost it, baby, when Cora came out. I was ready to throw you over my shoulder and run the other way with you." He pulled back and held her face in his hands. "I love you, Aileena Duncan, with all that I have." He kissed her lips gently.

She smiled and whispered against his mouth. "I love you, Owen Grey, and want nothing more than to be by your side for the rest of our lives."

He hugged her again then sighed. "Guess I better go apologize to Cora."

"I'm sure she'll forgive you." Leena snuggled into his neck, inhaling that scent that was only his.

Owen stood with her still in his arms then let her slowly slide down to touch her feet on the ground. Pulling her under his shoulder they turned toward the house. Both stopped and looked. In the back window stood the six friends who had become as much a part of their lives as they had each other's.

Kasey sighed and looked at Cora as she turned to Dade and smiled with tears in her eyes. "That was so beautiful, without hearing a word they said."

Dade put his arm around her. "Yeah, Owen's going to be a hard act to follow," he muttered.

Kasey leaned back against Chris and felt his arm go around her waist, his hand resting over her belly button. When he squeezed her back against him, she knew he could feel his little gift nestled against his palm and her skin.

"So, do we tell them we're sneaky witches now?" Steven asked quietly before they reached the house.

"No!" Rachel put her hand over his mouth and stared at him. "Never!" she hissed.

Owen stepped in the back door and grinned. "You guys have it all packed yet?" He almost hid behind Leena as the women moved quickly toward them. They were hugging him and kissing him and kissing him some more when she showed them the ring.

"Golden boy is at it again," Doc said loudly as a grin spread on his face.

"Better hand-fast him quick, Lee, so we get attention from time to time, too," Chris added as he clasped hands with Owen.

"Used all the sappy lines, didn't you, bro?" Dade asked as he sauntered toward him with a smile.

"Would have used anything it took, *bro*," Owen answered as he pulled Leena back against his chest.

Leena smiled up at him then turned. "We better get this stuff organized and packed so you can all leave and I can cuddle with my fiancé all night long." She winked up at him as everyone laughed and began to go through the bags he'd tossed on the table and floor.

No one spoke of what the gathering meant, of the murderer they knew would be there.

They just held onto the love and hope the engagement brought into their circle of friends.

He carefully placed the knife inside its case before wrapping it and putting it inside the bag.

It was time again.

Those that needed to be cleansed would come to him.

Setting the ring beside the Bible, he closed his eyes to pray.

Don't let me fail them.

Solstice

Heat

Book II

By Jacqueline Paige

❧ Chapter 1 ☙

Kasey had checked her bag four times now. What time were they supposed to be picking her up? She was tired from being awake all night working a spell. Nervous and scared about going to Solstice, where a killer was expected to be, she glanced at the clock again and tried to exhale slowly. She was even more excited and nervous about getting to spend some quality time with Chris.

Kasey had decided she was tired of waiting for him to make a move, but she had no idea how to make any move.

You can do this, Kasey girl, she told herself for the umpteenth time. Maybe, just maybe, if she could manage to get a midnight stroll with him, she could come back looking as thoroughly kissed as Lee had at Beltane.

Her stomach lurched. The thought of kissing Chris, other than a quick one, tied her stomach in a complete nest of knots, like a macramé planter.

Owen's Jeep pulled up, and she was halfway out the door before it stopped. She smiled at Leena briefly, but her eyes quickly caught the dark-haired man in the backseat as he pushed the door open for her. She stroked a hand casually over the fairy pendant hanging at her waist and then looked back to Chris to give him an inviting smile.

Chris glanced at his watch as Owen finally pulled out on the highway. Not bad, only a half hour behind.

Chris looked over at Kasey again, his mind still stuck on how she looked as she came running out of her house. Her hair actually hadn't been helter-skelter for once. She had left it so short, the choppy ends were soft and it flitted about with each movement of her head. She'd done something with the color too, it was darker than normal. He wanted to run his fingers through those short locks and see if they felt as silky as he imagined.

In the front, the newly engaged couple, of one-day were talking softly and holding hands. This only made him turn back to look over at Kasey again. What was this, the tenth time he'd glanced at her since she got in the Jeep? She almost looked sleepy.

"You look tired, Kase."

She nodded. "I am. I ended up staying up most of the night trying to charm a talisman, took me forever to work everything out."

He touched her hand softly. "We're going to recharge the gris-gris bags..."

"Oh, no, it's not for me. I made it for Cassidy, only she's going to think it's a gift, which works out with Solstice gift exchanges." She rubbed her eyes. "If I did it right, it will keep her safe." Her eyes were so sad when she looked back at him. "I don't want her to be the next victim. Ever since we saw her in that vision..."

Squeezing her hand, he grinned at her. "I'm sure you did it just fine, Kase. Your gifts are getting stronger with each day, soon you'll be able to take on anything you want."

"Thank you, Chris. Gosh, I am tired!"

He reached over and undid her seat belt. Without any effort, he slid her over to him. "Lie against me and catch a nap." He kissed the top of her head. "I'll keep you from slipping off the seat."

"Thanks." She slipped right down and rested her head in his lap. Shifting around until she fit her small body easily in the backseat next to his larger body, she closed her eyes.

Resting his hand on the bare skin of her exposed waist, Chris grinned down at her. She was already drifting off.

"So..." Owen said, drawing his attention forward. "What is this about gift exchanges at Solstice?" He glanced in the mirror at Chris, and then turned his head to look over at Leena.

Chris nodded. "It's an old tradition, exchange a magical gift or tool at Summer Solstice with friends."

"Oh." Owen's eyebrows moved down before he looked towards the road again. "I didn't get gifts."

"Yes, you did," Leena whispered quietly beside him.

"I did?"

"Uh-huh."

"Thank you, baby." He lifted her hand and kissed it.

"You're welcome."

Owen turned back to watch the road. a puzzled look on his face. He was most likely trying to figure out where to get something for Leena.

Chris studied the woman sleeping on him. She looked like a cherub when she slept. He stared intently at her face for several moments. Her small hand rested on his bare thigh by her head. She had perfect hands.

Lightly, he ran his hand over her hair and almost groaned out loud. It was like silk.

An ugly aggressive feeling came to him each time he'd thought of Kasey being at risk at this gathering. Were they all crazy to be going to another one if the killer from Beltane was going to be there? They did have advantages that few were aware of; hopefully the killer wasn't one of those few. He pictured how Leena looked when she and Owen returned from finding the bodies of those two women, he'd die before he ever watched Kasey go through that.

His eyes caressed her bare waist, imagining his hands doing the same thing. Having his long fingers lay across her belly button, and he could feel the fairy he'd given her dangling there and keep it still was taking a lot of self-control.

He'd had to curb the urge drop to his knees and kiss it when she came out dressed in a tight belly top and short skirt.

As she walked to the jeep, he'd seen her hand caress it and make eye contact with him, ensuring he would notice she was wearing his gift.

He had no fear she wouldn't like the Solstice gift he'd spent days deciding on for her, it was meant for her.

While allowing his eyes to wander leisurely over her bare legs, he noticed she'd kicked off her shoes. Her toes were painted at least four, no five he counted, different colors.

By the time they pulled into the gates at the gathering site, Chris wanted to jump out and stretch. He'd barely moved a muscle the whole trip, not wanting to disturb Kasey. Running a hand up and down her arm, he spoke softly. "Kasey, we're here."

She opened her eyes and turned to look up at him. His heart literally hammered in his chest when he looked at her sexy, sleepy expression.

"Thanks," she whispered with a raspy voice.

He touched her cheek with the back of his hand, brushing his knuckles lightly over the soft, glowing skin. "Anytime, sweetheart."

Kasey smiled as she pushed herself up. "I feel so much better." She brushed her lips against his cheek, lingering for a short moment. "You are quite a comfy pillow, Chris."

"You can use me anytime you need, little Kasey," he said in a low voice, almost drowning in her pale green eyes as she looked at him.

"Are you getting out sometime today?" Dade looked in the driver's window at them.

Steven winked at Kasey as she got out. "Kase, you look good enough to eat today." He walked over and hugged her, ignoring the glare Chris was giving him.

Chris was almost certain Doc was doing that just to annoy him.

"Oh! I love the belly ring, Kase! Where did you get it?" Rachel squeaked as she was bending down to look closer.

Kasey smiled up at Chris. "It was a gift."

Chris grinned down at her, liking the way she kept it between the two of them.

Cora walked over and looked too. "Oh my, those have to be real diamonds. Fake ones wouldn't sparkle like that." She reached out a finger to touch it and got a small zap. "Oh!" She put her finger in her mouth and laughed. "This dry weather is so awful for static charges."

Chris stuffed his hands into his pockets when he noticed Owen raise an eyebrow at the Doc, and then they both turned to stare at him. He glanced down at the ground, pretending he didn't understand the knowing looks they gave him.

Kasey chuckled. "I guess I'll have to call her my electric fairy." As everyone started moving towards the registration, she pulled him back a bit and looked up at him. "The stones are not fake, are they, Chris?" He just shook his head. "Great!" She puffed out her cheeks. "I need an insurance policy on my belly button!" He threw his head back and laughed as she headed quickly after the others.

Chris followed along behind, still close enough to hear Owen as he leaned closer to Steven. "Can he do that to an object?"

Steven nodded. "Yes, and I'd say he definitely did."

Owen laughed.

"Who did what?" Dade asked, pushing between them.

Steven glanced towards the women and then whispered to Dade.

"No way! Really?" Dade chuckled. "Sneaky bastard," he muttered and then immediately walked ahead of them when Cora turned to give him *that* look.

Leena stood by the registration, she noticed the site was even more natural and beautiful than the pictures had shown. There were herbs and grasses growing wildly around the whole camp. She couldn't wait to wander through the trees and along the creek to discover what was there. Harvesting herbs for her magic was very important to her.

She started a mental list of the herbs she most wanted to find. Wild catnip, of course, was always better. Would there be motherwort here? Oh, and the ground ivy would be at the perfect point to harvest. Grinning, she sighed and leaned back against Owen, now seemed as good a time as any to get him playing in the weeds. She was just turning to tell him of her plans when Gwen, in her vintage flowing hippy skirts, came flying out of the little registration building. She ran over to Leena and hugged her.

"Cora just told me. Congratulations!" She picked up Leena's hand and looked at the ring. She then kissed Owen. "This is so lovely!" She smiled at them both. "It makes my heart so much lighter to know something so wonderful came out of the Beltane gathering." She kissed both of them again. "Oh! You'll be dancing your first coupled union tomorrow night. Oh, this is wonderful!" She sniffled as she walked back into the building.

Owen looked down at Leena. "Coupled union?"

Leena laughed and started towards the building. "I'll explain later." Justin was walking over towards the group. She could see the strain of the past few months in his eyes.

"Justin, how nice to see you." She hugged him briefly.

The older man grinned back at her. "Gwen just told me the news, congratulations you two." He shook Owen's hand and grinned. "You're a lucky man, but you know that." He turned to nod to the others standing closer now. "It's great to see all of you here. Thanks for coming back." He rubbed his jaw and glanced around. "You'll need to meet Mr. Blaine, the detective they've sent. I'm not sure where he is at the moment, but stop by at dinner, and I'll point him out to you."

With that he offered a small grin. "It's certainly drier this time." He turned and went back into the building.

"Poor guy," Cora mused as she went into the registration building again.

When Chris walked out to where the others waited, he noticed a few tense stares.

"Chris," Kasey said in her sweet tone. "Did you happen to pay for all of our registrations and the cabin?"

He grinned down at her. "What could be more magical then the eight of us together at a gathering? My Solstice gift to you all." He looked at them knowingly. They couldn't refuse this gift.

Owen stepped forward until Leena put a hand on his arm and shook her head. "You can't refuse a Solstice gift, or you'll bring bad luck to the season." Unhappy blue eyes looked at Chris, and then Owen looked back at Leena and sighed in defeat.

Chris walked past them. "Shall we go check out the lodgings?"

Cora caught up to him and kissed his cheek. "Thank you."

Rachel did the same.

Kasey just looked up at him and frowned.

The outside of the cabin wasn't really cabin-like in appearance. It was a simple square building with dark siding and white trim. The deck, or the white boards that could be referred to as the deck, were large enough for two or three people to stand on, but not sit.

Once inside the cabin, they all stood in the small sitting area and looked around. There was a woodstove in the corner, doubtful it would have to be used judging by the sweat on everyone. The floor was well-polished wood that had seen many feet over the years, Chris decided.

There were two large armchairs, one faded blue and one red, a large brown wicker chair, comfort would be questionable, and the green couch that wasn't quite a couch, more of a loveseat that wanted to be a couch.

"Well, at least we won't *all* have to sit on the floor," Dade muttered as he walked over and opened a door. "And people, we have a bathroom. Okay, a tiny sink and a toilet." He turned and grinned at Owen. "You, big guy, might have to go in and out sideways, but at least it's not sixty feet away outside."

Leena stood there and looked at the closed doors. Sighing, she went and opened the first. "Double bed and a tiny TV-table-sized table. The wall is a foot from each side of the bed," she reported.

Opening the next, "Single, possibly a twin-sized cot-like bed, in this room. Nothing other than that, including space." She lifted her brows at the others as they peeked in the rooms after her. The next door revealed two cots and a tiny window more the size of a vent.

Chris looked in the last door over her shoulder. It had three narrow cots and almost a half-sized closet. "Well." Leena grinned at him. "We have four rooms, double bed, a single bed, two singles, and three singles, in addition to a closet-like space."

Owen grinned. "I'm calling the double bed that I'll be sharing with my fiancée." Everyone smirked, not arguing because it did make sense.

"I'll take the single then," Chris added as he stuck his head in and looked at the tiny space and realized Leena hadn't been exaggerating. He leaned against the wall beside the door.

Dade walked over and looked into the other rooms. "Guess Doc and I'll take the two beds in there, unless you ladies want to mix it up?" He lifted an eyebrow at the three women.

They laughed and walked into the room with the three single beds.

Leena dropped her purse on the chair. "Guess we'd better go haul everything in."

Dade shook his head. "I'll just drive the van over and park it beside the cabin. There's enough space."

It only took half an hour to get everything sorted out. Cora set the last package on the shelf they'd discovered behind a curtain they thought was a window. She looked over at Owen. "Were you expecting us to feed the whole camp?"

Owen shrugged and then grinned at Chris. "Just didn't want anyone to go hungry. You never know when those middle-of-the-night munchies will get you." Cora laughed.

Rachel was already putting some of the food back in bags. "If no one objects, I'm going to take this to the children's area. Munchies always come in handy there."

Steven nodded. "I'll go over with you and see if any of my fest kids are here."

Straightening from setting up the little travel table, Leena glanced at the women. "Before anyone goes anywhere, ladies, shall we cleanse and protect?" The women nodded and went into their room.

Leena looked around at the men. "A little tradition, although we could use this to recharge the gris-gris too, I suppose."

Cora nodded as she walked back out. "Yes, good idea." She stepped forward and placed a wooden carved mask on the table. "To watch over all," she said and stood to the side of the table.

Rachel stepped up and placed her large blue and black candles on the table. Holding her hand over them, they smoldered and then caught fire. "To protect and repel negative." She took her place beside Cora.

Kasey stepped to the table and set a large piece of raw jasper down. "To bring courage and tranquility to us all." She stepped to the side of the table.

Leena stepped up and opened her hand over a small dish. Herbs floated from her palm, then settled in the dish, immediately smoldering. She waited for the smoke to rise and then lifted her hands. "To cleanse and protect us all."

Chris watched as the smoke swirled around the small table and around each of them before circling the room and coming back to the dish. Cora motioned them to form a circle.

The four women joined hands with the men, as soon as the circle was complete, a warm tingle shot through his hands before everyone let go.

"That should also strengthen the gris-gris bags," Cora said as she went to sit down.

Chris raised his eyebrows at Kasey. "Tranquility?"

She nodded. "I didn't know if everyone else was as uneasy as I, after Beltane, so I thought it wouldn't hurt." She looked down at her clasped hands.

"A perfect choice, Kasey, thank you."

Dade sat on the edge of the little couch and sent Chris a determined look. "To test your stone out, Kase, now would be as good a time as any to discuss what Justin asked the men to do, before we all head in different directions." All eyes were on him at once.

Dade glanced once at Cora quickly. "Justin says this undercover cop asked if the four of us would help by making rounds off and on throughout the next few nights." The other three males nodded, but Chris noticed none were jumping in to help Dade explain.

"Alone?" Cora asked. Dade nodded and started to speak when she stepped in front of him and looked down at him, hands on hips. "I don't think so."

"Coralee, the killer isn't after men, obviously from that vision..."

"No," was all she said and then sat down, crossing her arms in front of her.

Chris looked around at the women. He had been sure this wasn't going to go over smoothly. "I have a suggestion." Everyone looked at him. "We could take turns going out as couples and wandering around. It would look less suspicious." He grinned over at Kasey. "I don't know about you, men, but I'd feel safer knowing little Kasey was there with me. If we saw anything, she could blast anyone up into a tree while I ran for help." Kasey laughed and put her hand over her mouth.

Owen chuckled. "He's right, well, for the most part. I'd feel better with Leena beside me than worrying about her."

Dade laughed. "You just want to sneak off and have sex in the bushes with her, bro. Tell the truth."

Owen grinned back at him. "Hadn't thought of that, but not a bad idea there, thanks." Leena lifted a cushion from the couch with a brush of air and tossed it towards him.

Ducking, Owen laughed and walked towards her. "Behave, woman." He grinned.

Steven stood up. "Other than the sex thing, which does have some merit, I agree with that idea." He looked over at Rachel and smiled. "Well, warrior woman, you want to protect me from the dark shadows?"

Rachel laughed and then shrugged.

Cora stretched. "I don't know about the rest of you, but I'm going to go try to grab a nap. It's going to be a long night, and getting up at dawn to light the Solstice fire will be even more difficult if we've all been in and out all night."

Dade nodded. "I'll head over and let Justin know what we'll be doing. I also want to see what this undercover cop looks like, so we don't attack him thinking he's the killer."

Leena sighed. "See if you can get the list of registrants too, Dade. We could check them with the Beltane list before dinner."

Dade saluted her and walked out the door grinning.

Rachel grabbed the bag of munchies and headed to the door. "You know where to find me."

Steven followed her. "Me too."

Leena grinned at Owen suggestively.

Owen held up a hand. "I know that grin says, 'Come get me,' but the eyes are saying, 'Owen, honey, I need a hand with something.'"

She laughed. "I do need your hand, to hold mine while we walk through the woods and meadow looking at the wild plants."

He shrugged. "I can do that." He took the bag she held out and opened the door.

KEEP READING FOR AN EXCERPT OF

SALVATION

By Jacqueline Paige

Chapter One

He watched the child in silence, not that he could be heard even if he wanted. If his math was correct, she was three years old now. Stepping into the room and away from the window, he watched her small body shake as she pressed an ear against the door. He couldn't see her face with the fall of wavy black hair covering it. But he knew the face under her messed hair was round and angelic.

From the other side of the door she was carefully leaning against, he could hear the yelling...again. Her parents spent most of their time screaming at each other and breaking things. He'd sat with the child many times in the last year while the adults in her world showed her all the wrong ways to live.

It worried him that she no longer cried; no longer curled her tiny body into the corner and tried to make herself invisible. At least the quarrelling adults had never brought it to her; he didn't know if he could stand to see her hurt in any way. He closed his eyes and cursed himself; what could he even do to help if they did?

A loud crash brought him back to the moment; he opened his eyes to see the girl remove her ear from the door. Her face was visible now and it pulled at his heart to see tears rolling down her round cheeks. It made her dark brown eyes seem blurry and vague. She hugged her tiny arms around her middle, trying to comfort herself. A small part of him wanted to take her in his arms and shelter her from the sadness, not that he knew how to hold a child.

She took two steps back from the door but still watching, as if she was afraid it was going to fly open. She sniffled once and raised her face, then looked right at him. Did she actually see him? He was tempted to look behind to see if there was something there that would catch her attention, but he was afraid to look away and go back to being invisible to all.

She blinked and cleared the tears from her eyes yet continued to look right at him. With her chin up she used her sleeve to wipe across her face, then raised her chin with a determination he knew all too well. Her eyes appeared as if they were looking right into his, causing his heart, if he truly still had one, to jolt inside of his body.

Finally, she turned from him, went to the little table in the corner, and sat on the small chair. She opened a book, took colored sticks from a messy carton, and scribbled in angry motions over the outline of the picture in front of her.

Sighing, he closed his eyes. She would be fine. He really did need to stop coming here.

He had tried to stay away, as he knew he should, and had been able to watch from a distance. But the child lay on the bed with her face hidden, shaking and distraught. He didn't know what he could do, but he liked to believe his presence would be sensed and she would somehow be comforted.

Glancing away from her, he noticed papers crumpled up on the floor. He couldn't pick them up to look at them, but he could read part of one. *"Happy 7th birthday."* She was seven already? Had not only a few months passed since she was that tiny cherub-faced child? He frowned. How had he lost track of four entire years? What did he have to keep track of except time? All he *had* was time, endless expanses of time.

Shaking his head, he stepped closer to the bed. If only he could offer a calming touch to let her know she wasn't alone. But in truth, she was; he could hear the screaming outside of the walls of her room, and knew that she was very much alone in this world.

She rolled onto her back, clutching something to her chest. With an angry swipe she wiped across her face and took a long shaky breath. He leaned down to see her better and was surprised to see how she had grown since he last let himself get this close. Gone was the childish softness. In its place, the beginning of a more mature form was now visible. He sighed and stepped back; this small one was going to be a world of trouble for some man in the years to come.

Looking back he found her eyes looking right at him, as only she had ever done. He stepped back in shock. He told himself she was just staring into space and it happened to be in his direction, but her eyes moved over his body in a slow, measured way. If he spoke would she hear him? He clenched his jaw; hadn't he spent years trying to be heard by others? He wouldn't waste one more ounce of energy on that ever again.

When she stood up, he almost stepped back again, afraid she'd go right through him and make him feel undetectable. Instead, she stopped in front of him to look up at his face. Inside his head he smiled at her, but the movement did not show on his face. She couldn't really see him; he must be creating this from years of desire. She turned and walked to a shelf in the corner. He hesitantly took a few steps to follow her.

He was astounded when she turned and motioned to a ship sitting on the top shelf. He looked at her for a moment and then moved his eyes to the ship. He smiled; it was a small model of a galleon. While it looked quite like a real one, very majestic and formed well enough, he frowned. Why would she want him to see that? Why would a young girl of seven even want a scale model ship? He looked back to see she had calmed and wasn't the distressed child she'd been just moments ago. He noticed the tilt of her chin and recognized that determined glint in her eyes. He smiled at her and hoped by some fanciful miracle that maybe he was partially responsible for this.

So he was a completely spineless man, he thought as he entered her room yet again. He had not lost track of time and knew she was twelve years older now. He had only allowed himself to come this close while she slept over the last few years though, for he was uncertain of what her ability to see him actually meant. She stormed past him, opened her door, and screamed obscenities that he'd only ever heard from older, weathered males. She shocked him, made him wonder whether he should really be here. The door slammed, and he turned to see her take a leap and flounce onto the bed.

She had definitely lost that helpless, angelic look. Her dark eyes turned to him and he had no choice but to stand there and watch her look at him. She bounced off the bed, straight up as if she were pulled by a rope, and walked past him to the shelves along the wall.

He turned slowly. Gone were the childish toys and trinkets. There were no more coloring sticks in this one's life. His eyes moved over the top of the shelf. She had, over the last several years, added to her galleon, and it now held a detailed frigate and shebec model. If he were the size of a mouse, he could have lived on them, they were that detailed. She had associated him with the ships, and he supposed she was observant to have done so.

With a hesitant movement he raised his eyes away from the ships he'd last seen in their real and true form to look back at her. She smiled at him, or possibly it was a snarl; it wasn't easy to distinguish, but the point was she could really, truly see him and he was once more left to wonder what it meant. He heard a door slam downstairs and watched her turn quickly to the window.

Stepping closer so he could see, her mother was leaving, and with her was a man. Even though he had never seen this man before, he knew it was the sort of man any woman was better not getting close to.

Hearing her heavy sigh he turned. She had walked back over to the bed and was putting tiny drops with wires attached to them in her ears. He'd noticed most children of her age walked around with wires coming from their ears. Somehow he doubted it was to lessen the sound of cannon fire. He watched her for a moment longer, decided she was well enough for now, and left without further hesitation.

The sound of sob haunted him once again, without intending it, he found himself inside her room. In the last four years he'd managed to stay away, but in an odd moment of weakness, had spent a few brief moments here, just to assure himself she was well enough. The room had undergone enormous change; it now assaulted his senses to be in it. It was a mix of bright and dark, contrasting with each other in ways that it made him dizzy. Gone were the pretty pinks of childhood; in their place was black with blood-red splatters.

He stopped beside the shelf and wanted for one moment to touch the ships. Two more spectacular replicas displayed on the top shelf. A caravel, which, he thought with a smirk, looked as pieced-together in this size as he had always thought they were in the real versions. The man-o-war filled him with longing, just as the real thing had once done. There wasn't anything that could compete with the force of it, the sheer threat its appearance on the horizon had wrought. Bringing himself from memories of a past long gone, he turned to find her sprawled half on, half off the bed. She was talking low into a phone; yes, he knew what a phone was—now.

"I hope he falls and breaks both of his legs and has to spend the rest of the year hobbling around on crutches! He's such a loser; I don't know why I even bothered." She sniffled.

Pausing, he raised his eyebrows and tried to understand what she talking about. A male was no doubt involved; he was not so long gone that he didn't recognize the tone that every female adopted when a male had done wrong. What he didn't understand was the word *loser;* had there been a race? He shook his head and decided he needed to observe more television in his wanderings. It had been his only way to discover a world outside of his confinement. The only link that let him feel as if he were still part of the human race, not a lonely drifter who felt no peace. Of course, the first time he saw the wondrous thing they called a television, he was intrigued by such a puzzling contraption.

"Yeah, okay, later!"

Turning, he watched her hang up the phone and hop off the bed. He knew his eyes bulged when she stood up and walked over to close the door. He felt like he'd just been broadsided! What was she wearing? He seriously doubted she should even leave the building. Her shoulders were bare, as was her midriff, and his throat practically seized shut when he realized she was no longer a child in any sort of way. She had breasts! When had she gotten those? His eyes traveled down to see bare womanly legs beneath a short skirt. If he actually had such a thing as saliva left in his body, it would have dried right up inside his mouth.

She walked over and touched the man-o-war ship with a feminine hand, and he suddenly felt like an extremely old man. Turning with her hand still on the ship, she looked directly at him, and he froze, not knowing how to react. She was past sixteen years now and more than womanly, but he felt saddened to realize that she had never been allowed much of a childhood.

His eyes traveled the length of her again, noting that she was just a little more than a hand's span shorter than his own height, but it was her eyes that swallowed him. Her dark hair hung to her shoulders, untamed waves of thick silk. Her deep brown eyes had been highlighted with coloured powders, and the result completely robbed him of air, or would have if he still breathed. A child of this age should not know how to look at a man the way she was looking at him.

He watched without movement as her hand ran over a sketch of a face propped behind the ships, he would swear it was a likeness of his own face—himself in a looking glass, the way he remembered looking. He moved a hand to touch the scar that ran from his temple to cross his cheekbone. The sketch was of him, including the scar. He glanced back at her and had so many questions, but none he would ever ask. She could see him, but how? And why?

Inclining his head to her, he turned to leave before he could change his mind, making a silent vow he would not return again.

~

Miranda got out of her faded, rust-covered car and slammed the door. "Great!" She looked down the dirt road only to kick the tire as she walked to open the hood. "You couldn't die where there are actual people or traffic, could you? It had to be in this scenic, stupid, middle-of-absolute-nothing spot!" She propped the hood open and leaned on the front of the car, looking in. "Nothing's smoking, sizzling, or hissing...which means I am so screwed! I can't even fiddle with anything to make you start again, you stupid piece of—" She took a deep breath and tried to calm down. With a sigh she turned around, feeling defeated. "Okay, Randy, you just need a little reflection time here to come up with a new game plan." She walked across the shallow ditch, and headed toward a large tree. "No need to stand in the sun and bake your brain while you do."

Dropping to the ground, she sat with her back against the tree. "This has not been one of my better days." An orange butterfly fluttered down to sit on the top of some weeds a few feet from the tree. She watched it for a moment. "It started out bad enough. Can you believe he dumped me? I mean, seriously, he was hardly the catch of a lifetime or anything, but to leave me a message, breaking up with me on the phone? That is so low!"

The butterfly's wings flitted a few times, making her feel as if it were responding to her dilemma. "Apparently, I'm too

266

blunt, and that bothers him." She snorted and shoved her heavy hair back from her face. "I just tell it like it is. It's not my fault most people prefer to be lied to." The butterfly moved to another plant a few feet away.

Randy sighed. "I should have taken that as a sign and just stayed home, called in and played dead, or something... Going in to work in the mood I was in was such a huge mistake." She beamed at the frantic fluttering from the creature. "But you won't tell anyone I screwed myself right out of a job, right?" She shrugged. "The job sucked anyway. I should have left there a long time ago. I mean, really, I was hired to work in the art department...which for some silly reason I thought might have something to do with art...but, nooo, was I wrong or what? I spent all my time being the flunky and running this here and that there... I don't think I was even allowed to contribute to more than a handful of projects the whole time I was there"—she huffed out a breath—"and the boss...what a chauvinistic asshole!"

The butterfly seemed to pause in its movement, and Randy nodded. "Yeah, you're right. Telling the boss man that I was not his personal gopher was probably not the best way to go about it." She pulled her knees up and rested her chin on them. "I'm single and unemployed all in one day. Oh, and let's not forget that stupid piece of crap sitting over there." She looked at her car on the road. Looking back, she watched the insect flutter up and hover for a moment at her eye level before it flew off in the direction of the car. "Yeah, I better see if it will start...not that I have anywhere to be, but I'd rather sulk at home than in the middle nowhere." She got up and brushed off her pants.

She tried looking under the hood again. "Maybe you just needed a break, huh?" she said to the car. "I'm going to try to start you now, and if you can just be nice and get me home, I promise I'll call someone to fix you up." She patted the car gently before climbing in behind the steering wheel. "Impress me," she whispered as she turned the key.

Three times she tried and although it made noise like it wanted to start, it didn't quite seem to have the energy to complete the task. "Well, at least you're not completely dead. I'll just give you a few more minutes to get it together." She got back out of the car and leaned against the side, peering down at the motor. "I should have taken shop in school instead of art," she mumbled to herself.

Sighing, she closed the hood with a loud bang. She glanced up at the sky to see dark clouds rolling in fast on the breeze, covering the sun. "Oh, that's just what I need to complete my—" The rain began so quickly she had to close her mouth to stop from swallowing it. It pelted her, soaking her before she could get to the door of her car.

Hopping in quickly, she slammed the door shut and brushed wet hair out of her face. "Perfect!" It was hitting the windshield so hard she couldn't even see the road. She wiped her wet hands down her drenched pants a few times before she realized it was useless; they weren't going to dry. "I have seriously pissed off the world today, haven't I?"

Waving her hands around she tried to dry them before she dug into her purse for her phone. She held it in her hand and squeezed her eyes shut as she opened it. Opening them slowly she almost laughed. No signal. "I'm shocked," she mumbled without emotion as she tossed the phone over her shoulder into the backseat. The rain ended as fast as it had begun.

Grasping the steering wheel, she slowly lowered her forehead to rest on it. A strange, yet familiar feeling prickled across the back of her neck. She didn't raise her head, just smiled into the steering wheel. "You could do something to help."

She lifted her head slowly, afraid to move too fast, and turned to look beside her. She watched the image of the man she'd been seeing for years become clearer. If she focused hard enough, he almost appeared to be real. Many times over the years she thought she was seeing things, possibly ghosts, but it was only ever him.

He gaped at her, his shock more than obvious. "How...you can see me? Truly?"

Randy sat there wanting to reach out and hug him. Hallucinations didn't talk—did they? His voice was rough and deep, and she'd never been happier to hear someone speak. "I more or less sense you most of the time, but if I focus hard enough I can see you." She looked at the scar across his left cheek. "You're very clear today."

He frowned. "And you can hear me?"

Randy tried not to grin. "I'm answering you, aren't I?"

"That's impossible..."

"And yet, here we are talking and being all visible-like." She looked at him, from his long ebony hair down to his black worn boots. "I have a lot of questions, mostly pertaining to whether I'm sane, but right now...I don't suppose you know anything about cars?"

Dark eyebrows shot up, he opened his mouth and then closed it for a moment "I have never actually been inside one until this moment."

"Ah. I figured as much." She reached around and grasped the key. "If this happens to start, I'll be driving like a speed demon to get home ASAP, so will you be able to chill right there and come with me or am I gonna watch you poof away again?" Serious pale blue eyes looked over every inch of her face.

"I don't think I comprehend the meaning of what you just said." He said it softly, still frowning.

Randy laughed. "Sorry. I want you to come to my house with me, is that possible?"

He opened his mouth then closed it for a moment, a serious look in his eyes. "I am not certain I will remain with your car when it's moving, but I will come to your home later on if I cannot."

She bobbed her head a few times, smiling. "Cool." She let out a quick breath. "Cross your fingers."

Frowning again he looked down at his hands. "For what purpose?"

Randy chuckled. "Never mind!" She turned the key, it groaned a few times, a bit faster than before. She tromped on the gas and the car roared to life. Without looking beside her, she threw it into drive and slammed her foot on the gas, trying to get home as fast as she could just in case it died again.

"I believe I will meet with you at your home. I do not like being in this thing while it is moving," he murmured between clenched teeth.

Randy glanced beside her and swore her ghost was slightly green and suffering from motion sickness. "Okay... Hey, what's your name?" She looked back at the road and gunned the gas pedal again.

Closing his eyes briefly, he opened them again quickly and swallowed. "Jareth Blackwood." He inclined his head to her. "Until later."

She glanced over to see him gone already. "Jareth," Randy whispered. Her ghost had a voice and a name; maybe today wasn't such a sucky day after all.

KEEP READING FOR AN EXCERPT OF

After
the
Silence
Volume 1

BREE

By Jacqueline Paige

Chapter One

I was nineteen when the world went crazy, nothing that was would ever be again.

Remnants of a familiar world remained, but not enough to instill those warm, fuzzy feelings you get when life is comfortable and predictable.

I'm Bree Taylor. This is an account of what I remember, how things happened when life changed forever and I managed to survive. There is so much to tell, a thousand pages wouldn't be enough to explain it all, but someone has to tell it. There needs to be a record so if we, as a planet survive, others will have the history. If we don't, then the next species to invade earth will know what we did wrong.

It is now just a few days after my twenty-second birthday, I'm standing looking out the window and wishing my brother, Shawn, well in the afterlife. A seemingly small laceration on his leg became so much more and took him away from me, leaving me to figure out this world on my own. If I have relatives left living, I wouldn't know. All that I cared for are now ashes spread over the dirt and just memories inside my head.

I am alone.

"Bree?"

I turned towards Darren, one of my adopted brothers, and gave him a look to tell him we were done discussing my decision. He didn't heed the warning.

"Are you sure this is what you want to do?"

His voice was filled with grief and worry. *Was I? Yes, at least eighty percent certain.* "Darren, I can't stay here. Being in the city is dangerous enough as a family, never mind a single girl."

A desperate look appeared in his eyes. He was probably wishing at this point that some of the other brothers were still alive, but only Bobby and Darren were left out of my six older brothers.

"We'll move you closer to us, keep you safe."

We, being his very old mother and wheelchair bound brother. I gave him my most stern look. "I think you have enough to worry about, you don't need me to add to that list."

Darren's eyes strayed to the picture I still held. The one of my family and me before life was forever altered.

"Shawn would have wanted me to. I feel like I'm letting him down."

I offered him a smile that said I had accepted it, even though I really didn't. "Shawn is gone and I have to go and try to find my own place now. You guys did all you could to prepare and teach me to fend for myself, your job is done.'

He stuffed his hands in his pockets and leaned back against the wall. "Where will you go?"

I turned and looked out the window. "I think the mountains."

A sound came from him that told me he thought I was too much of a girl to survive that. "The crazies hide there."

I chuckled and slowly turned back, rolling my eyes at him. "And they don't in the city?" His expression pleaded with me. "Darren, I know you have always been close to my family, you're like family. So I know that Shawn probably told you I changed after the virus." The fear in his eyes confirmed my suspicions. He knew the truth. "I have to find out what I've become, before others do. I need to know if I'm a good thing or a bad thing. And I need space and solitude to discover this."

"Bree, you could never be bad."

My heart warmed from his words. "I hope you're right."

He sighed loudly. "Fine, but you're taking Tremor and Shawn's weapons – otherwise I'm going with you."

I knew he wouldn't, we both knew it, but it was his way of feeling like he had done all he could. "I don't have to take Tremor. I can walk."

He shook his head sending his black hair scattering around his face. "We have LadyBell and her colt; we don't need any more than that. Tremor's fast and loyal and he'll get you through the bad times."

I was hoping the bad times would be few, naive I know, but I could hope. My heart strained as I fought to keep my resolve. He loved his horse and to know he was sending him out there with me meant more than I could express. "Thank you." I wanted to hug him, I really did, who knew when I'd have any friendly human contact again. If I hugged him now I knew I would fall apart, and I needed to keep my head out of the emotional whirl that was already threatening to suck me in. "I should get ready. I want to leave early enough so I can be out of the city before darkness falls."

Darren nodded, even though his entire face told me he didn't agree. "I'll go get Tremor. You get your stuff packed up." He looked at me for a long silent moment before he rushed back out the door.

I stood there looking at the door long after he'd gone. In my head I wasn't at all sure this was a good plan. I was following my heart and it was telling me to get out of town and find out where I was meant to be. Of course my head was saying that was a load of crap, but I was still going to do it. I couldn't explain why I needed to be outside and away from all the buildings and people, it just felt right.

Darren didn't know I was already packed. When I knew Shawn wasn't going to recover I started to gather up what I would need. Before Shawn was too far away from me, we had discussed my plan. He agreed I needed to leave. He had also said he was coming with me as soon as he was on his feet. I think by that point we both knew he would never recover.

I swore to follow the least traveled path. I promised to stay away from crowded places. I vowed to him I would survive and then I tucked the blanket around him and went off to cry by myself until my eyes felt like they were going to split in half.

I'm done with the crying and ready to take on what's left of this planet and the series of trials I know it will throw in my path. Tale of a colony of peaceful people live high in the mountains, it's my plan to find them. I hope the stories of the crazies that live between here and there are just that, a farfetched creation of some idiot's imagination.

Going into my room, I quickly headed to the closet to pull out the packs that had been sitting ready for me. I didn't need a lot. I could live off the land if needed, but one entire bag contained dehydrated food, just to be safe. As I swung the largest pack up onto my shoulder I caught a glimpse of myself in the mirror. Would this be the last time I saw the woman looking back at me? I looked into my now green eyes, a leftover from the virus. I stared until I saw it; determination, hidden just under the surface. Sighing, I ran a hand through my choppy red hair and debated, very briefly, if I should dye it a dull brown and tone it down. I knew that would never happen. I wouldn't trade in my brilliant hair for anything. It was a statement and if I couldn't do anything else I was definitely going to make one.

Closing my eyes, I prayed for my spirit to stay strong. When I opened them I didn't look at the mirror again, just picked up the other two bags and walked out of my home for the very last time

Darren stood outside holding the reins and crooning softly to Tremor. I couldn't see his face, which was a blessing, I didn't have to see his eyes begging me not to go again. The large horse's ears flicked as he listened attentively. No doubt he was receiving instructions to keep me safe and out of harm's way. Darren lifted his face away from the animal and looked over at me. "He's quite happy you're getting him the hell out of this city." A half hearted grin appeared on his face. With a tilt of his head he motioned to the other side of the porch. "We're going to walk with you until you're outside the city limits."

I turned and looked to see Bobby leaning against the side of the house. I couldn't help but smile when he wiggled his eyebrows at me. Bobby was the clown of the group that grew up together. I often wondered if anyone else ever sensed he was too serious inside and that was why he joked around as much as he did. Bobby was my first crush when I was thirteen. It never went anywhere, for obvious reasons, but I still had a secret place for him in my heart. I was grateful he was coming along; it would prevent Darren from pleading with me to change my mind, again. "Hey, Bobby." He pushed away from the wall and sauntered in his easy way towards me, his long leather jacket making him look like he floated.

"Hey, Brat. You didn't think you were going to sneak off without saying bye did you?"

"Wouldn't dream of it."

He pulled the bag from my shoulder. "Good to know."

Darren came over and took the bags, taking them to secure to Tremor's saddle. "I think you should walk with us for a while and then he won't be too tired to haul ass when you need him to later." He didn't look at me when he spoke.

"She'll be fine, Dare, we taught her." Bobby's tone sounded annoyed.

Silently I hoped he was right.

Stepping in front of me, he looked me over. Without a word he moved and took off the coat that I couldn't ever remember him not having. "You're going to need something to keep you dry and warm." He held the coat out to me.

I opened my mouth to say something, but nothing came out. Pulling my hands out of my pockets I took the jacket and looked up at him. Bobby was a good six inches taller than my five foot five making me wonder if the leather was going to drag on the ground when I put it on. He continued to stand there and say nothing so I put my arms quickly into the sleeves. It hung about three inches off the ground. He gave me a triumphant grin and then moved around behind me, pulling at the material muttering about straps as he did. When he was finished the coat didn't gape away from my body as much as it had.

"There's a nice custom pocket on the inside left." Leaning around me, he flipped the coat open to point to it. "And this…" Bending down to the cuff of his jeans, he pulled up the material to reveal a knife handle sticking out of his boot. "Fits in it perfectly." I knew my eyes were wide as he slipped the knife into the pocket.

He stepped back quickly and jammed his hands into his pockets like he was afraid of grabbing me if he didn't. As he looked down, just before his shaggy blonde hair covered his eyes, I thought I saw a tear running down his cheek. "Find a better place, Bree," he whispered, so softly I almost missed it.

I swallowed the lump that lodged in my throat and nodded. "Thanks."

"Let's go." Darren urged from where he stood. "I want you to have more than enough time to find somewhere to stay when it gets dark.

I wanted to take a huge breath and build the courage to take this final and first step, but I couldn't bring myself to do it in front of them.

"Mom sent a bag of things." Darren patted the small one tied to the back of the saddle. He didn't elaborate what kind of things. Running his hand to the front of it, he flipped open the small pack. "Shawn's hand-gun is in here and there's enough ammo on the other side to last a long time." He looked down at the ground and said nothing further.

I moved around to the front of Tremor and looked up into his big eyes. 'We're going to be just fine aren't we?" I ran my hand down the blackness of his coat over his neck and picked up the reins. His ears flicked and he brought his mouth down to nibble at my shoulder. As far as encouraging signs went, that one worked for me.

I couldn't stand the looks Bobby and Darren were giving each other, so without prolonging this any further, I turned and started to lead the way down the street, thankful we weren't far from the nearest border.

I kept Tremor at an easy trot until we were far enough away that I wouldn't be tempted to go back. Stopping, I turned him and looked back to the two men that stood exactly where I'd left them a few minutes earlier. I waved my arm at them, silently thanked them and wished them well. Turning the animal in the opposite direction, I prodded him with my heels to get us out of here. He complied without hesitation and carried us quickly away from the city that was filled with nothing but heartache that I could no longer face

About Jacqueline

Jacqueline Paige lives in Ontario in a small town that's part of the popular Georgian Triangle area.

She began her writing career in 2006 and since her first published works in 2009 she hasn't stopped. Jacqueline describes her writing as *all things paranormal*, which she has proven is her niche with stories of witches, ghosts, physics and shifters now on the shelves.

When Jacqueline isn't lost in her writing she spends time with her five children, most of whom are finally able to look after her instead of the other way around. Together they do random road trips, that usually end up with them lost, shopping trips where they push every button in the toy aisle, hiking when there's enough time to escape and bizarre things like creating new daring recipes in the kitchen. She's a grandmother to nine (so far) and looks forward to corrupting many more in the years to come.

Jacqueline loves to hear from her readers, you can find her at:
http://www.jacquelinepaige.com/
where you'll find her social media links and upcoming projects